Conspiracy of Bones

(And the Beat Goes On)

by

Tracy Krauss

Fictitious Ink Publishing
Tumbler Ridge, BC

ISBN: 978-1-988447-36-0 (epub); 978-1-988447-37-7 (kindle); 978-1-988447-35-3 (paperback)

(1st edition published as *And the Best Goes On* by Strategic Book Group, New York, NY, 2009)

FOREWORD

This book has a special place in my heart. It was my first novel to get published, and was the result of many years of writing and revising, sometimes through difficult circumstances like temporary blindness. It was also the result of much research into intelligent design and creationism as a scientifically viable alternative to currently accepted theory about the origins of the planet.

I am grateful to Strategic Book Publishing for taking a chance on this story back in 2008. It released in 2009 under the title *And the Beat Goes On*. Since then, my writing has grown and developed and when the rights reverted back to me, I knew it needed revision. Among other things, I wanted a title that better suited the actual subject of the novel. Thus, *And The Beat Goes On* became *Conspiracy of Bones*.

The story itself remains the same. It is as ancient as its beginnings and as relevant as the belief in an all powerful Creator. Enjoy.

"And God saw that the wickedness of man was great in the earth, and that every imagination of the thoughts of his heart was only evil continually."

Genesis 6:5 KJV

PROLOGUE

Tom-tom... tom-tom... Pulsing... throbbing... the earth reverberated. Dancers leapt to the ancient rhythm, their half naked bodies, glistening with sweat in the firelight, twisted and arched as the primal beat called to the pulse within. Overhead, the display case of heaven sparkled, the diamonds large and brilliant against their black velvet nest. Accompanying this was a symphony of sound; a full choir of heavenly voices carried on the solar winds through the crystalline canopy of heaven to the sons of earth below.

The heavy scent of giant orchids, which bloomed along the outer perimeter of the temple gardens, mingled with the spices and perfumes that were thrown into the fire by the priestess. High above the ornate altar around which the dancers poured their carnal worship, a handsome, young, would-be king watched from his seat of honour. His heartbeat quickened, for he knew what was coming next. He had witnessed the ancient ritual as a child, when his own father had been crowned king. Had become a god.

Abruptly, the drum ceased. A hush swept through the crowd of onlookers who circled the stone platform. The dancers scattered. From out of the shadows marched twelve beasts. They were human in appearance except for the gigantic wings, leathery like those of a bat, which were folded across their backs and whose tips nearly touched the ground. Each man was tall and well muscled - the finest and bravest in the kingdom. They were the king's guard, especially chosen and groomed from boyhood; a privilege for only the strongest and bravest. They would accompany the king wherever he went - even to the grave. As descendants of the Nephilim - the race of giants born from the union of the gods and mortal women - they feared nothing; not even death.

The guards lined up on the large platform, facing the king, as the chief among them solemnly ascended the flight of stone steps that led from the altar to the king's throne. From here he had a good view of every spectacle. The guard saluted, turned, and gave the signal to the others.

With precision, the guards stepped back to form a corridor. The heretofore silent crowd could not help but murmur. A wave rippled through the masses as six burly slaves led the captive forward, shackled, hobbled, and muzzled. Even then, it was a struggle to get the huge beast prostrate upon the altar of sacrifice. Its beady eyes glistened as its leather wings twitched.

A priest came forward, gilded knife held high over the creature's heart. A slave released the muzzle that had kept the creature silent and the knife plunged directly into the heart of the animal as a piercing scream echoed through the forest, seeming to rebound from the canopy of the brilliant sky.

Other skilled workers moved quickly into place, and with a few precise cuts, the huge leather wings were removed. Next the head was severed, the brains neatly extracted, leaving only the long pointed beak, majestic red crest, and beady eyes intact.

Blood dripped from the newly hewn crown as it was placed reverently in the hands of the chief guard. With dignified solemnity, he carried the grisly trophy up the long stairway to the king. The priest followed closely on his heels. The prized headpiece was placed on the king's head, even as blood continued to drip from its depths onto his hair and beard. The priest, who had brought with him a goblet of the animal's blood rendered from its jugular vein, presented it to the sovereign. He whispered the ancient words of the deity into the king's bloody ear - an incantation not meant for mortals. Slowly the new sovereign raised the goblet to his lips. Without wavering he took a swallow from the cup, letting the blood trickle from the corners of his mouth. Lowering the goblet, his handsome face was suddenly spoiled by a malicious grin.

The priest stepped back as four others came bearing the wings, still attached as one piece by the skin of the creature's back. They were strong men, but even they let out a grunt as the heavy cape was settled onto the shoulders of the monarch. He thought for a moment he would not be able to bear the weight of it. Once the wings were properly cleaned and tanned, they would weight much less and he would be expected to wear them for all public ceremonies. But for this night, he must bear the full weight of the mantle, blood and all.

The blood, which the priest had mixed with some special herbs, was giving him new strength, however. And the words... those secret words passed down from the outer world of his ancestors... words which no human could hear... these also gave him power. He was one of them, now. A god among men.

He straightened majestically in his seat, as if the weight on his shoulders was nothing more than an ordinary cloak. He smiled a bloody smile, flashes of white peaking through the glistening red, and raised his hand in salute.

A cheer went up from the crowd. The heartbeat of the tom-tom was revived. People rushed forward to clap and dance around the flaming torches that skirted the perimeter of the platform as the dancers resumed their gyrations around the altar of incense. The tempo increased, as did the frenzied dancing. Some of the spectators began screaming and wailing; others tore at their clothing. Just when it seemed the festivities were about to turn into a full-fledged orgy, a trumpeting signal brought the writhing crowd to a standstill.

The guards remained steadily at their posts, circling the outer edge of the platform. The tom-tom took up another beat, this time methodical and solemn, as a priestess, waving a fragrant branch of flowers before her, led a procession from the darkness of the forest into the light of the torches and then up into the centre of the platform. With her were twenty-four maidens, all beautiful in their delicately fluttering garments; all virgins, never having set sight on a member of the male gender before this moment. They had been raised for this purpose; innocent, yet knowing that their lives held great significance. Now was the time of fulfillment.

The air was heavy with perspiration and heat, laced with tension and anticipation. The priestess finished her brief words of blessing. One word from the King now was all it would take.

With relish the newly crowned king surveyed the virgins. Beautiful, innocent and ripe, every one. His own lustful desires rose up and he grinned widely. He would have his pick at a later time, in the privacy of his own chambers.

Suddenly, a flashing sheet of light swept across the sky to the east, followed by a deep rumbling much like the mighty cascading noise of a waterfall. The crowd gasped in fear.

Perhaps it was a sign of approval from the gods, he thought. He hoped. Somewhere deep within he heard another voice. His father had told him once about a man - a lunatic - who had been building a boat from before his grandfather's time. He was a self proclaimed prophet and said that the earth was to be destroyed by a flood. It seemed ridiculous then and even more so now. The crazy man had been giving his warning for hundreds of years and nothing had happened yet. Besides, he was a god himself, now. He was absolute ruler, at least in this part of the world. His own ancestors had left the area where the lunatic lived long ago, partly in search of treasure; partly to get away from his teaching. They had settled far away in a prosperous and fertile land. And here they had been met by the gods.

As if in answer to his thoughts, another amazing spectacle lit the sky. This time it was a giant forked bolt of light, followed by an even louder crash. The people gasped again; someone even screamed. He must take control. With a lion like roar, the king lifted his arm, giving the signal. "The gods are pleased! Let the ceremony continue!"

The guards, who had previously been standing at attention around the perimeter of the platform, suddenly jumped into action. Without any delicacy or ceremony, they charged at the group of maidens, grabbing their chosen prey and proceeding to rape them with violence and brutality right before the gaping crowd of onlookers. The mob cheered on encouragement as the fetid orgy continued before their eyes on the platform. Potential escapees were thrown back into the arena for more, as each man exercised his rights to the full. Before long, many onlookers joined in the debauchery; some willingly, others not. It did not matter. This was one night when anything and everything was acceptable. The king looked on in sadistic pleasure, hungry lust burning within his own loins. But gods had control over their desires. He must remember that. His time would come later.

Another sheet of lightning crashed along the horizon, illuminating the spectacle below. This was followed by a forked bolt, spectacular in its intensity and brilliance. Some of the people started to scatter in fear; others seemed to be spurred on. The king ignored the uncertainty in his own heart. With another roar, he stood with outstretched arms and shouted his approval.

"And God looked upon the earth, and, behold, it was corrupt; for all flesh had corrupted his way upon the earth. And God said unto Noah, the end of all flesh is come before me; for the earth is filled with violence through them; and, behold, I will destroy them with the earth."

Genesis 6: 12-13 KJV

CHAPTER 1

The African sun beat down on the open jeep as Dr. Mark Graham and his companion bumped along what could hardly be called a road. A local man from the Nbedele tribe, hired on as part of the archaeological team, drove the jeep along the hazardous path up the mountain. Hair raising switchbacks and steep inclines didn't seem to faze the driver as he manoeuvred the vehicle with one hand. Some pebbles cascaded off the trail's edge to the ravine below. Good thing he was used to it, Mark decided, or he might be tempted to bail.

As he braced himself for the next jarring pothole, Mark thought about yesterday's meeting with the Zimbabwean government officials. Everything had gone well - on the surface, at least. They had agreed to continue their sponsorship. Yet there was this nagging sense at the back of his mind that something rippled beneath the surface - something hidden either by neglect or design of which he was not aware. It was an uncomfortable feeling. Probably just his general distaste for dealing with administrators. It rankled when unnecessary red tape got in the way of progress.

His crew had been meticulously digging under the site of an

ancient temple - a sacred site stringently protected by the government. The temple site itself had been unearthed decades before,
but legend had led to speculation that an even older civilization
had once used the spot. Mark had been honoured when asked to
assemble a team of specialists to investigate the possibilities
without compromising the original excavations. It was
painstaking work. But already, after only five months, the team
was rewarded with signs that the legends were indeed rooted in
fact. Under the temple mound they had discovered an even more
ancient burial ground with an intricate system of tombs that
seemed oddly more advanced technologically than the layer of
simple graves directly above. This was not entirely unexpected;
history often spoke of a more barbarous people supplanting a
superior civilization. But there was more. So much more. There
was a sense that they were on the verge of something big - monu-
mental, even.

And then the authorities had the audacity to question
whether there was any use continuing! They said they were
running out of budget and it was taking too long. Fools! Didn't
they know there was no way to unearth secrets that had been
buried for millennium in just a few short months? These things
took time and care. And money.

That was the bottom line. Always was. Mark wished he had
the benefit of some nice multi-trillionaire benefactor. Oh well.
For now he had managed to secure another four month contract,
having convinced the officials of the importance of the find to
the economic development of the region. But in the end, he
doubled it would be enough time. He was a scientist, not a
magician.

As the jeep rounded the last corner, Mark spotted one of the
tents that had been set up on site as a lab. The archaeological site
extended over a fairly large area. Several tents and simple wooden
structures had been erected to house the necessary workstations
and accommodate the crew. Square sections had been roped off

for the painstaking process of uncovering tidbits of information, one grain of sand at a time.

Mark jumped from the jeep into the cloud of gathering dust and strode directly to the quarters where he expected to find his co-worker, Laura Sawchuk. He left his bags for his Nbedelian assistant.

He had left Laura in charge during his brief absence. Laura Sawchuk, Doctor of Anthropology, was very knowledgeable in a wide field and was also very capable at giving direction and leadership. She had been his colleague on more than one job and he trusted her judgment and skill for the task at hand. She was also, at present, his girlfriend.

Girlfriend had a somewhat adolescent ring to it, Mark decided. His 'partner' would be a more appropriate phrase - it was the terminology Laura used, anyway. Mark wasn't quite sure how their relationship had advanced to more than just colleagues. Close proximity did that to people sometimes. And loneliness.

He found Laura examining a fragment under a microscope. She didn't look up when he entered. At 36 she was a couple of years older than he was. Her career always came first; a fact that suited Mark, since he shared her passion for work.

He strode to where she sat and tried to get a glimpse over her shoulder at the tiny fragment. "What have we here?"

"Hello to you, too." She didn't look up. "I thought you were going to be back yesterday."

"I was delayed an extra day in Harare." Mark pulled up a stool and sat down beside her.

"Oh? That good news or bad?" she asked.

"Good. I managed to convince them to give us another four months."

"Four months?" Laura straightening and looked at Mark for the first time since he had arrived. "We can't possibly be finished in four months." She reached over and flicked a stray twig from his unruly mass of dark curls.

"I know that." Mark ran a hand through his hair, creating a small cloud of dust. "But I had to take it or leave it."

Laura leaned forward and placed a quick kiss on Mark's nose, her streaked brown and blonde ponytail bobbing. "Good to have you back, in any case. Mnanga didn't kill you, I see, with his reckless driving."

Mark grinned. "Still in one piece, miracle as that is. What you looking at, anyway?"

"A fragment from some of the plaster leading into the antechamber I told you about." Laura turned back to the microscope. "It seems to have some kind of metal alloy embedded in it."

"Plaster?" Mark's brows furrowed.

Laura nodded. "I'm not sure what else to call it. A coating of some kind. Unusual, I know."

"Very," Mark agreed. "Most tombs are simply hewn from the rock, not plastered over. Mind if I take a look?" Laura relinquished her seat and Mark took his turn peering into the microscope. "Hm. I see what you mean. I've never seen anything like it." He couldn't help keeping the disappointment from his voice. He had wanted to be the first into the chamber.

"Don't worry. We haven't made a breakthrough into the chamber itself yet. I knew you'd be disappointed not to be here, so we've held back a bit."

"Thanks. I appreciate it." Mark continued to peruse the tiny fragment.

"Besides, there's been plenty of other excitement to keep us busy."

"Like?"

"The bone fragments."

"Still no word from the lab?" He already knew the answer. He'd checked back in Harare.

"No, but we're starting to see a pattern."

Mark's curiosity was really pricked now. He looked up. "What kind of pattern?"

"Come and see," Laura said, leaving the plaster fragment behind for the time being. She led Mark to a computer station. She sat down in front of the screen and clicked several icons with the mouse. A large blueprint of the dig appeared on the screen. "The strange bone fragments we found first were located here." She pointed to the location with her finger. "Alongside the human remains that appear to have been disturbed - either by some type of seismic activity, or by other humans."

Mark nodded. "Mmhm." It was nothing new to him. He had been present during that discovery. "Go on."

"The next grave we uncovered also contained unidentified bone fragments. Only this time..." she paused for effect. She glanced over at him, ready to gauge his reaction. He raised his brows in question. "I'll bring up a digital photo," she said, clicking the mouse deftly once again. Several windows opened. "Ah, here we are." She punched one more key and a colour photo came up of a long curved bone. It was broken in two places, with part of the inner section missing. She hit another key and a second picture came up. This time it showed Laura and Rocco, one of the crew managers, holding the bone between them.

Mark whistled. "That's one big chicken wing."

"Then you agree that it looks like part of a wing?" Laura asked, surveying him closely.

Mark blinked and peered at the image again. "Yes... it does, doesn't it?"

"The humorous is almost entirely intact, with parts of the ulna attached. It looks to be from a very large winged creature. The parts that are left clearly seem to have been placed with the body, intentionally."

"How large?"

"Pretty darn big, that's all I have to say. Bigger than an albatross or any present species of bird that I know of."

"You know what this means, don't you?" Mark looked over at Laura, obvious excitement burning in his eyes. "We've discovered another Troy - an ancient legend thought to be nothing more than myth." He pounded the computer table and the monitor flickered momentarily.

"Watch it," Laura warned with a smile. "Our power supply isn't the most stable."

"What else you got?" Mark asked.

"Rocco's team has been continuing on those same graves. He may find the other 'wing', so to speak, and by the look of the placement of those two graves, we're speculating there could be a whole ring of graves surrounding the entrance to the antechamber." She paused. "Providing you want to disturb them."

"Hmm. Like guards." Mark rubbed his chin, two days worth of stubble rasping under his fingers.

"Right. Here's another interesting find from the same grave." Laura pointed to the next photo. "It appears to be some kind of head piece or mask, probably worn expressly for burial. It's pretty badly decayed and was in danger of disintegrating into dust if we tried to remove it."

Mark just stared at the screen.

"I know what you're thinking." Laura interrupted his thoughts. "About that legend. Don't go spreading rumours until the lab has done a full analysis. I've had a hard enough time convincing Rocco to keep his feet on the ground. You know how he can be. We could all be discredited if we aren't careful. First we need solid lab work on both the human and non human fragments."

"No need to remind me about procedure, Doctor," Mark stated in a business like tone. "I am still chief archaeologist on this dig."

"Of course." Laura gave Mark a sideways glance. "I wasn't trying to offend you. You seem awfully touchy."

Mark sighed and ran a hand through his unruly hair. "I guess I'm just tired after the trip."

"Your nerves shot after Mnanga's driving?" Laura offered.

"Right," Mark agreed with a chuckle. "Plus, I hate being out of the loop. I feel like all the important discoveries are being made when I'm gone."

"You need to relax." Laura stood up and moved to stand behind him. She began kneading his neck with her fingers.

"IIᴜ... that feels good." Mark closed his eyes.

"I can make it feel even better later," Laura said with a suggestive smile.

"Oh? Definitely worth coming back for." Mark allowed her fingers to do their magic on the stiff cords in his neck. Suddenly he opened his eyes. "I'd like to take a look, myself." He straightened, all business again. "At that bone. It's been stored and numbered with the rest of the artefacts?"

"Of course." Laura dropped her hands. "I just thought you might want to wait and start fresh tomorrow."

"With only four months grace, I don't think we can spare the time." He rose and turned to leave.

Laura stopped him with a hand on his shoulder. "Mark?"

"Hm?" He turned.

"I missed you."

His nod of acknowledgement was barely perceptible as he headed out the door.

———

Mark strode to where he hoped to find Rocco Cortez, one of the project's crew chiefs, making his way past various aspects of the site. By far, the dominant feature was the ancient temple ruins. It had been reconstructed in places and consisted of an outer and an inner courtyard, with the chambers of the temple itself in the centre. The building had been made from rock quarried from the surrounding area. Mostly what was left, after being uncovered, was the foundation, with only a few walls remaining intact. But the location of the altar and several other important features could be clearly identified. The original archaeological excavations had taken place over thirty years ago. What Mark and his team were interested in now was not the temple itself, but what lay hidden far beneath it.

This type of excavating was very painstaking and precise. In order to get at the layers beneath without disturbing the top layer, the team had to tunnel underneath using an elaborate system of braces, all the while ensuring that they did not destroy a potentially important find. They started well away from the temple mound itself, creating a crater like moat around one side of the site. From here they could open up the side of the hill underneath, exposing subsequent layers as they went. It was backbreaking work with an element of risk, but the thrill of discovery outweighed the drawbacks.

"Rocco!" Mark called when he spotted the other man. Rocco was a short, somewhat stocky man of Puerto Rican descent. He wore his greying hair in a haphazard ponytail, and sported a thick black moustache. "I hear there have been some exciting discoveries in my absence," Mark said once he had reached his colleague.

"She showed you the photos?" Rocco asked.

"Yeah. Pretty amazing."

"See the real thing yet?"

"Just heading over there now." The two men started walking together toward the storage and cataloguing compound. "So what do you think?"

Rocco shrugged noncommittally. "You probably don't want to know."

"I trust your judgment."

"At least someone does," Rocco muttered.

Mark slapped the older man across the back. "Don't let Laura scare you. She's just cautious. It's her way." He smiled. "She even warned me about keeping the discovery under wraps until the final analysis report comes in. So, what do you think?"

"It's obvious. In keeping with local legend, plus the size, shape and wing span..." Rocco paused and surveyed his boss out of the corner of his eye.

"So you seriously think we've unearthed the remains of a long extinct variety of flying dinosaur?"

Rocco nodded. "Very Pterodactyl like. I've seen them before."

Mark let out a small disbelieving laugh. "No wonder Laura is so paranoid. The sooner we get a positive ID, the better. I just wish I'd been around personally to document the whole thing."

"You don't trust us?"

"I didn't say that. It's just that this could either be the biggest scientific discovery of the century or the biggest hoax. We'll either be famous or look like laughing stocks." Mark glanced over at Rocco's unsmiling profile. "Any slip in procedure and we could be completely discredited."

"They'll try it, don't even fool yourself into thinking they won't."

Mark raised an eyebrow. "You sound pretty sceptical. And who are they?"

"The establishment."

"The establishment," Mark repeated, his tone flat.

"Yeah. In this case, the scientific community. They accept only what fits into their own preconceived theories. Anything outside the box gets tossed."

"That's hardly fair." Mark shook his head, a smirk creeping unbidden to his lips. "If that's the case, we might as well pack up right now and go home."

Rocco pointed a finger at Mark as they continued to walk. "You laugh now, my friend, but you'll find out soon enough. The capitalist regime that rules us all. Money. Profit. Bottom line.

That's where the real power is. We're all just pawns in a big game of chess."

"Someone definitely put something nasty in your cereal this morning," Mark said with an outright laugh.

"I'm serious." Rocco stopped walking and crossed his arms over his chest.

The grin faded from Mark's lips. "I know. That's what worries me."

Rocco's eyes twitched; his countenance remained grim. Without another word, he strode forward. Mark followed in silent contemplation until they reached the compound, a large canvas structure. Rocco stopped at the entrance and gestured for Mark to enter first. Mark greeted the guard with a perfunctory nod and bent his head in order to clear the low doorway. Rocco followed closely on his heels.

"It's numbered and documented right along with everything else from my quadrant. I did it myself." Rocco pointed to the right in the dim interior of the make shift compound. It consisted of rows of metal shelving lined with labelled trays and clear plastic bags of artefacts. "Right there." He searched the area with his eyes, squinting. "What the... it was here yesterday. I knew you'd want to do the preliminary lab work yourself. What did she do with it?" He let out a string of expletives in Spanish.

"Who do you mean? Laura?"

"Has anything been crated for transport to the States yet?" Rocco demanded, ignoring the initial question.

"Is that what she suggested?"

"Yep. I told her to wait until you got back. I told her you'd want to see it for yourself." Rocco shook his head.

"I take it you two had some disagreements on the subject." Mark crossed his arms.

Rocco frowned, flashing Mark a quick glance. "You could say that."

"What else has been going on in my absence?" Mark's mouth

formed a grim line. He wasn't feeling too happy at the moment. Laura had just finished telling him she had saved the bone for him to look at. Why would she lie to him about it?

"Go ask your second in command. She'll tell you whatever you want to hear, I'm sure."

"I don't like the sounds of this. The last thing I need are my two most valuable crew members at logger heads with one another."

Rocco just shrugged. "I just did my job. Numbered and documented, just like it's supposed to be. Talk to her if you want answers."

"I intend to," Mark ground out.

He turned and strode from the compound.

CHAPTER 2

"We need to talk," Mark announced as he stomped into the lab where Laura was working.

"About what?" Laura asked casually, continuing with her work. She was calibrating some measurements on a chart that was spread open before her.

"I think you probably already know." Mark stopped beside her desk and folded his arms. "I just came from talking to Rocco."

"And what kind of hype is he spouting now?"

"He seemed surprised that you'd sent away the bone sample. He said he'd already catalogued it and had advised you to wait for me." There was just a hint of accusation in his voice.

"Sent away the sample? What are you talking about?" Laura looked up questioningly.

"You didn't send the bone away for detailed testing?"

"No. Why would I do that? I knew you'd want a look at it." Laura shrugged. "Besides, that's not procedure. We'll crate the items we think can't wait and send them together. Although I'm not sure I want that particular item to get out of my sight." Her eyes narrowed in sudden understanding. "I suppose Rocco's been making up nonsense again. That man has an authority issue."

"Really? I hadn't noticed."

"Because you're a man. He doesn't like taking orders from a woman." Laura gave Mark a withering look.

Mark pulled out a stool and sat down, some of his earlier anger dissipating. "I heard you two had some disagreements while I was away."

"Nothing I couldn't handle." Laura flipped her ponytail. "Although by the sounds of it he hasn't let it go. What's he accusing me of now?"

"The wing bone. It's not in the compound." Mark eyed her closely, gauging her reaction.

"What?" Laura's eyes widened and her gaze swung to Mark. "Where is it?"

Her surprise seemed genuine, which only made him feel more unsettled. "I was hoping you could tell me."

"And he said I sent it away?" Her eyes narrowed and she shook her head "Figures. Thanks for believing in me, by the way."

"Sorry." Mark broke eye contact. He sighed and rubbed his chin. "There must be an explanation. I'll go back through the compound myself with a fine-toothed comb. He probably just forgot where he put it." Somehow Mark doubted it. Rocco was always thorough and professional. A mistake of this magnitude was not typical of him. But what other explanation could there be?

Laura interrupted his thoughts. "He's gone way over the deep end this time. He was carrying on about dinosaurs and the coexistence of people. Then he got on to international conspiracies and cover-ups - it was starting to freak some of the crew. You know how tenuous our position is here. One bit of bad press and we'll be shut down."

"It would never come to that." Mark said it as much to convince himself as Laura.

"No? Well, I don't trust Rocco. The guy is nuts. I seriously have doubts about his stability - and his credibility. As head of this thing, you might want to look into it." She challenged him with her eyes.

"Are you suggesting I fire him?" Mark asked.

"You do what you think you have to," she stated firmly, her gaze not wavering from his.

Mark looked away and rubbed the back of his neck. "Rocco's an important part of this team. He's experienced and knows his stuff. I'll bet he's worked on more digs that you and I combined - and seen a lot more, too." He glanced back at Laura but her features hadn't softened.

"He's seen too much. In fact, I think he's starting to see things, as in hallucinate."

"You mean all the dinosaur stuff," Mark stated.

"Exactly. Who in their right mind would even entertain something so ridiculous?"

"Well, Rocco says -"

"Stop!" Laura interjected, putting up her hands. "Dinosaurs and man did not coexist. We know that. It's been proven. So don't even go there." She crossed her arms over her chest. "You're scaring me," she added.

"Hey." Mark stood up and went behind her. He rubbed her arms with his hands and felt her stiffen. "I didn't say I believed it. But I'm not afraid to test my own theories. It's what science is all about." He kissed the top of her head.

"We'll let the evidence speak for itself." Laura looked over her shoulder at him and then launched off the stool and strode from the room.

"Exactly what I intend," Mark said with a sigh.

———

The sun rose and set abruptly in the mountains. And darkness meant one thing. Suppertime. Mark crunched his way over the sand and gravel to the large, army style tent that was the kitchen and dining hall. A string of electric light bulbs, hanging limply in front of the tent, helped light the way. The pulsing of diesel generators was a constant sound in the background. It disturbed the peace of the otherwise remote location, but was necessary to keep power up and running.

Mark greeted several crew members as he took his place in the cafeteria line. Local cooks had been hired for the task, and the food was not fancy; standard backwoods fare that filled your stomach and kept you going through the long, physically taxing days.

He found a spot at one of the long tables beside Laura. She glanced his way but kept on eating without greeting him. She was still angry and he couldn't blame her. He dug into his own plate of food.

Rocco joined them a few minutes later. "Hello, boss." Rocco eased in beside Mark. "Laura," he added with a nod.

Laura barely acknowledged him with a flick of her eyes.

"So, did you hear that Sam is getting married next week?" Rocco said before shovelling some mashed potatoes into his mouth.

"No," Mark replied, taking a bite of his own rather watery potatoes.

A wily grin appeared under Rocco's bushy moustache. "I guess he only had to promise two cows instead of the traditional three for the bride."

Laura leaned forward to peer past Mark at Rocco. "You're kidding, right?"

Rocco just laughed. "You know what they say about these local girls."

"That is so racist and you know it," Laura objected with a disgusted tone.

"What about you, boss?" Rocco asked slyly. "Why don't you

pick yourself one of the locals for a bride? With your reputation, you could probably get away with only one cow."

Mark tried to smile, not really enjoying Rocco's obvious sadistic pleasure in the turn of the conversation. "I'm not ready for marriage." He avoided Laura's gaze and concentrated instead on his meal.

"I don't know," Rocco said reflectively. "I always figured if I was to fall in love it would just hit me. Smack!" He clapped his hands together. "Right between the eyes and I wouldn't know what happened."

"Trouble is, who in the world would return the sentiment?" Laura raised an eyebrow.

"Hey, look at this face. Who wouldn't fall for this face?" Rocco looked from one to the other. "What? It could happen."

"The idea of love at first sight is absolutely ridiculous." Laura pointed at Rocco with her fork. "It's a myth."

Mark furrowed his own brows. "I don't know about that. That's the way it happened for my folks, or so I'm told."

"Really? I can hardly believe it – with you for a son." Rocco said.

"Thanks," Mark said with a rueful grin.

Laura smiled for the first time. "He has a point. You're about as romantic as the bones you study."

"I thought you liked my bones." Mark grinned.

"Speaking of bones," Rocco said, "tomorrow I'll get my men to open up another Joe." Rocco was referring to the human remains still encased in their burial cells.

"Is that necessary?" Laura flipped her hair back off her shoulders. "You know the policy to leave as many graves undisturbed as possible."

"I think, under the circumstances, it is necessary," Mark said. Rocco beamed.

Laura shrugged. "You're the boss. And keeping that in mind,

maybe you should be the one to open the 'Joe', as Rocco so eloquently puts it. At least with you in charge, there shouldn't be any questions about procedure." She gave Rocco a scathing glance.

"Agreed. Although, I want to be present when we break inside that chamber for the first time, too."

"Fine." Laura went back to pushing her food around on the plate. "The place has been there for a few thousand years already. I'm sure a few extra days won't make much difference."

Mark decided to leave the subject at that. "We'll decide on a plan of action in the morning. I've made too many miles today to make any more decisions tonight."

———

Later that night, as Mark lay beside Laura on his narrow cot, he was surprised by his inability to sleep. He had been physically exhausted before they'd made love, but now he was wide awake. He eased his arm out from under Laura's head, and carefully hoisted himself from the cot. He was just pulling on his jeans when she stirred.

"I guess I should go back to my own tent," she mumbled, turning over. She didn't seem in any hurry. Everyone knew about their relationship, and even though things were a lot more casual out in the field, they still maintained their own quarters.

This change in the status of their relationship had only recently developed. They had been acquainted for a number of years. The archaeological field was a fairly tight community, even worldwide. Laura came from Australia but they had met first at a site in Arizona. It was a Navajo burial site - Mark's personal specialty. They remained connected through conferences and various other job related functions until Mark had requested Laura's expertise on a particular dig in South America. She had agreed and now this was the third job site that she had joined him on since.

They'd been together so much in the past few years it seemed inevitable that their relationship take on a more personal nature. He just hoped she wouldn't read too much into it. Then again, this was Laura he was talking about. If anything, he should be more worried about his own sense of emotional attachment.

Mark sat down on the one folding chair and reached for the saxophone case that sat propped against the tent wall. He gently removed the instrument and fingered it fondly in the darkness.

"What you got there?" Laura asked, sitting up half way.

"Hm?" Mark asked absently. "Oh. My saxophone."

"I didn't know you played."

There was a lot she didn't know, Mark brooded silently. "I don't really. At least not well. It belonged to my grandfather. Jack Burton." He checked to see if the name meant anything to her. Apparently not.

"So you keep it around for sentimental reasons?"

"I guess. It's my one connection to home." Mark carefully placed the instrument back in its velveteen bed and shut the case with a click. "You never heard of him?"

"Who?"

"My grandfather. Jack Burton. He used to be a pretty famous jazz musician in his day."

"I was never really much into music," she said. "He still alive?"

"Last I heard," he replied with a wistful smile. It struck Mark suddenly how very little they knew about one another outside the field. He looked over at the woman sitting on his cot, wearing nothing more than a sheet. "What's your take on marriage? Commitment?"

Laura blinked in surprise. "Where did that come from?"

Mark shrugged. "I'm not sure. Maybe thinking about Jack got me thinking about home which got me thinking about my folks..."

"Ah." Laura nodded. "The love at first sight pair."

"Yeah." Mark laughed and looked down at the case in his lap.

"I can hardly believe they spawned the likes of you," she teased. She sat up and hugged her knees.

"Well they didn't, really. Deanie is my stepmother. My Dad married her when I was about twelve. It was just he and I before that."

"What happened to your own mum?"

Mark shook his head. "I'm not quite sure. Apparently she took off when I was quite young. Never met her."

"Oh. I see." Her gaze flickered away.

"What about your family?" Mark set the case on the floor by the chair. "Any brothers and sisters?" He was amazed they had never had this conversation before. What kind of a man expected sex but didn't even know anything about the woman who shared his bed?

"Just me," Laura said. "My Mum and Dad were quite a bit older when they had me, so I don't have any other known living relatives. Maybe a cousin in Sydney, but I've never really kept in touch. You?"

"I have one sister, Harmony. She's quite a bit younger than me, obviously. I did my share of babysitting - her and the other musicians' kids while they were out doing concerts."

"Concerts? What do you mean?"

Mark smiled, remembering. "My stepmother used to be in a band. I used to get stuck babysitting a lot while they were out rehearsing or performing."

"Interesting."

"I spent a lot of time with Jack in those years, too. My Grandpa. Well, my step-grandfather. We became very close, though." He paused. He had treasured those days. Now they seemed a million years ago. He hadn't had much time for family recently. Too busy digging into the past.

"You're scaring me with all this sentiment," Laura said with a slight laugh.

"Sorry." Mark tried to smile and glanced back at Laura.

"You're still worried about that missing bone." It was more a statement that a question.

Mark latched on to the excuse gladly. "Shouldn't I be? It's not like Rocco to be so careless."

"I told you. Rocco's beginning to slip in more ways than one."

Mark cocked his head to the side. "What if it is some kind of conspiracy, like he says? What if someone is out to sabotage the site?"

"I really doubt that." Laura shook her head. "Although, I have heard some of the local workers talking about the dangers of tampering with the dead. Maybe someone is trying to scare us off for superstitious reasons."

"I hadn't considered that. But who?"

"It's probably nothing." Laura rose from the cot, pulling the sheet around her like a toga and strolled around behind his chair. "You're way too tense." She massaged his shoulders and then bent over and kissed his neck.

Mark turned his head and gave Laura a quick peck on the cheek, then disentangled himself from her hold as he rose from the chair. He wasn't in the mood for any more tonight. "What about the fact that that wing bone looks a lot like a Pterodactyl? Found with human remains?"

Laura sighed, coming around to sit on the chair herself as she reached for her errant clothing. "There's probably a very logical explanation for it." She pulled on her jeans. "Whoever belongs to those human remains probably also had access to some dinosaur bones. They were probably used as part of their burial ritual and are not contemporaneous. Dating will clear it all up, I'm sure."

"I hope." Mark rubbed the back of his neck and lowered himself onto the cot. He opened his mouth in an over exaggerated yawn. "I'm beat."

Laura's eyelashes fluttered downward. "Right. I'd better get back to my own bed and get some sleep."

Mark flopped onto his back after she'd gone and crossed his arms behind his head. Too many conflicting feelings were running around inside of him. Laura, Rocco, dinosaur bones... What was really happening here?

CHAPTER 3

At six am sharp God turned the light bulb on. At least that's how it seemed. There were no drawn out dusky shades to the morning. Near the equator it was either night or it was day. Mark rose at his usual 5:45 and met Rocco shortly after he'd had his breakfast.

"Hey, Boss. You're up and ready, I see," Rocco said.

"Absolutely. Your team ready to go? I'm anxious to get started. Show me where you uncovered those first set of bones."

Rocco led the way into the side of the crater that had been created beside the temple mound. Elaborate cross beams held the hill intact as they went deeper into the wide tunnel that led below. Legend had it that a mighty race of kings had been buried here, long before the ancients that had built the temple. It appeared they might have found evidence to prove it was true.

The team had uncovered an elaborate system of tombs, carved deep into the side of the mountain. The main tunnel had been blocked off by what appeared to be a mudslide. A thick layer of sediment had hardened over the entrance and it was only by chance that Mark and Rocco had noticed enough irregularity in the pattern of the swirling layers of rock to investigate further. Once this had been cut away, the tomb appeared to be part of a natural cave, the height and breadth of which varied substantially from one part to the next. Branching off from this main artery were several smaller tunnels, only high enough to crawl through. These all led back to the main tunnel, but within each were carved shelves upon which human remains had been laid and then sealed with tightly fitting rock plugs. Rocco and his team had opened the first encasement while Mark was away. It's where they'd found the surprising contents.

Rocco led the way to the open grave. The remains had not yet been removed, lying in grim testament to a former life long since expended. Mark wasn't ready to make an estimate on the age of the find yet, but the skeleton was in surprisingly good shape, considering. He took note of the large frame; at least seven feet tall; and the strange headdress, which, as Laura had pointed out, was very fragile.

"You've taken all the measurements?" Mark asked, barely above a whisper. A sacred stillness enveloped them and he felt the need to keep his voice down.

"Naturally."

"Just checking. And the wing bone? Where was it?"

Rocco pointed. "Here. You can still see the depression of the wing in the dust. I've taken all those measurements, too."

"Good." Mark peered more closely at the indentation the bone had made and the soft markings around it that implied more than just a bone had rested there. "Nothing seems to be disturbed. Like there hasn't been a breath of wind in here for millennia."

"You ready to open the next one?" he asked.

"Ready when you are," Rocco said.

Rocco, and Mark worked together to unseal another tomb, chiselling away at the mortar around the stones used to block the opening.

Mark stopped to wipe his brow with his sleeve. "Tell me more about your theory, Rocco. What do you think we've actually discovered here?"

"It's obvious," Rocco stated without hesitation. "Those wings bones are from a Pterodactyl."

"Dinosaurs died out long before humans," Mark countered.

"Maybe, maybe not." Rocco shrugged.

"What makes you say that?"

"I've been on digs before. Seen things. Things that nobody wanted to face up to." Rocco held Mark's gaze.

"Give me an example." Mark started chiselling again.

"Okay. Like the time I was working on a dig in Texas. Found dinosaur tracks and human tracks in the same valley."

"I heard about that." Mark huffed as he continued working. "I thought it was established that the human tracks were a fraud. Somebody carved them."

"That's what they want people to think." Rocco pointed his chisel at Mark. "And who knows, maybe some funny guy thought he'd sabotage the dig that way. Maybe it worked, too."

"And your point?"

"That was only one set of tracks. I saw others with my own eyes. I helped uncover and measure them." Rocco eyes had a glint, even in the relatively dim light. "But who is left to believe it except those of us who were there? Too many sceptics were just looking for a way to discredit the site."

"Okay, so that's one example," Mark conceded. "There could be any number of explanations. Certainly not proof enough on its own."

"There are others. Lots of them."

"If that's the case, why aren't they documented?"

"They are," Rocco replied, "but nobody in the scientific community wants to touch them."

"I can see why," Mark said wryly.

"Which is exactly what happened the last time."

"What last time?"

"The time they found actual skeletal remains along with dinosaur remains."

"You mean human skeletal remains." Mark gave Rocco a sidelong glance, his muscles still working to carefully break the seal.

"Of course. What'd ya think I meant?"

"Just checking."

"I've been doin' my research. Ever since the time in Texas, I've been keeping track. There are a lot more of these types of finds than you'll ever read about in a scientific journal." Rocco hesitated. "I can see you think I'm nuts. Loco in the head. I'm no religious wing nut, you know."

"Never said anything about religion." Mark shrugged.

"Most people do. The two seem to go hand in hand."

They worked silently for a few more minutes. Rocco was agitated, of that Mark was certain. He'd never seen the other man so passionate before.

"I think this is loose enough to move," Rocco said with a grunt.

Mark and Rocco carefully shimmied the block from its resting place and set it on the dirt at their feet. Mark knelt before the freshly opened tomb, the stale air reaching out to greet his nostrils. He shone the light from his high beam torch into the cavern and his breath caught in his throat.

"Pretty impressive wing span, eh?" Rocco peered over Mark's shoulder.

It was just how Laura had described it. The human skeleton lay perfectly intact, horizontal with hands folded over the rig cage. It was a very tall specimen, Mark noted; even longer in length than the last had been. Perhaps even eight feet tall. Remnants of a headdress clung to the skull; bits of tanned leather, and a long, fragile armature that could have been a beak. Most impressive, though, were the set of wings, long since disintegrated to nothing more than bones, that had been obviously folded over the body like a shroud. They would have covered the man, as large as he was, from chin to toes.

Mark finally found his voice. "We'll remove the remains in their entirety for analysis. I think this is unusual enough to warrant opening more tombs, as well. All of them if we have to, to get to the bottom of this."

Rocco reached into the opening with a long set of tweezers. "Check this out." He lifted a gold chain and pendant from the chest cavity and gingerly pulled it out. He held the piece of jewellery up for examination. Though covered with dust, it was definitely gold.

Mark scrutinized the pendant then looked into Rocco's eyes, which were shining with vindication. It looked like a perfectly fashioned flying reptile, wings outspread and beak open. "It doesn't prove anything. We'll wait for the analysis."

"You'll send these away?" Rocco asked.

"Not till after I've examined them thoroughly myself," Mark assured, "and not until I have another set locked away somewhere for safe keeping. I'm not letting anything else get out of my sight."

Rocco agreed with a nod.

"And Rocco," Mark added, "just for security sake, in case this does turn out to be something... unexpected... let's not sound any alarm bells. I want everything perfectly and precisely documented until we know for sure. Got it?"

Rocco nodded. "Gotcha."

Later, Mark had time to examine the bones himself. They were hollow, like a typical bird's, but had the distinctly elongated fourth finger of a flying reptile. They were also very large, with an estimated wingspan of 20 feet, although in comparison to the human, 'large' was a relative term. Maybe things just grew big back in those days. As to the age of the find, that was still a mystery. So far no other artefacts lined up with any other known eras in human civilization. He was anxious to do his own set of dating tests as well.

Laura entered the lab and sauntered to Mark's workstation. "I hear you're opening up the entire burial site, wholesale."

Mark glanced her way and then back at the bones spread out on the table. "Considering the unique quality of what we've found so far, it would be negligent not to."

"The government might not see it that way." Laura lifted her chin. "Part of the agreement was to keep disturbance of the original temple to a minimum."

"I'm well aware of our agreement," Mark stated, "and so far have complied. We're digging under the temple, not through it."

"But the agreement also states that graves must not be unduly tampered with beyond what is reasonable - "

"I know what the agreement states." Mark set the tweezers he was using on the table with a distinct clack and held her gaze until she looked down. "And under the circumstances, I feel I'm doing only what is reasonable." He sighed and removed his surgical gloves, slapping them down beside the tweezers. "This could be the biggest find in the history of modern archaeology." When she didn't respond he stood up and placed his hands on her upper arms, forcing her to look at him. "What if those are Pterodactyl bones? The people of Northern Zimbabwe have a long-standing oral tradition that includes reptilian like flying creatures. What if they didn't die out with the rest of the dinosaurs? What if some dinosaurs did survive to coexist with men?"

She pulled away from his grasp and turned her back. "You can't possibly believe -"

He cut her off again. "Think about it. Every culture has legends about giant reptiles; dragons and such. What if there's some truth to it? Most legend has at least a small basis of truth to it. We'd never have discovered the ancient city of Troy without believing the legend first."

"Sounds like you're trying to convince yourself." Laura's tone was sceptical.

"What if the lab results come back and verify Rocco's claims? What if they are Pterodactyl bones?"

"Rocco!" Laura fairly spat the name. "The man is a lunatic. If not for him and his crazy ideas, nobody would have even considered anything of the kind."

"If that's the case, the lab results will clearly show it. Once those bones are sent it's out of our hands, anyway."

Laura's eyelashes fluttered nervously. "Then why bother opening more tombs? We've got all the evidence we need."

"All the evidence you need, you mean. But not near enough evidence to satisfy this cowboy." He held her gaze for a moment, his mouth a straight line.

Laura's arms flopped to her sides and she let out an exasperated sigh. "Why are you being stubborn about this?"

"Why are you?" he countered.

She turned on her heel and scurried from the lab, her ponytail flying out behind her.

Mark watched her retreating figure and then turned back to the bones. Maybe he was being stubborn, but sometimes truth demanded it.

CHAPTER 4

Several more tombs were opened, revealing a distinct pattern. Each grave housed a very large human specimen with the same 'wing bones' and headdress carefully placed with the body. A few other pieces of gold ornamentation were also found, usually depicting a winged creature of sorts, either in flight or standing at attention.

Progress had also been made at unblocking the entrance to the inner chamber. It appeared as if an earthquake or some other natural disaster had blocked the entrance itself. Several members of the team had been working diligently around the site with brushes and baggies, lest they find any tidbits worth bringing to the surface. The day finally arrived when they were ready to break the final seal to the entrance and investigate the inner room itself.

A reverent hush enveloped the crew as the last stone was carefully removed. Laura, Rocco and Anthony Vanguard, the resident expert on legends of the South Western regions of Africa, stood ready. Mark stepped carefully over the portal and shone his lantern into the depths of the room.

"Look at the walls," Laura gasped. They gave off an eerie glow, similar to the florescence of white walls under black light, only green in hue. Elaborate paintings covering every surface jumped forward.

"What's making it glow like that?" Anthony peered through his wire-rimmed glasses. His hair stuck out at odd angles, fuzzy in the glowing light.

"Must be the metallic alloy we found traces of," Laura said. "I never did identify it."

Mark touched the surface of the wall, not wanting to cause damage, but unable to stop himself. It was indeed plaster, applied masterfully to create a remarkably smooth surface. When he removed his hand, traces of the green glow had transferred to his fingertips.

"I knew it," Rocco said under his breath. "Just look at these pictures."

They all turned to examine the story depicted on the wall to Rocco's left. A monarch of sorts, clearly wearing royal attire, and sitting on a throne, was presiding over a throng of ordinary subjects. Startling, however, were the numerous guards surrounding this kingly figure. Humanoids with massive wings outstretched and long, pointed beaks. Certainly not the primitive cave paintings they had expected.

"Kingly guards," Anthony stated. "Just like we suspected."

Other parts of the mural showed Pterodactyl like creatures flying through the air, while others were being sacrificed on elaborate altars.

"So these creatures, whatever they are, were part of an important religious ritual," Laura noted. "Obviously symbolic, but there's still no proof about what they were."

"I'd say the artist's rendition is pretty clear," Rocco said cryptically.

They turned to another wall.

"Our lanterns seem to be activating this illuminating effect." Mark pointed to some ceramic jars placed along the perimeter of the room. "What do you suppose these are?"

"Boss, check this one out," Rocco said, embarrassment evident in his voice.

Mark and the others turned to look at the opposite wall. Anthony whistled. It was a graphic depiction of grotesque winged creatures having sexual intercourse with human women. The whole scene was presided over by another Pterodactyl like creature.

The room itself was not that large - only about ten feet square. On the far wall, covered by more of the glowing plaster, was the clear sign of another door. "The king himself?" Mark asked.

"Probably." Laura squinted at the wall. "We'll need a specialty team to open the door without damaging the plaster."

"What do you make of it, Anthony?" Mark asked.

"It clearly supports the local stories of a mighty race of kings that inhabited the area." Anthony cocked his head to one side. His somewhat rumpled appearance belied the intellect beneath. "Notice the ornamentation and signs of superiority. And the guards... Well, I think we've seen evidence enough that they were more than just legendary." He looked at the rest over the tops of his glasses and grinned.

"And the flying creatures? What do you make of them?" Mark asked.

"Clearly reptilian," Anthony mused. "You know, Doc, I'm not so sure that Rocco's so off base on that one. Of course, legend abounds, especially to the north, about Pterodactyl like creatures living in the Jiunda Swamps. *Kongamoto*, they're called. Locals have reported sightings as recently as a hundred years ago." Laura let out a grunt, but Anthony continued. "Now this one here has some interesting possibilities." He pointed to the last depiction. "There are numerous accounts from various cultures all over the world of godlike beings coming to earth and copulating with humans. It's often a way that ancient cultures justified a certain line of rulers. If the king descended from the gods, ordinary folks were afraid to question him. It's interesting that this particular one also includes the strong reptilian bird imagery that is so prevalent."

"Seems logical, given the reverence and symbolism the creatures seem to evoke," Mark said with a nod.

"True," Anthony agreed.

Mark surveyed the walls and let out a sigh. "Well, we'd better get busy gathering our stats. I want detailed photos from every possible angle. I also want another sample of that plaster, as well as the pigment, for further analysis. And one of these ceramic containers. We'll want a crew down here as soon as possible to open that next door."

"I'm on it, boss," Rocco offered, already heading out into the narrow passageway that led to the surface.

"Laura, you'll look after the photos?" Mark asked.

"Don't I always?" she shot back.

"Good. I have a couple of ideas I want to check out."

Mark did have something to check on - a hunch, really. The ceramic jars that had been placed around the perimeter of the antechamber brought back some vague recollections of something similar he'd seen in a museum somewhere. It took some time to locate the information on the internet, but, sure enough, it was there. Several years back, similar ceramic jars had been found in an ancient Mesopotamian site. Encased in the jar was a smaller copper cylinder suspended within its mouth. Inserted into the length of the cylinder was a length of iron ore. Apparently, when grape juice was added to the jar, an electric current was generated.

The jars recovered from this site were similar in design, although more sophisticated in appearance. Perhaps they were a power source to help illuminate the chamber. Imagine! Early electric lamps!

Now he just needed to find out what was in that plaster to make it glow. He'd already sent a sample, along with some other bones and artefacts, to a personal friend and colleague who worked in New Mexico. John would know what to do with them.

For some reason, however, Mark decided to keep that little bit of insurance a secret.

CHAPTER 5

"Here's something that you might find interesting." Anthony pushed his glasses up on the bridge of his nose. "I've catalogued over 250 stories, from every continent, about gods coming down to earth to sleep with mortal women. Seems they don't make them as good looking in the 'ether' world. Either that, or the gods are always horny."

There was a round of ribald laughter. A group had gathered under the shade of one of the tent flaps, taking a break from the African heat. Besides the expert on folklore and legend, Anthony Vanguard considered himself the resident entertainer.

"Hey, Doc," Anthony called, as Mark walked by. "Did you know I even found just such a reference in the Bible?"

"Huh? What's that?" Mark stopped in mid-stride. He'd been on his way to talk to Laura and hadn't really been listening.

"In the Bible. A story about gods getting it on with our women."

"Really?" Mark shook his head. "I don't recall anything like that."

"Sure. It's in Genesis. 'The sons of God had relations with the daughters of men'. Started a whole race of giants, who were apparently very evil, since after that God sent Noah's flood and killed them all. Part of His judgment on the earth, so the story goes."

Mark nodded absently. "Interesting."

Anthony continued with another story as Mark moved on. He found Laura sitting in front of her computer. "I was wondering if you'd made any progress with the photos."

"It's coming along fine." She closed the email she was composing, and looked up with an unnatural smile.

"Well, it's just that I was looking for them in our photo folder and I didn't see anything. I thought you were making some hard copies as well."

"I am. I just haven't gotten to it yet." Laura swung her ponytail. "They should be there. I downloaded them myself."

"Well, they aren't," Mark repeated, more irritably.

"Are you sure?"

Mark gave her a murderous look and crossed his arms. "Check for yourself."

Laura brought up the photo folder on her screen and opened it. After a few moments of scrolling, she shrugged. "That's funny. They were here yesterday."

"Look what else is missing." Mark pointed. "All the photos of the wing bones are gone, too. Somebody is sabotaging our data."

Laura looked up sharply. "Are you accusing me?"

"I haven't ruled anyone out."

Her eyes narrowed. "I may not agree with Rocco's assessments of those bones. In fact, I admit I'm a little uncomfortable with the way this whole dig is progressing. But I'm a professional. I don't go around sabotaging sites."

"Then who is?" Mark asked.

"I don't know. Maybe it's just a computer glitch. They probably got put somewhere else and we'll find them later. In any case, I'll go down and take more pictures immediately, if it'll make you feel better." She lifted her chin.

"Don't bother. I'll do it myself," Mark muttered. "But from

now on I want everything, and I mean every scrap of information, to personally pass my inspection. I want everything backed up in triplicate." He turned on his heel and strode from the room.

The missing photos were just another in a line of problems. The lab in Harare had apparently sent an important package almost two weeks ago. No one on site remembered receiving the registered package. Not even Laura. She suggested that it got lost in the mail. After all, this was Africa.

It could happen, he supposed, but too many such slips were more than coincidence. He kept looking over his shoulder, like he couldn't trust anybody any more. He had already started compiling notes and evidence on the side that he was emailing to himself, as well as to his friend John Bergman at the university in New Mexico.

He sat down at his workstation with a heavy sigh and flipped open his laptop. Good. There was a message from John, now.

"Analysis complete on those bone samples. One of the most perfect examples of a Pteranodon I've seen. Probably dates to the late Cretaceous period about 65 million years ago. Like to know where you found him. As to the human sample, we did Carbon dating only, since you sent no other reference info. It is definitely male and appears to be about 40,000 years old, give or take a few thousand. As to Carbon dating the Pterodactyloid, we were not able to get an accurate reading. The sample was contaminated and was giving a much younger reading than is possible. Analysis also came back on the metallic alloy samples you sent. Although, I'm not a specialist in geochemistry, it is apparently a very unique combination of copper and tungsten. All the official specs are being sent, both by web and hard copy via registered mail. Just thought you'd be interested in a sneak peek. JB."

Mark let the contents of the message sink in. It was confirmed, then. The strange bones were Pterodactyl. As to their age, Mark had to laugh. Naturally, the scientists at the lab would not have accepted their findings as accurate. Dinosaur bones could not be dated contemporaneously with human remains. It was unthinkable, even when the evidence was staring them right in the face. Wait until he proved that the two sets of bones had been found together - placed there on purpose. But he realized from the opposition that he'd been facing on site, as well as the easy disregard in his friend's email message, that he must be very careful about how the facts were presented.

As to the metal that was suspended in the plaster, Mark had some other theories that were developing. Tungsten was used in the filaments of electric light bulbs, while copper wire was the main conductor of electricity used in most modern appliances. What if the ceramic jars were small generators, like the ones found in Mesopotamia, and were used to actually power up the wall itself? It would be an astounding example of advanced technology never before seen from an ancient culture. Then again, nothing should surprise him about this dig anymore. The real dilemma now was, how much should he share with Laura?

Laura swung around on her stool. "You sent specimens to New Mexico?" Her voice rose several decibels. "That seems a bit unorthodox. Besides, you need more than one signature to verify the location from which the specimens came. You can't just go sending off bone samples without anyone else knowing about it. No matter what your friend's conclusions, if you can't prove where you found them in the first place his findings are useless."

"I'm getting the feeling that you're working against me, here, Laura." Mark widened his stance. "What do you mean 'verify where I got them'? You were there! You saw them with your own eyes, placed along with the human remains. So was Rocco. And Anthony and I don't know how many others."

"Of course I'm not trying to deny that fact," Laura huffed. "I was just pointing out that you didn't follow procedure, and therefore, if it came to it, your findings could be considered suspect. There might be plenty of people out there who would like nothing better than to sabotage this dig and make us all look like fools."

"So that's what you're worried about. Your reputation."

Her gaze flashed to his. "And yours."

"Thanks." Mark looked up at the canvas ceiling, mostly to avoid Laura's haughty gaze. "But I think I can look after myself in that department."

"I'm worried about you," Laura said quietly. "You're becoming - obsessive."

"You would be, too, if every time you turn around something else went missing."

"Look, I already apologized for the photos and for the delay in getting the sample results. Although, neither one of those was my fault. What more do you want? A pound of flesh?"

"Of course not. Just forget it." Mark ran a hand through his hair. He really didn't know who to trust any more.

The mental stress was starting to take its toll. Mark lay awake, unable to relax. He turned over on the narrow cot, considering whether to sneak over to Laura's tent. They hadn't renewed their physical relationship since their last disagreement. He wondered what she would say if he just showed up on her doorstep.

Things were too complicated as it was, without making them worse. He thought again about the tests he'd been running in the lab with the ceramic generators. He'd had some success and was anxious to try his theory in the antechamber itself.

The whole camp was asleep as Mark emerged from his tent and looked around. The sky was inky black and clear with the moon at half-mast. He used his pocket flashlight to illuminate the path to the lab where he retrieved some supplies and then continued toward the entrance to the tomb, careful to listen for wild animals along the way. It felt eerie entering this home for the long dead so late at night. Alone. Although it was pitch black inside, even during the day, there was something about the still-ness of the night that sent a shiver up his spine.

Once inside the cave, Mark switched on his headlamp. He passed by the various tunnels leading off to the resting places of the guards, and approached the entrance to the antechamber. Suddenly he heard a noise. He stopped dead in his tracks, listening intently. After a few seconds of silence he continued until he heard it again.

"Is someone down here?" he called.

Nothing. The noise had come from within the antechamber. With measured movements, Mark sneaked forward and peeked around the narrow entrance.

"Laura!" Mark expelled a rush of air, his heart pounding.

"Mark! What are you doing down here? You scared me half to death." Laura's hand was over her heart.

"I could be asking you the same question." He emerged fully into the glowing interior of the chamber.

"I couldn't sleep," Laura replied. "I thought I'd come down and take those pictures we lost. A peace offering."

Mark looked around, but didn't see any camera. As if reading his thoughts, she pointed to the backpack resting on the floor. "Camera's still in my pack. I was just admiring the artistry when I heard something. I must say, you pretty much had me freaked there for a second. I thought I was in a bad horror film."

"That thought also crossed my mind," Mark admitted with a grin.

"And what are you doing down here at this time of night?" Laura placed her hands on her hips. "The boss needs to get his sleep so he can deal with all the crisis that happens in a day."

"Couldn't sleep, either. Come over here, for a second." He began extracting some items from his own backpack.

"Wine?" Laura asked in surprise when he pulled the bottle from the pack. "Planning a romantic dinner party?"

"Closest thing I could find to grape juice," Mark replied. "I've been working on this theory. Based on some artefacts found in the Fertile Crescent. The ancient Babylonians were able to construct simple generators made out of iron ore and copper, fuelled by nothing more than simple grape juice." He uncorked the bottle with a pop.

"Really? Fascinating."

"My hypothesis goes something like this. We have here several examples of potential generators - ceramic jars that also contain iron ore and copper filaments." He swept his arm in a wide arch, still holding onto the bottle in one hand and the cork in the other. "Thus, we have our power source. Also note that the plaster in the walls contain a delicately balanced mixture of copper and tungsten."

"You figured it out?" Laura asked.

Mark nodded and continued with his discourse, lecture style. "Potential 'light bulbs', if you will. Witness that the jars are all connected to the wall by this small, almost imperceptible, copper wire protruding from the base of the jar and imbedded in the plaster itself. 'Plugged in'. Now, when I fire up the generator..." He carefully poured the wine into one of the ceramic containers. The wall nearest to the jar began to glow a brilliant fluorescent green. Mark blinked. "It works," was all he said.

"You're a genius." Laura stood next to him, staring at the glowing walls. "But why were they glowing to begin with?"

"I haven't figured that out yet. Maybe just some residual effects. Maybe the electricity coming off our gear, or even our bodies. It does appear that the elements used in the plaster are very sensitive to any energy source. Certainly different technology than anything I've ever encountered."

They stood back, looking at the mural for several minutes.

"You gonna drink that?" Laura asked suddenly, pointing at the half empty bottle of wine.

"Huh?"

She lifted a shoulder. "Well, it just seems like a waste, now that it's open."

Mark shrugged and handed her the bottle. She took a long swallow and then handed it back to him, wiping her mouth on her shirt sleeve. "Not bad. Nice atmosphere, too. Although the company's not very talkative." She smiled in his direction.

He returned the smile and followed her lead. The wine was full bodied with the taste of ripe, juicy grapes. Or maybe it was the setting that made it taste all right. They both sat down on the floor and shared the rest of the wine in silence as they surveyed the glowing room.

"You know," Laura said, "I do realize that I need to apologize for all the stress I've caused. I've been meaning to bring it up for days, but I'm rather proud, you know."

"I know," Mark agreed, but cracked a smile.

"I mean, the screw up with the lab results and then the photos. I don't blame you for thinking the worst. You just need to know that none of it happened intentionally. And if I've been a little uptight, well... it's only natural. When you see someone you care about being put under so much pressure... " Her words trailed off as she placed her hand on Mark's thigh.

"I guess we've all been under a bit of pressure."

"We need to relax, I think. Let off some steam." She was rubbing his leg now, coming dangerously close to his privates. "I've missed you." She leaned forward for a kiss. When their lips parted, she breathed huskily, "I think it would be exciting to make love here. Don't you?"

Mark felt his libido surge in response. He was about to acquiesce when his eye caught a glimpse of the grotesque demonoids, swooping in the act of possession over the helpless women. He froze. "It's getting pretty late. We'd better get some sleep." He disengaged himself from Laura's arms and stood.

"Suit yourself," Laura said tightly. She jumped to her feet, grabbed her bag, and led the way from the chamber. It only took Mark a minute to gather his things and catch up.

"About those photos," he said from behind her. She stopped in her tracks, but didn't turn around. "Don't worry about it. I came and took plenty earlier on today – just in case."

Laura's back stiffened but she continued on without further comment.

CHAPTER 6

The next day arrived and with it the moment they had all been straining toward. The inner chamber would be opened. Once the work crew had carefully chiselled their way around the sealed off entrance, the door swung in with surprising ease. "This is it," Mark said under his breath. He, Laura, Anthony and Rocco entered, leaving the rest of the crew outside in the main antechamber with all the paintings.

Mark had to duck his head to get in, although once inside it offered just enough room for him to stand. The roughly ten feet by ten feet space was empty except for a large casket sitting in the middle of the room. Mark ran a hand over its smooth surface and was surprised by the resin like feel of the material. There were a few markings, probably script, but little else in terms of ornamentation. Not what he'd expected.

"Well, let's see what we've got," Mark said. It took all four of them to lift the heavy lid and slide it off to one side. He frowned. The container seemed to be full of black dust.

Laura nodded her head slowly. "Charcoal. A common method of preservation."

"I want every bit of it bagged and sent to the surface for analysis," Mark ordered.

With surgical precision, the charcoal packing was gently swept into storage containers and passed out to the waiting crew for transport to the surface where it would be further sifted for arte-facts. Mark watched the entire process while Laura documented it with her camera. About two hours later a fabric shroud appeared.

"Stop." Mark held up a hand. "Let's be careful here, folks. Maybe we can lift the veil and get a peek at what's underneath."

In slow motion, Rocco and Mark lifted the fragile shroud.

Gasps echoed through the chamber. Before them lay not the skeleton they expected, but a perfectly preserved human face. His olive complexion appeared pliable, with only some slight recession around the mouth where a hint of gleaming teeth could be seen. His dark hair was intact, seemingly still attached at the scalp. It was a handsome face, probably no more than thirty years of age.

"The Nephilim," Anthony breathed.

"What?" Rocco looked sharply over at his colleague.

"A race of giants. Born of the union between gods and men," Anthony chanted in a dramatic tone.

Laura ignored his theatrics. "I wonder what embalming tech-nique was used. The preservation is remarkable."

"We could make millions selling it as an anti-aging cream," Rocco said with a laugh.

"The layers of charcoal are probably a factor," Mark noted. "We'll do a thorough analysis above ground. For now, let's get the preliminaries. Rocco, Anthony, let's remove a little more of this shroud. See if the king, here, has a crown."

Using sterile tongs, they gently peeled back more of the shroud. All eyes widened.

This was no crown of gold and jewels. Tucked along the top of the casket, lying on its side, was a ceremonial headdress similar to the remnants found with the guards. However, this specimen was perfectly preserved. Dark leather, pointed skull, gleaming eyes, long, sharp beak... a textbook Pterodactyl head.

"What have you got to say now, Doc?" Rocco directed at Laura with satisfaction. She remained speechless.

Mark blinked, not able to take his eyes off the treasure. "There's no denying it, now."

"Just like the legends say," Anthony offered with a whistle.

"I'll get some photos," Laura finally spoke. Mark gave her an intense stare. "Don't worry," she added icily. "I won't let anything happen this time."

"Good," Mark stated, his tone no nonsense. "I won't let this one get away from me." He turned to the rest. "We better get to work gathering our stats. I want this entire casket removed to a safe location as soon as possible."

The specimen was wearing a suit of leather armour, and clutched a sceptre of bronze intricately carved with images of various animals. Included with a lion, boar and elephant was the now familiar Pterodactyl. Rocco whistled as he and Anthony took some measurements. "Here's proof of that legendary race of giants you were talking about."

Laura snapped several photos. "There are probably basketball players just as tall."

"True," Anthony conceded, "but the average height has increased over time, not the other way around. For this time period, these men would have been giants."

"We haven't established a time period yet," Laura pointed out. Her camera whizzed again.

"What did you call them, again?" Rocco asked Anthony as they continued to record their data.

"Nephilim," Anthony replied.

"I don't recall hearing that reference before," Mark mused. "At least not in the Nbedele legends."

"Oh, it's not from this area." Anthony looked over at Mark and smiled as he talked. "It's a Biblical reference."

Mark's brows rose. "Really? Fill me in."

Anthony peered into the darkness of the cave, as if in a trance. "And the sons of God saw the daughters of men that they were fair; and they took them wives of all which they chose. There were giants in the earth in those days; and also after that, when the sons of God came in unto the daughters of men, and they bear children to them, and the same became mighty men which were of old." Anthony stopped and blinked, directing his gaze at the rest of the group who had all stopped working as well. "Some manuscripts say 'Nephilim' instead of 'giants.'" He smiled and went back to work.

"How do you do that?" Rocco asked.

Anthony looked over the tops of his glasses. "What?"

Rocco shrugged. "Repeat it like that. Like you were saying it word for word."

Anthony tapped his temple. "Photographic memory. Anyway, the story goes that people became very wicked in the sight of God. And it was at that point -"

"That he sent the flood," Mark finished for him.

"Exactly," Anthony verified with a grin. "I'm proud of you, Doc. You must have attended Sunday School after all."

"A few times," Mark agreed dryly, but he smiled none the less.

"So it all comes back to a fairy story about gods coming down to earth to have sex with the local women," Laura said with disgust. "That's the best you can do?"

"Hey, don't shoot the messenger." Anthony put up one hand in defence.

"As enjoyable as your story was, we need to get to the facts," Laura stated. "Who were these people and where did they come from?"

"I think the pictures on the walls speak plainly enough about what they believed," Anthony said.

"Or what a few powerful people wanted them to believe," Laura countered.

"That's true," Anthony conceded. "I think we all realize that those in power have to have some kind of hold over their subjects. Being a descendant of the gods would be a good way to keep your opponents in check."

"I think there is more to it than that," Laura said. "Notice how the power is in the hands of the males, which only goes to show that males have consistently felt the need to prove their dominance over females, especially sexually. It's a basic insecurity built into the male gender."

Rocco grinned. "Them's fightin' words."

Laura tossed her ponytail off her shoulder and took another photo. "Men overlook the fact that females have the real power."

Anthony smiled. "Fascinating. Do tell."

"They've historically been able to make men do whatever they want simply by enticing them with sex. Men just don't have control of themselves in that department, so they've had to make up stories with themselves portrayed as super human in both strength and power."

Rocco raised a brow and looked over at Mark. "Any of that true, boss?"

Mark just shrugged. "No comment."

Rocco nodded. "Smart man."

"What you say has some truth to it," Anthony said. "Women have been the downfall of many great men. Napoleon and Josephine; Samson and Delilah."

Laura held her camera aloft. "It seems to me the real downfall was in the weakness of the men. The women were just proving the point." Whiz.

Rocco leaned toward Anthony with a staged whisper. "Give up. You can't win."

"No, I agree with much of what Laura is saying," Anthony

said. "But to get back to the legend. There might be a connection between the Biblical account and what we have here."

Laura rolled her eyes before taking another picture. "You think that these people are the real thing? Descended from gods who came down and raped the women of the area? Please. This is even more ridiculous than dinosaurs and humans coexisting."

"Which looks to be true," Rocco pointed out.

Laura ignored him. "If we were worried about our credibility before, this is sure to take the cake."

"I never said I believe that actual gods came down," Anthony continued talking. "Maybe it was a race from a different place - another part of the globe with different technology - that seemed god like. Certainly these are not typical proportions for human beings."

"There are other African tribes that are unusually tall," Laura offered.

"But not in this area. The legends all clearly point to a race of men from 'elsewhere'," Anthony stated.

Laura shook her head. "I think you put too much weight on your legends."

"Most legends have some basis in fact."

Laura flashed a glance at Mark. "So I've heard."

"And this is one site where we actually have more than just the legend," Anthony pointed out. "We have actual specimens of giants, however they were 'begotten'. We also have the very unique location of the burial caves. Not only were they far underground, but if you recall, we had to dig through a layer of sediment and fossilized material, which suggests a catastrophic flood of some kind. Pre Noah. Get it?" Anthony grinned.

Laura rolled her eyes. "Now I've heard everything."

Anthony let his eyes sweep the room. "These tombs were buried and preserved by some such natural disaster. You can't deny that."

"We dug through and catalogued it just like that. 'Cat-astrophic flooding'," Rocco said.

"Now, I'm not saying it had to be Noah's flood." Anthony quickly raised a hand before Laura could say anything else. "Or that such a worldwide event even took place. But we have evidence that clearly follows the Biblical legend: giants inhabited the land before the flood."

"I'm surrounded by people who are supposed to be scientists - experts in their field! And all I keep hearing is fairy stories." Laura snapped the lens cover onto her camera and began stuffing it into its case.

Anthony continued. "There are also Biblical accounts of dinosaurs roaming the earth. Most scholars think that the story of Job takes place chronologically before that of Noah. It's in this account that we find references to dinosaur like creatures - the Behemoth and Leviathan, to name two. For those interpreting the Bible in a literal fashion, this makes sense, since God created everything. It stands to reason that he also created dinosaurs."

"I see where you're going with this," Rocco said. "If this cave dates back to pre-flood days, then the presence of Pterodactyl bones would be nothing strange."

"Exactly!" Anthony slapped his thigh. "Even if there was a worldwide disaster, miraculously, evidence got preserved in these caves. This could be the greatest find in history. It could prove much of the Biblical mythology as true."

"You sound like you're already convinced." Laura noted scepti-cally. "Next you'll be asking for an altar call."

"There have been some interesting finds already," Rocco said. "An ark like structure was found grounded on a mountain in the Middle East."

Laura swung around to meet Mark's gaze. He had been silent for most of the exchange. "What kind of operation are you running here?" she demanded.

Mark shrugged. "Anthony's just offering another possible angle. I don't think there's any need to be so defensive."

Anthony agreed, "Right. It was just a thought." He laughed. "You know me, always ready to delve into a good folk tale."

"That does it, I think." Mark looked around. "You three clear out so the guys can get in here with the harnesses. I want this fellow safely out of here as soon as possible."

"You don't have to do that, boss. I can do it," Rocco said.

"I'm not letting him out of my sight."

"Suit yourself. I'll head up if you're sure." Rocco ducked to step through the opening into the other chamber.

"Get those harnesses in here!" Mark ordered. Anthony and Laura squeezed through the opening and the four waiting crew with the harnesses stepped in, one at a time. They skilfully loaded the now closed casket, and balanced it between them on shoulder harnesses.

Mark was about to say something when he stopped and held up a hand. "What was that?"

They all heard it this time - a distinct rumbling. Suddenly, sediment sprayed down from the ceiling as the earth emitted another distant groan.

"Could be a cave in," Anthony called from the other room.

"Let's get this thing out into the main room," Mark said to the moving crew, ignoring Anthony.

"Leave it behind," Laura's voice reached him. "We need to get out of here."

"No! I'm not leaving it behind." Mark hollered. He was answered by another tremor and more rocks.

They managed to manoeuvre the heavy load out into the antechamber and readjust it for the trek through the tunnels. "Get going," Mark said to Laura and Anthony. With a nod, Anthony grabbed Laura's arm and they scurried ahead, out of sight.

The crew moved forward as quickly as possible with their

precarious load. They were halfway through the tunnels when a large rock tumbled from above, hitting one of the men squarely on the head. He let out a surprised exclamation and momentarily lost his balance. The casket swayed on the shoulder harnesses. The sheer weight of it caused another man to bump against the tunnel wall.

"Steady!" Mark yelped. "Ron, let me take over that harness."

But it was too late. The heavy treasury landed with a crunching thud on one corner, crushing the man's foot beneath. He let out an agonized cry.

Mark jumped forward. "Steve, help me get this harness off. Ron, take some deep breaths."

They worked quickly to take the harness off the injured man. There was another rumble, only this time closer. Another barrage of rocks and pebbles rained down. Mark shielded Ron with his back, and then continued with the last buckle. "Now on my signal, lift."

Ron let out a gasping groan as the men hoisted the heavy burden off his shattered appendage. They shuffled their way a few more feet and carefully set the cargo down with a unified grunt.

"I hate to do it, but it looks we'll have to leave it for now." Mark was interrupted by another spray of sediment. "Come on. We'd better hurry."

Fumbling now with desperate fingers, the harness was undone and left with the casket. Ron was helped up and limped as quickly as possible down the tunnel with the assistance of two other members. Mark and the other crewmember followed as fast as they were able down the tunnel toward the entrance. Here and there fallen debris made their passage more difficult. At one point, Ron had to be lifted through an opening while the others had to crawl on hands and knees. Mark noticed several beams that had been used for bracing, leaning drunkenly or fallen all together.

Finally, Mark could see a circle of natural light, and strained more urgently toward the goal. He was the last to emerge, just as another rumbling crash sounded. The tunnel filled just yards behind them. He looked back and covered his face with his T-shirt as billows of dust clouded the entrance. All of the men were covered from head to toe in grey, powdered earth.

"Mark! You're alright!" Laura ran forward to embrace him.

Mark turned to shout some orders, disentangling himself from her embrace. "Get a stretcher! Ron's been hurt."

"You could have been killed!" Laura persisted. "You scared me half to death."

"Not now." Mark pulled himself to his feet and pushed past her. "Just a cave in," he called, trying to sound unconcerned. "Let's move away from the entrance, everybody. Give them some room. Ron's going to be all right. Come on, back to camp. We'll start in first thing tomorrow and dig our way back in."

"Are you serious?" Laura scurried after Mark's limping form. "After what just happened you'd risk going back in?"

Mark gripped Laura's arm and manoeuvred her toward the camp. "I'm not just going to leave it there."

"But it might be too dangerous." She stopped and shrugged her arm free. "You have to think of the lives of your crew. One dead king isn't worth the life of a living crew member."

"No one else is going to get hurt. I'll triple the bracing, if necessary, although it was supposed to withstand unexpected seismic activity. I'll have to speak to Joey about that."

"You mean, speak to Rocco," Laura said.

"Rocco? That's not his department." Mark squinted in confusion.

Laura shrugged. "I overheard him telling Joey he would handle it."

"That explains it, then." Mark's eyes narrowed. "He had no business. I have experts in place for that job. Joey is an engineer, for goodness sake. Somebody could have been seriously injured or worse, down there. I'll have to speak to them both about it. There have been way too many glitches on this job."

"Could be a bad omen. Maybe you shouldn't go back in."

Mark looked at her with disbelief. "That coming from the least superstitious person on the crew? What happened to all your scoffing at Anthony's legends? Don't tell me you've become a believer?"

Laura laughed. "Hardly. But as you say, there have been a lot of problems since we first discovered those bones."

"I'm not giving up," Mark stated emphatically. "I don't care how long it takes. We're getting that casket out of there."

"Who is going to finance that? "Laura asked. "With our time constraints and now this, you might not be able to." She crossed her arms.

"Once we show our sponsors the photos you took today, there should be no question about continued support." Mark stopped and looked at Laura. She had become suddenly still. "The camera. Where's the camera?"

"You don't have it?" Laura asked weakly.

"No! Of course I don't have it! You were the one taking the pictures!" He cursed loudly and swung away from her, running both hands through his hair.

"I guess I left it behind in all the commotion."

"That sounds rather convenient," he ground out.

"Are you implying that I left it on purpose? Is that it?"

"I just can't believe you would be so negligent," Mark countered.

"Negligent? Me? Who's the one risking the lives of the crew? You're more concerned about your big find than about the safety of human beings."

Mark could have gladly throttled her. He was about to make another scathing remark but he thought better of it. He clamped his mouth into a tight line, and strode away in the direction of his own quarters. Maybe this dig was cursed.

CHAPTER 7

Mark stayed in his tent alone until darkness fell like a curtain over the African mountain. He knew he had things to do. He should be checking on Ron; confronting Rocco; talking to Joey. Apologizing to Laura. But for some reason he couldn't force himself to face any of them. He wanted to go to bed and wake up the next morning and find that it had all been a dream; that they had gotten the casket up to the surface safely. He should be on his way to New Mexico the day after tomorrow, accompanied by the most astounding archaeological find imaginable.

Instead he was sitting here. Alone. In a dark and dusty tent with no one to talk to, while a whole crowd of people waited outside for his next order. He wondered what his next move should be. Of course, he wasn't even going to consider leaving the casket and its precious contents behind. They had to re-dig that tunnel. There was just too much valuable evidence lost down there.

He had some slight misgivings about the safety factor, despite what he'd said to Laura. There were risks involved. But he had to remain confident, not only for the psyche of the crew, but also to keep any government officials off his back. He didn't need Laura's reminders about the tenuous agreement they had with the government. He needed to keep a low profile; get back in and get out before his permit to excavate got yanked.

Confronting Rocco was going to be another thing. He was a trusted colleague and a good friend. He knew his stuff. And he had a good rapport with the other crew members. He was able to maintain productivity without dampening their enthusiasm for discovery. But he also had the humility to know when something was out of his league. Mark just couldn't believe that Rocco would have been so careless as to go over his head and take care of the bracing himself. Or that Joey had let him. Getting the facts sorted out tomorrow was not something he was looking forward to.

Mark sighed and glanced around the darkening room. His eyes rested on the saxophone case. He wondered what advice his grandfather, Jack, would give. Jack was never one to give up. He was the very embodiment of tenacity. Mark did not relish the thought of having to dig back into the tombs again. But he knew he would do it. There was no other choice.

He went over to the battered instrument case and picked it up. He clicked it open and gently lifted the saxophone from its crushed velvet bed. Attaching the reed, he put the mouthpiece tentatively to his lips, but did not blow into it. He closed his eyes and fingered the pads in a silent song from the past, one that Jack had taught him long ago. Someday, when he had the privacy of more than just canvas walls, he would attempt to play in earnest. For now, he must be content with the memory of the song as it played in his head.

There was a 'knock' on the outer flap of his tent. There was no hiding, Mark realized. If he didn't take matters into hand, matters would come to him. "Yep," he called gruffly.

It was Anthony. He bent to step through the inner door flap, letting it fall behind him as he straightened. "Sorry. Hope I'm not interrupting." He gestured at the saxophone still sitting on Mark's lap.

"Oh, no. That's alright." Mark nestled the sax back into its case and set it on the floor.

"I didn't know you played the sax." Anthony gestured at the instrument case. "The way sound travels around here, it's funny I never heard it before."

"I don't play, really," Mark admitted. "The sax belonged to my Grandfather. Sometimes, I just like to hold it. Helps me think."

"Hmm. And I guess you've got plenty to think about right now," Anthony said. "Rocco's going to be in pretty deep, I would imagine."

Mark frowned. "Who told you that?"

"It's common knowledge. I must admit, I had doubts about Rocco taking charge of the refit in the first place. But I figured you were the boss, so you must have had your reasons."

"I never gave Rocco any such instructions," Mark stated emphatically. "Safety and engineering is Joey's portfolio. Why would I change that?"

Anthony shrugged. "Beats me. Sorry, man. I just assumed..."

"I'll get to the bottom of it first thing tomorrow." Mark waited, eyeing Anthony closely. "Is that what you wanted to talk to me about?"

"Actually, if you've got a minute, I came here to talk to you about something else."

Mark raised a brow. "Oh? What?"

Anthony took a quick look around and then seated himself on the cot. "It's about what we were talking about earlier, in the chamber, before the cave in."

"We talked about a lot of things. I'm afraid you'll need to be more specific."

"Right. Well, about the legends surrounding the site, and how they seem to line up with our findings. More specifically, the Biblical ones - about the Nephilim and the Flood and that." He stopped, waiting for a comment from Mark. When Mark gave none, he continued. "See, it's like this. I've studied hundreds, possibly thousands, of manuscripts from every culture and country. But there's something about this particular story, this Bible account. It's different, somehow, but I can't quite put my finger on it. It's farfetched - way out there - yet I find myself wanting it to be true. Almost believing that it is. And then the evidence we've found - it's almost too much. Not to mention all the weirdness. Techno glitches, cave-ins, artefacts gone missing... like we aren't supposed to tamper with it. Like the whole site is cursed, or something. It has me feeling spooked."

Mark narrowed his eyes. "What do you mean, artefacts gone missing?"

"You know. That first set of Pterodactyl wing bones. Then no results came back, records went missing..." Anthony trailed off.

"Did you just say 'set'?"

Anthony nodded. "From the first find."

"I was told that first site contained only one wing. It's what made the subsequent tombs so important."

"Pretty sure there were two wings."

Mark leaned forward. "How can that be? I saw the photos from that first excavation. There was one, badly damaged and incomplete. And Laura and Rocco both clearly stated there only was one specimen."

Anthony shrugged. "Hey man, I know what I saw. I was there during the initial opening of that tomb. The first one was damaged; a cave in, I guess. But we definitely dusted two wing fragments. The indentations made by the bones were right there after we removed them. You must have noticed it yourself."

Mark thought for a moment. He recalled the stillness of the shallow tomb and the perfect indentation left in the sand of a large wing. It had filled him with awe. But there had only been one. The sand on the other side of the body had been perfectly smooth. Too smooth, perhaps. He frowned. "You're sure?"

"Photographic memory, remember?" Anthony laughed,

tapping his head. "Ask Rocco. He'll verify it. He and I were together."

Rocco again. Mark felt an uneasiness rising in the pit of his stomach. Rocco's name was connected with a few too many incidents.

"Anyway, about that legend thing," Anthony picked up where he left off. "I just needed to bounce it off someone. To talk about it out loud instead of play it over in my head. Kind of de-mystify, so to speak, so I could sleep tonight. Sounds kind of crazy, I know, but -"

"No. It's not so crazy," Mark said. "I must admit, I've been entertaining some of the same speculations myself."

"Yeah?"

"I mean, I've always been one to look at the evidence. Verifiable facts, only. But some of what we've uncovered does not fit in well with what I've assumed to be true up until this point. There's the rub, for all of us. If we take the evidence before us, it means throwing out a whole lot of other evidence that we've come to believe as fact. The new evidence doesn't fit into the old framework. The two simply don't mesh."

"So what do we do about it?"

"Create a new framework," Mark suggested. "I just haven't figured out how to do that, yet. But I know for a fact that I can't deny what I've seen. Which is why it's so important for us to get back down there and recover that body. It could be the key to the whole mystery."

"Or not. Maybe it's like I said, and we're not supposed to know the truth."

"Back to the curse thing?" Mark asked wryly.

"Precisely."

"I'm not willing to go that far. It's taken a leap of faith for me to accept that dinosaurs coexisted with man."

"Hm. Rocco's been telling me some interesting things about that. I thought he was off his rocker at first, but now that I've seen it with my own eyes... I guess that's why it suddenly doesn't seem so farfetched to just jump in and believe the whole thing. The Bible thing, I mean. Noah's flood, everything. The works."

"I know a lot of people who believe every word of the Bible as the literal truth. They wouldn't be at all surprised by what we found here," Mark said.

"Oh yeah?" Anthony surveyed Mark for a moment. "You another one of those prodigals?"

Mark's eyebrows shot up in surprise. "What do you mean?"

Anthony laughed self depreciatingly. "It's okay. Takes one to know one. I'm the son of a preacher man, myself."

"No kidding," Mark said.

"Mmhm," Anthony replied. "The fire and brimstone variety. You?"

"My family are all believers." Mark looked down at his lap and then up again.

"But not you," Anthony stated.

"The prodigal son," Mark laughed dismissively. "You said it yourself."

"Why? What happened that you don't believe the same way your family does?"

Mark shrugged. "I don't know. I mean, I definitely saw a positive change when my own Dad got 'saved', as they say. But it was like I was on the outside looking in. I just never really felt the need for that kind of thing." Mark caught Anthony's gaze. "What about you?"

Anthony laughed. "Mine's a real prodigal story. I had to try extra hard to play the part of the bad boy so that the other kids wouldn't think I was a wimp. You don't know the pressure of being the preacher's kid. Everybody expects you to be perfect all the time. And then of course, I had to endure the double retribution of my father's shame. He kept warning mc I'd cross the line someday. I guess I believed him. We haven't spoken in eight years."

"Eight years?" Mark blinked. "That's a long time. I haven't seen my family in three, but it's not because we aren't speaking."

"Good to know I'm not alone in my waywardness." Anthony slapped his thighs and stood up. "Thanks for the ear. I suppose I'd better head back to my own tent, now. Think of a way to reconcile what I think this is all about and what people want to hear." He stood up and ducked out through the canvas flap.

Mark sighed. How did one present these facts and not be lumped with a raving bunch of religious fanatics?

"I want round the clock digging to get at that casket," Mark informed in his most commanding tone. The entire crew was gathered for a meeting. "That's got to be number one. And this time I want double the bracing under Joey's direction. You got that?" He held Rocco's gaze pointedly.

"That was a misunderstanding," Rocco defended. "I thought -"

"I don't want to hear your excuses." Mark held up a hand. "It cost us big time. Now we're under the gun. All I expect from you is to deliver. Get me that casket."

Rocco nodded, his gaze downward. "Gotcha." Apparently he wasn't going to stick around for any more. With a salute, he turned and scurried away. The rest of the crew followed.

Mark watched them for a moment before turning in the direction of the lab.

"Mark, wait a minute," Laura called. He stopped in his tracks, waiting for her to catch up. "So, you're still going ahead with the dig?" she asked, almost accusatory.

"Of course. You don't think I'd leave a find like that buried, do you?" He didn't slow his strides.

"But the safety issues -"

He cut her off. "Taken care of. I'm still the boss out here, remember?"

"Of course," she said coldly. "I'm not questioning that. I just thought -"

"Don't you have work to do? Cataloguing? Analyzing data? Something?"

She looked at him mutely, setting her mouth into a grim line. She turned and strode off in a different direction.

Mark sighed and ran a hand through his already unruly mass of dark curls. This was going to be one bad day.

Mark squeezed his eyes tight, resting his forehead against the coolness of the saxophone. What was he supposed to do? Leaving the site now was unthinkable! But...

Jack.

He'd just received the email that morning. Jack Burton, jazz great, had passed away peacefully in his sleep. Jack Burton, mentor, grandfather, confidant. Dead.

Mark drew in a shuddering breath, willing himself to get control. He had a job to do. The biggest discovery of his career - perhaps of all time, lay buried under a pile of rubble deep in an African cave. And time was not on his side. He couldn't afford to go gallivanting halfway across the globe to Winnipeg. No, he would just have to take it on the chin - another one of life's left hooks - and carry on. He rose from the rickety folding chair, stroking the gleaming metal instrument with gentle fingers before placing it reverently back in its carrying case.

Mark entered the mess tent. It was later than usual and there was no line up, so he was able to fill his plate quickly and walked to where Rocco and Anthony sat. "You have another crew working the night shift?" he asked without greeting.

"As we speak." Rocco kept his eyes on his plate as he pushed some food around with his fork.

"Good. I want back in there in less than a week. Tell your men I'll be checking their progress myself."

"It might take a little longer, considering the damage done to the bracing. But don't worry. Joey's on it this time." Rocco looked up. "By the way, Joey says there was nothing wrong with the initial bracing. That level of seismic activity could have damaged almost anything."

Mark looked down at his plate, his stomach suddenly rebelling at the thought of food.

"Say, did I tell you about the latest theory Rocco and I were discussing this afternoon?" Anthony piped up.

"Um, no. What about it?"

Laura sat down beside Mark with a clatter. "Where have you been hiding all day?"

He didn't look at her when he answered. "Why? You need something in particular?"

"There were a few inconsistencies in some of the lab work that came back from Harare," she explained. "Plus, I've made some progress on those photo comparisons from the antechamber. I thought you'd like to know."

Mark nodded. "I'll take a look as soon as I'm done here."

"I thought you were going to check on the progress at the excavation?" Rocco reminded.

"Right. Of course." Mark nodded absently. Anthony said something else, but Mark didn't hear him. He placed his utensils on the untouched plate of food and pushed his chair back from the table.

"Boss? You alright?" Rocco followed his boss's abrupt movements with his eyes.

"I'll be fine," Mark clipped. "Let's have a look at that information right now," he said to Laura.

Anthony and Rocco exchanged a bewildered glance as Laura scurried after Mark's retreating figure.

It took about half an hour for Mark to look over everything Laura had to show him. He rubbed his neck wearily as he clicked the laptop shut.

"Thanks," Laura offered. "I'm glad things aren't looking as bad as I feared. After so many problems, I was really beginning to think this project was jinxed. I guess I over reacted to what I thought were more glitches in the lab reports."

"It's okay," Mark said. "Better safe than sorry."

Laura surveyed him for a moment. "You look beat."

"I most certainly am," he replied without hesitation. "But, it's off to inspect the dig." He pasted on a false smile and stood up.

Laura frowned up at him with concern. "You're working yourself to the bone. You'd be a lot more useful to the entire operation if you got a good night's rest."

"I doubt that. Besides, I wouldn't be able to sleep anyway."

"Mark, what is it?" She placed her hand on his forearm. "And there's no use saying 'Nothing'. What aren't you telling me?" She waited a moment before letting her hand slip to her side. "Stubborn," she mumbled.

Mark allowed a slight tug at his lips. "I know."

"And if it's us... you know, what's been going on between us, I don't want that to stand in your way. I'm your friend first and I'm also a scientist. This dig is as important to me as it to you. You've got to know that."

Mark let out a sigh. "You're right. It's not just the dig."

"Go on." Laura folded her arms.

Mark shut his eyes for a few seconds, squeezing tight, then

expended another burst of carbon dioxide. "I got news today from home."

"Oh? What news?"

"About my Grandfather, Jack Burton. Remember I told you about him?" Mark asked and Laura nodded. "He died."

"Oh Mark! I'm so sorry!"

Mark shrugged, feeling a certain amount of release now that he had told someone. "My father emailed me this morning. He died peacefully, in his sleep. So that's a blessing."

"But it's still hard," Laura said. She rubbed down the full length of his arm.

Mark nodded.

"Are you going to the funeral?" she asked.

"Of course not. How can I? I couldn't leave the site now. Not at this critical time."

"Why not? You think we can't handle it?" She cocked an eyebrow.

"Of course not. But the cave in. The casket. The tight time frame..."

"Exactly why you should go," Laura reasoned. "It'll be at least a week until they get back into that tunnel. In the mean time, you'll be roaming around like a caged lion making it difficult for the rest of us to do our jobs. You'd be better off taking that week to visit your family. Grieve with them."

Mark furrowed his brow. "You really think so?"

"Of course," she replied. "You'll get the closure you need and arrive back just in time to open the casket. After that we'll still have some time to finish everything up here, crate what we need to send, maybe even get an extension once the government sees what we're sitting on."

"Hm... You really think you can handle it?" he asked again uncertainly.

"Of course," she said confidently. "Trust us for a change. You've got a great team assembled here." She paused. "Well, except maybe for Rocco. But other than that you've just got to trust us. Trust me." She went up on tiptoe and placed a kiss on his lips.

What she said made sense. Maybe he did need some closure if he was ever going to be able to continue on this project without going crazy himself.

CHAPTER 8

Mark glanced out the tiny porthole. Nothing but swirls of cottony whiteness could be seen far below. The jet flew too high above the earth for there to be any other sites in view. They were somewhere above the central plains of the North American continent by now. It had been a long and physically taxing trip from the dig, first by jeep, then Cesena 185, and finally jet, making several transfers along the way. It was quite a trek from the backcountry of Africa to Winnipeg, Canada.

It seemed like forever since he'd seen them last. How long was it anyway? Three years? It had been for his sister's graduation from high school. Harmony was almost twelve years younger than he was. In many ways he felt like he'd been part of the parenting team, rather than just an older brother. It was hard to believe she was now twenty-one. It would be good to see her again - and the rest of his family.

Well, almost the rest. Jack wouldn't be there. The realization hit him again, in the gut like a punch before tightening one's muscles against it. Of course it was bound to happen one of these days. Jack was getting old. But for some reason Mark had always thought he'd get back one more time before...

"Excuse me, Dr. Graham," a pretty flight attendant with a French accent interrupted Mark's thoughts. "The Captain has asked that all electronic devices be turned off. I will have to ask you to shut off your computer."

Mark blinked at her absently for a moment. "Oh, of course," he acquiesced as her words registered. He may have heard just such a request over the intercom only moments before, but he couldn't be sure.

He scanned the screen of his laptop once more before shutting down, then clicked the lid shut with finality before zipping it into its carrying case. He sighed heavily. Jack Burton had been more than a grandfather. He had been his mentor and his friend.

The familiar monotone melody of the seat belt sign broke into his thoughts, and Mark concentrated on the changing view out the window as the airplane began its descent. They broke free from their cottony cocoon and were suddenly thrust into a clear expanse of blue sky. The curvature of the earth stretched out beyond the horizon of flattened landscape. A patchwork quilt of brown and gold and green pocked frequently with small, irregular ponds that spoiled the precise grid of man's claim to the land.

On the table flatness of the prairie he could already see in the distance the heart of the province of Manitoba, its capital city of Winnipeg. The downtown core rose like a multifaceted steeple among the sprawling parish of suburbia. At its core, the meeting of two mighty rivers, the Red and the Assiniboine, sliced the city. The forks of these two water highways had been the centre of commerce during the early days of the fur trade, the birthplace of a revolution, and afterwards, the seed of a province.

He felt bone weary as he joined the other passengers in the tunnel leading out of the plane. The travel home had been long and arduous, and the emotional stress that he was sure to face, already had him feeling drained.

As he walked through the gates from International arrivals, he scanned the crowd for the familiar faces of his family. Then he spotted them. His father, Russ Graham, an older version of himself, stood beside two red haired women. When they made eye contact, his sister Harmony and his stepmother Deanie both came rushing forward.

"Mark! Oh, Mark, you look terrific! So tanned!" Deanie burst out, squeezing the daylights out of him. "Look, honey! Isn't he tanned?" she directed at her husband. "It must be all that hot African sun."

Harmony joined in for her share of hugs and the two women chattered excitedly for a few more minutes while Mark's father, Russ, held back. Finally Mark was able to extract himself from their embraces and turned with an outstretched hand to his father. "Dad."

"It's good to see you, son." Father and son shook hands firmly before Russ pulled Mark into a quick embrace, slapping him on the back. There had been a day when the elder Graham would not have showed such a public display of affection. His wife had been working for over twenty years to free him from that reserve.

His parents had not changed all that much in the past three years, Mark noted. Russ Graham had aged slightly, adding a little more grey at the temples to his dark hair. He still kept it closely cropped in an effort to keep the unruly curls in order. Mark's hair had the same propensity, but Mark usually didn't have time to worry about such things, and at present his hair was rather bushy, curling over his collar. Both men had dark and intense blue eyes, well chiselled features and solid builds. There was no mistaking the resemblance, except for the quarter century difference in their ages.

His stepmother, Deanie, looked almost as young as ever. She was close to fifteen years younger than her husband, but regardless of that fact, she looked younger than the early forties that she was. People often mistook her and Harmony for sisters, rather than mother and daughter.

"I'm so glad you came, Mark," Deanie was saying as they gathered his baggage and headed for the exit. "Jack will be pleased, I think, looking down from heaven. It's such a comfort to know that he's gone on to be with the Lord."

"That it is," Russ agreed.

"I mean, when I think of how he used to be so sceptical about spiritual things, it's so awesome to know that he came to know Jesus before he passed on." Deanie smiled.

Mark felt a familiar tightening in his chest. Naturally. His family couldn't pass up an opportunity to talk religion. He had kind of forgotten how much it irritated him sometimes.

Deanie continued, "I guess we have your mother to thank for that, Russ. She just wouldn't give up on Jack. He didn't stand a chance!" Even though she was Jack Burton's daughter, she had always called him by his first name. It was something Mark was also used to. That's just the way it was in this family. His father's mother was 'Grandma' or 'Mother', depending on who was addressing her, but Jack had always just been Jack, even to his own daughter.

"Grandma Graham can be stubborn," Harmony said.

"Probably as stubborn as Jack ever was," Russ agreed with a fond grin.

"You're a fine one to talk!" Deanie laughed, giving her husband a playful nudge. "If I recall, you wrote the book on stubborn. You're as immovable as they come."

"Hardly," Russ scoffed. "I married you, didn't I?" He slipped an arm around Deanie's still slim waist and she leaned into him.

"You've got to be stubborn in order to survive in this family," Mark cut in. "And Harmony, here, got a double dose from both sides of the family."

"Thanks," Harmony shot back. "Nice to have you back in the country, big brother. And when were you leaving again?" she asked with sarcastic humour.

They continued the good-natured banter as they reached Russ's sedan and piled in.

The warmth of the summer sun beat down on the heads of the mourners, as they gathered to pay their last respects to friend, father and grandfather, Jack Burton. Mark scanned the graveside as the minister pronounced the benediction. There were more people here than he would have imagined, including some people from the press. Jack had more friends and followers than Mark had realized. He was once again struck by the simple humility of the man that was also known as one of Winnipeg's favourite sons. He would be sorely missed.

The minister talked about Jack's faith in Christ at the church service. It was surprisingly upbeat, considering that someone had just died. The surviving members of Jack's band played a musical tribute and dignitaries gave short testimonies about Jack's life and character. Mark's own father, Russ, read the eulogy. He could tell that it was difficult for him, but Russ was a man of stalwart disposition, and carried it through despite the eruptions of tears coming from Deanie and Harmony.

Now they stood huddled together at the graveside, along with Jack's closest friends. They continued that way for several more minutes as the general mourners began to disperse. "Good bye, Daddy," Deanie said softly, blowing a kiss toward the lonely coffin. She'd never called him that. Russ's arm encircled her shoulders a little more tightly.

The intensity was almost too much for Mark. He let out a pent up breath and stepped back for a little more air.

"Mark," someone addressed him, hand out stretched. "So good to see you. I didn't get a chance to say 'hi' earlier. It's been awhile, eh?" Brent Walters pumped his hand vigorously. Mark was glad for the friendly diversion.

"Good to see you, Brent. How are Holly and the kids?"

"Great, just fine," Brent responded. "Around somewhere."

Brent waved vaguely. Mark caught a glimpse of Brent's wife, Holly, hugging Deanie.

Brent and Deanie went back a long ways. Brent was the son of Jack's best friend and fellow band member, Benny Walters. He and Deanie had grown up on the road together, more like siblings than anything else. They had quite a history, both good and bad. Mark had been awe struck by Brent in the early days when he had led a rough looking rock and roll band. Twenty years later, Brent no longer looked like the Bohemian artist. He was a regular looking middle-aged man with trim, greying hair and a moustache.

The rest of the band had pretty much gone their separate ways, but Deanie and Brent had remained connected, partly due to their long history, but mostly due to their mutual faith in Christ. Apparently, there was a time when Mark's father, Russ, had been jealous of Brent's friendship with Deanie. But Brent's conversion to Christ had been a factor in bringing both Russ and Deanie to the Lord, as they put it. The two men had become solid friends since.

"Here's Bryan, now," Brent said, waving his son over. Mark was surprised at the difference in the young man that stood before him. Last time he'd seen Bryan, he was a gangly teenager with a cracked voice. Now he was a young man of about eighteen, who was filling out in muscle and stature, and who addressed him in a decidedly mature tone. Certainly not the same kid whose diaper he'd had to change on occasion!

"I didn't see your dad around," Mark said to Brent.

"Nope. He passed on about two years ago. Cancer," Brent replied.

"Sorry to hear it," Mark said with genuine sympathy. "He and Grandpa Jack made quite a team."

Brent laughed. "Kind of like Oscar and Felix," he noted.

"Who?" Bryan asked.

"The odd couple," Brent explained. "Oh, never mind. You're

too young. In any case, there's only Toby and Mike left of the old group."

Mark nodded. The aging musicians had played their tribute at the service, and had been gathered with the family at the grave. They still stood talking with Russ and the others, Toby Rantt's white head starkly contrasting against his leathery black skin, while Mike Colinsky's gangly height stood out above the rest of the group.

Mark saw his sister in the tight embrace of another young woman, as they rocked back and forth for a few minutes. When they stepped back from one another, he was surprised to recognize Brent's daughter Amy. If he thought that Bryan had changed, he was shocked at the transformation in the older sister.

Last time he'd seen them was at Harmony's graduation, three years ago. He had flown in especially for the occasion from an archaeological site that he'd been working on in New Mexico. He'd only been able to spare a couple of days, and what with the necessity of spending the majority of the time with his immediate family, he'd had little more than a quick re-acquaintance with the Walters family. What he remembered was a small, unremarkable adolescent; a shy girl who was somewhat underdeveloped and had dirty blonde hair. She was only one year younger than his sister, but at the time she was still the annoying little girl whom he'd had to read the same story to over and over again in order for her to go to sleep.

What he was presented with now, was a very pretty young woman; still petite, but certainly not underdeveloped. Her blonde hair was piled loosely on her head in an attractive style, and she wore just enough makeup to enhance the green of her eyes without covering the sprinkling of freckles across her nose.

"Mark, you remember Amy?" Harmony asked, slipping her arm through the crook of Mark's elbow.

"How could I forget?" Mark smiled at Amy.

"Excuse me," Russ interrupted the exchange. "A few people

are going up to the house. I wonder if you and Harmony could catch a ride over with Brent and meet people as they arrive? He said he wouldn't mind squeezing you in. I think Deanie would like to spend a few more minutes here alone."

Mark looked around. More and more people were leaving the cemetery. He nodded. "No problem."

Mark, Harmony and Amy walked across the grass to the tree-lined driveway where Brent's car was parked. Brent, Holly and Bryan sat in the front, with Holly in the middle, while the other three squeezed into the back seat. Harmony sat in the middle between Mark and Amy.

"So I hear you've been in Africa this last while," Brent said conversationally.

"That's right."

"It must be fascinating," Holly said, glancing over her shoulder. "What exactly is it that you're working on?"

Mark went into a simplified explanation of the temple site and the layers of burial sites that had been hidden underneath.

"Mark's always liked rocks and old pottery better than people," Harmony teased when she got a chance.

They arrived at the Graham house just minutes before the first visitors. Deanie had arranged for a caterer to provide refreshments, so all Mark and Harmony had to do was act as host and hostess.

Mark's Uncle Ken and Aunt Kathy arrived first. They had escorted Ken and Russ's mother, Dorothy Graham, to the funeral, but due to the elderly woman's mobility, they had not gone to the cemetery. Mark allowed Harmony to open the house, while he helped his uncle get his grandmother out of the car. They proceeded along the sidewalk and up the wide front steps at a snail's pace.

"You were always such a good and helpful boy," Grandma Graham said. She was panting once inside the house, quite out of breath.

"A long way to come for a dead man," Ken commented to Mark with a grunt.

"Ken! That was rather unfeeling, don't you think?" Kathy scolded.

"What was that?" Dorothy asked. "I can't hear out of my right ear."

"It was nothing, Gran," Mark assured her. Mark could see that his Aunt and Uncle hadn't changed much since last time he'd been home. Still bickering and complaining. There had been a time when the whole family thought they would change. It was true, they had both gotten help with their alcohol problems, but AA hadn't been able to fix the negativity and bitterness that still seemed to define their lives together. It was a wonder they bothered to stick it out, especially now that their two children were well away on their own. Perhaps for some people the familiar, no matter how unpleasant, was preferable to the unknown.

"So what are Sam and Greg up to these days?" Mark asked conversationally once they'd gotten Grandma settled in a comfortable chair.

"What's that?" Dorothy asked loudly.

"I was just asking Uncle Ken and Aunt Kathy what Sam and Greg are up to," Mark repeated, loud enough for her to hear.

"Oh, I'm still praying for your cousins," Dorothy responded.

Ken rolled his eyes. Kathy piped up, "Samantha lives in Brandon now. She moved there last year and is doing quite well in real estate. I'm sure she would have come to the funeral if she wasn't so busy all the time."

"Finally left that stiff of a husband," Ken added. "About time, too. The guy was no good."

Mark found it ironic that the same thing had often been said about his uncle Ken.

"No need to bring that up," Kathy chided her husband. "Sam is doing very well these days. She's got the children in a very nice daycare. They're benefiting so much from the extra socialization."

"Learning how to swear, cheat and steal," Ken muttered. "I couldn't wait for them to go home last time they came for a visit. At least now we don't end up babysitting them all the time like before, though."

"There you go again!"

"What's Greg doing?" Mark interrupted before his Aunt and Uncle could fan the argument into a full-fledged fight.

"Who?" Dorothy asked, straining to be part of the conversation.

"Greg," Mark said loudly.

"Greg's doing very well in the oil patch," Kathy said proudly.

"So you think," Ken muttered, taking a sip of his coffee.

"He moved out to Alberta a couple of years ago," Kathy explained. "Of course, we don't hear from him very often. You know how young men are about calling home."

"I don't know about that," Ken mused, looking at Mark. "Mark, here, flies half way around the world to attend a funeral. Bet he calls his folks a little more often, too."

"I haven't been home much these last few years, either," Mark said, trying to deflect some of the attention from himself. The last thing he needed was to have his relatives start an argument over comparisons between their own children and himself. He'd been down that road enough times as a child. As he recalled, his cousins had always caused their parents their fair share of grief. They had been irresponsible and ungrateful, even then, and apparently things hadn't changed.

Harmony was greeting more people at the door and Mark used it as a way to excuse himself. "I'll talk to you a bit later, Gran," he said into his grandmother's ear before departing.

Several people whom Mark recognized from his parents' church had arrived. As well, Toby Rantt, the drummer from Jack's jazz ensemble, had arrived with his wife, children and grandchildren. They had all been close with Jack Burton over the years. Mark shook hands with various people and made some small talk as he made the rounds with the ever-increasing number of guests.

Finally, his father and Deanie arrived. Deanie didn't appear to be in any shape to play hostess, and Harmony was engaged in conversation with one of the younger members of the Rantt clan. With a sigh, Mark went to see if his Grandmother needed anything. His time for grieving would come later. For now, he needed to be strong for the rest of them.

He sat quietly beside his grandmother for a few minutes watching the rest of the people chat. She reached over and grasped his hand with a surprisingly strong grip. Her skin was very soft and fragile; paper thin and loose on the knotted chords beneath.

"Did she tell you about how your Grandpa came to accept the Lord Jesus?" Dorothy asked. Mark didn't respond right away, and she went on. "I'd been witnessing to Jack for years. Ever since his heart attack, oh, twenty years ago, at least."

Mark remembered the time well. He had just gotten close to Jack, and felt like he had finally found someone who really understood him. Then Jack had suffered a heart attack and Mark thought that he would never see him again. He'd cried many nights into his pillow when nobody else was around. Jack had eventually recovered, although a much weaker man, and he and Mark had renewed their relationship. It had made Mark appreciate him even more, knowing that he'd almost lost him.

"Stubborn man, though, he was," Dorothy mused, "he'd always just laughed and started in on one of his own stories, as if he hadn't really heard what I had to say."

Mark smiled. He could see Jack doing just that.

"Then, about six months ago, he startled me with a question. 'Dorothy,' he said, 'Where do you think a man goes when he dies?' It was an open invitation for me to share the gospel once again. But this time he really listened. He never said anything, which was unusual for your Grandpa Jack, as you well know. He just listened like so." She demonstrated by cocking her head to one side. "He must have known something; that his time was coming soon. He never said any more to me about it. Probably didn't want to hear me say I told you so. But he told Deanie just a week before he died that he had accepted Jesus as his Saviour. My, what a blessing for her to hear those words, once he passed on. Just died in his sleep, real peaceful like. It's a good way to die, I think. In your sleep."

Mark was more affected by the short discourse than he was willing to admit. Once again he sensed a growing uneasiness. It was fine to talk about God and Jesus in relation to anyone else. For most of his family it was the way they defined themselves. But Jack... he had been such an independent thinker... such a free spirit. To know that he had put his faith in something so illogical was unsettling somehow.

Mark excused himself and went out onto the back deck for a breath of fresh air. There were a few other people out enjoying the late afternoon sun, conversing in small groups of two or three.

Mark leaned against the railing and surveyed the rooftops of the neighbourhood. This was the home of his boyhood. He used to know every family by name for blocks around when he'd had his paper route. Now he doubted there were any familiar faces left.

"Hi," a female said, joining him. He looked down to see Amy Walters, at least a head shorter than himself. She looked soft and feminine. Laura was tall and athletic; hard and tanned from working in the African sun. He felt embarrassed that his mind had made the comparison, unbidden.

"Hi, yourself," Mark replied with a friendly smile. He turned back to stare at the rooftops.

"I know you were probably much closer to Jack than I ever was," Amy began. "I mean, he was your grandpa, not mine. But sometimes I felt like he was my grandpa, too. He and my real grandpa were so close."

"You probably saw more of him in these last years than I did," Mark said. "And he wasn't really my grandfather. Not by blood, anyway. But he was one special guy. I'll miss him."

"Me too," Amy agreed.

They were silent for a few moments before Mark picked up the conversation again. "So tell me, Amy. What do you do now that you're all grown up?"

"Nothing as exciting as the infamous Dr. Mark Graham." She laughed.

"Hardly."

"Oh, I don't know about that. Harmony's got a whole scrap-book of articles about you and your discoveries."

"Really?" Mark was genuinely surprised. "From where?"

"Science journals, or 'Archaeologist Today', or something." Amy shrugged. "Pretty impressive for someone so relatively young."

Mark laughed. "The operative word is 'relatively'. Compared to you, I'm pretty ancient."

Amy just shrugged again.

"So you still didn't tell me what you're doing these days," Mark prodded.

"I just finished my second year of nursing," Amy said.

"Following in your mother's footsteps." Mark nodded. "Makes sense."

"I guess it's what people expect."

"You don't sound all together pleased."

"It's okay," Amy said. "I mean, I'm not musical like my dad. Harmony and I used to pretend that someday we'd start our own band when we got old enough. Kind of like our parents and our grandparents. Carry on the family tradition and all that. Only an all girl band, since we didn't want Bryan involved - my stipulation! But when we finally got big enough, I had to face the truth that I couldn't carry a tune and had a terrible sense of rhythm."

"A terrible fate for someone with your lineage," Mark stated with a grin.

"Exactly! So my next best alternative was nursing."

"A fine and noble profession if it's what you want."

"What I really want to do - what I dream about - is going into missions," Amy said. "To go to some remote part of the world where they've never heard about Jesus, and teach them to read the Bible and pray..."

"Do places like that still exist?" Mark asked doubtfully.

Amy shrugged. "You tell me. You're the world traveler."

"In my line of work, our only contact with locals is with some of our preliminary work crews or in dealings with the governing authorities. We're more interested with the cultural aspects of past civilizations, not the present one," Mark explained. "In any case, if that's what you really want to do, you should go for it. It's what Jack would have said."

Amy smiled. "I suppose he would have, wouldn't he?"

"Sure he would have."

"I just keep telling myself that nursing could be a useful skill if I ever did go into missionary work."

"True. It would probably be very practical," Mark agreed.

"Although I really don't like the sight of blood," Amy mused.

"Hmm. That could be problematic," Mark said dryly.

"Ya think?" Amy laughed. "My mom keeps telling me I'll get over it."

"Remind me to keep an eye out for you, just in case I end up in hospital before you've conquered that one." Mark smiled.

"Amy! There you are!" Amy's mother, Holly Walters, came through the sliding glass patio doors. "I think we're going to get ready to leave soon. Deanie's looking awfully tired. I think she needs some solitude. Nice to see you again, Mark," she added before retreating back indoors.

"Nice talking to you," Amy said as she turned to follow her

mother back into the house. "Hope it all goes well for you back in Africa."

"Thanks. And likewise. It was nice talking to you, too. You've grown up a lot since last time we met," Mark said. "Hope you figure out what it is you want to do." He watched as she stepped through the opening and closed the glass behind her.

Amy Walters had indeed grown up.

CHAPTER 9

All of the guests had gone home. Deanie was in the family room listening to some of her father's old LP's, Harmony was talking on the phone, and Russ was loading some glasses into the dishwasher. Mark decided it would be a good time to check his emails. He wondered if any new developments had occurred at the site.

He scanned through several messages before opening one from Laura.

"Bad news. You need to hurry back. The government wants to shut us down due to risk factors. Sorry to rush you."

Russ frowned. It was just like Laura to make it short and to the point. No details whatsoever. He knew his family would have a hard time understanding, but he would have to take the next flight back to Harare. He couldn't risk not getting the casket out of that tunnel.

Harmony found him in the study a few moments later, still in deep contemplation.

"Looks like some serious thinking going on," she commented, perching on the arm of Mark's chair. She put her arms around his neck and gave him a quick squeeze before standing up and sauntering to a row of framed family pictures on a shelf. "What's up?"

"Just work." Mark shut off his laptop and snapped the lid down. "All that same old stuff you find so boring."

"Did I say that?" Harmony asked, picking up a picture of herself and Mark. He was wearing a cap and gown; she was at least half his height. "Remember that?" she asked, showing him the photo.

"Of course. It was my graduation day." Mark smiled.

"Obviously." Harmony laughed. "I mean what you told me that day. Remember?"

"Refresh my memory."

"I was worried because you were going off to university in the fall and I thought that when you moved out I'd never see you again. You said that no matter where you went in the world, you'd always come home again. You said that family was family forever, no matter what."

"Hmm. Pretty sage advice, if I do say so myself," Mark said. "I guess I haven't quite kept up my end as well as I should have."

"You've done okay. Your work is pretty important to you. I'm fairly proud of my big brother."

"So I've been told. Amy Walters tells me you've kept some kind of scrapbook. I might like to see it sometime. Just to see what the experts are saying about me."

"I can go get it now, if you like," Harmony offered. She left the room and came back a few minutes later with a large, hard covered album.

Mark flipped through the pages. He was surprised by the in depth discussion of his life and work. He vaguely remembered talking to some reporters at the various sites portrayed, but hadn't really paid much attention to what was being done with the information. He was also dismayed by the misrepresentation that he caught on occasion.

"I don't recall making that comment," he said under his breath, flipping to the next page. "I was hardly implying that my discoveries rivalled those of Machu Picchu. If they would have checked my own final dissertation on the topic, they would have seen that." He closed the book.

"So what had you looking so puzzled a few moments ago?" Harmony asked, taking the album from her brother's hands. "They can't hold down the fort without you?"

"I've got an excellent crew," Mark replied. "It's just that we're running into some issues with the government authorities. I'm afraid I'm going to have to leave as soon as possible."

"But you just got here!" Harmony protested.

"I know. Sorry, kid."

"So tell me more about this great archaeological dig of yours that you have to go back to so soon."

"We've come across some pretty spectacular discoveries, if I do say so myself," Mark said.

"Like what?"

Mark stopped for a minute, considering just how much he should tell her. Finally he leaned forward in a conspiratorial fashion. "Actually, little sister, we've found some dinosaur remains. Pterodactyl to be exact."

"So what's the big deal in that? There've been lots of dinosaur bones found."

"Not among a human burial site." Mark smiled, waiting for her reaction.

"Really?" she asked, her eyes getting wide. "Now, that is cool!"

"I thought you'd think so."

"Well, that just proves it, then," she said triumphantly.

"What?"

"Since God created all living creatures, it follows that dinosaurs and people lived at the same time. Believe me, I've had this discussion with my Biology teacher more than once. Now, thanks to you, we have scientific proof!"

"Hold on, there," Mark cautioned. "You're forgetting that's it's also been scientifically proven that dinosaurs died off long before human life existed. Though I am very excited about this discovery, we're still waiting to piece together all the information. There's got to be a plausible explanation. Maybe one type of flying reptile survived in isolation. We don't know. But don't go jumping to conclusions."

"Proven by who?" Harmony asked. "Some scientist somewhere that doesn't want to entertain the existence of a supreme being? There's been plenty of evidence to show that dinosaurs and people coexisted. The scientific community just doesn't want to take a serious look at it because it would blow all their precious beliefs in the theory of evolution out the window. They've spent too many billions brainwashing the general public to admit that they could be wrong after all."

She was beginning to sound a lot like Rocco, Mark decided. "They, as you say, are also highly educated professionals, trained in scientific methodology. You also forget that I'm one of them."

"Hey, nothing personal. I'm just laying it on the line for you."

"And where did you get all your wisdom?" Mark asked.

"You sound kind of defensive," Harmony noted. "I've been reading up on it. It was a subject that always kind of bugged me. Somehow what I'd been taught in school didn't sit well with my personal convictions about God. But I never really found any very satisfying answers."

"Until?" Mark prodded.

"Well, I found several sites on the net," Harmony explained. "Mostly all trained professionals and scientists, too. They've got all kinds of scientific evidence that's never made it into any major scientific journals."

Mark was sceptical. "There's probably a good reason for that."

"Hey, what happened to you?" Harmony asked. "I remember a day when you had as much faith in God as I do. You're one of the people who said I had to be myself, who God created me to be."

"I guess I grew up," Mark said. "It's all well and good for you, if that's what makes you happy. Personally, I prefer to put my faith in things that can be seen, not some invisible benevolence."

"But that's just it, Mark. Don't you see? You can't see, or prove evolution any more than you can prove creation. None of us were there to witness it firsthand. But the evidence is overwhelmingly in favour of intelligent design. It takes a lot more faith to believe that this whole world, so delicately balanced right down to the minutest detail, could have happened by chance. I'll send you some information some time."

Their father walked into the study. "It's been a long day," he said before sitting down himself.

"Where's Mom?" Harmony asked.

"It's been a pretty stressful day for your mother," Russ said. "She went to lie down. She'd got a bit of a headache."

"I'll go see if she needs anything." Harmony gave her father a kiss on the cheek, and then turned to her brother. "Think about what I said, Mark. 'The heavens declare the glory of God; the earth proclaims the work of His hands.' It's all right there for you to see, if you'll just open your heart to see it."

Both men watched her exit. Russ looked amused. "Your sister been lecturing you?" he asked.

"You could say that," Mark replied with a smile. "She's certainly not lacking in conviction."

"She never was," Russ agreed. "She's like her mother. Once she's decided on something, she goes for it one hundred percent. What was she trying to convince you of?"

"We'd been talking about some strange discoveries at the site I've been working on." He almost didn't want to say anymore. His father was sure to side with his sister on the matter.

"What kind of discoveries?"

Mark swallowed. How was he ever going to explain this to the scientific community if he couldn't even tell his own father? "We've found something pretty - unusual, Dad. Human remains purposely buried with the remains of what appear to be Pterodactyl." He waited for the response.

Russ didn't say anything for a moment, then rose and went to his bookshelf. He took down a volume and handed it to Mark. "Here. You might be interested in this."

Mark scanned the cover. Great. A book about God. Just what he was afraid of.

"I'm not asking you to believe what I say," Russ said. "Read it for yourself. With an open mind. It's written by a scientist who'd made some discoveries himself that he couldn't at first explain. In the end he came to one conclusion. God created the heavens and the earth. He's put years of research into that book. I think you'll find it fascinating, if not enlightening."

Mark turned the book over and read the back cover. He raised his eyebrows at the author's credentials. Maybe he would take a peek later, just to satisfy his curiosity.

"Yep, your sister has her mother's enthusiasm for adventure, and the ability to see the silver lining in everything. Now you, you're more like your old man. Don't take anyone else's word for anything. You want to figure it out for yourself - to test all the angles and mull over all the possibilities. I wish I could convince you to see things my way based on my own experiences. But I know that's not the way you tick. I understand that perfectly, and I respect it."

Father and son sat silently for a time until Mark spoke up. "Ever wonder what our lives would have been like if you'd never met Deanie?"

"Sure. Lots of times. And I've come to the conclusion that I'd still be stuck in my own self-righteousness and bitterness over your mother. It's because of Deanie that I gave my life to Christ."

Mark thought of the woman who had given him birth. He'd never met her and his father did not talk about her. From the bits of information he'd been able to piece together, she had abandoned them when Mark was just a baby. Apparently it had been a marriage of necessity, which she was not ready or willing to commit to. She had never attempted to contact him or establish any kind of relationship. Mark had only seen one picture of her at his grandmother's house. It was taken the day of the wedding. His father had not kept any reminders of that painful period in his life. His baby pictures started at about four months of age, shortly after Miranda Graham had left. Mark had held secret resentment toward her as a child, as well as a sense of inadequacy. What mother would abandon her baby unless he didn't measure up in some way? Now, as an adult, he was over those feelings. He felt nothing but remote apathy that occasionally bordered on the curious.

"So what are your plans, now, Son?" Russ asked.

"I need to get back as soon as possible," Mark replied. "I know it hasn't been much of a visit, but there are some important developments and I really need to get back."

Russ nodded, understanding full well the driving need to keep one's commitments.

Later that night, in his bed in the spare room, Mark flipped through the book that his father had given him. Petrified tree trunks running directly through several layers of the geologic record; human and dinosaur footprints found side by side; evidence of catastrophic flooding throughout the earth; countless flaws in carbon dating and cover ups galore, some of which never got removed from science text books. Fascinating, if not credible. He might enjoy reading the book after all.

A light tapping sounded at the bedroom door. "Come in," Mark said, setting the book aside, and sitting up a bit in the bed. It was Deanie.

"Your Dad tells me you're thinking of leaving sooner than expected," she said, sitting on the edge of the bed.

"Yes. There are some - problems on sight that need my attention. I really can't stay," Mark explained.

"I understand," Deanie said. "I just wanted to say how much

it's meant to me, for you to come all the way for Jack's funeral. I was a bit out of it today, and I just wanted you to know that I really appreciate it."

"Jack was pretty important to me. I wanted to come."

Deane smiled. "He always looked on you like his own grandson, you know."

"And he was, and always will be, my Grandpa," Mark offered.

"You know, he said some things before he died that I think he wanted you to hear."

"Like what?"

"He said that he was sorry that in all the times you spent together, he never gave you any real advice that mattered."

"That's not true. He always gave me lots of good advice. Why, I came to him with everything, and he always delivered."

"I think he meant about spiritual things," Deanie said gently. "He never was one much for religion, you know that. And I think toward the end he felt bad about that, like he had somehow turned you off God because he had never believed. You were always so willing to listen to whatever he said."

"I think I eventually grew up enough to make up my mind on most things. No need for him to worry on that account."

"But he realized he was wrong, near the end. That he did need Jesus. I think that's what bothered him the most. That now he knew Jesus and maybe you didn't."

"So my whole family thinks I've turned away from God," Mark stated quietly.

"Have you?"

"I don't know. Maybe I never really belonged to Him in the first place."

CHAPTER 10

Mark had plenty of time to ponder the question on his flight back to Africa. He had believed in God as a child because he'd seen the evidence of change in the lives of the people around him.

Mark remembered the turbulence of those early years well. His father, normally a conservative and self controlled individual, had veered off course in an uncharacteristic fashion and begun a relationship with Deanie, an ex rock and roll junkie and daughter of jazz great, Jack Burton. When Deanie ended up getting pregnant, she and his father had married. The early days of their union had been anything but peaceful.

Mark recalled the harsh words that were exchanged when they thought he wasn't listening, covered by pretence when they knew he was. He remembered the times Deanie had snuck him over to her rock and roll friends' rehearsal studio to listen to them play. His father hadn't been pleased. Then Deanie had run away for a short while. It wasn't until she went into premature labour and she almost lost her own life in the process that things started to turn around. Through it all, Grandma Graham had been praying, and apparently her prayers had paid off.

After that, his parents turned to God and started attending

church. The change in their behaviour and outlook was truly remarkable. Not to say that they never had problems, but somehow they managed to work it out. His father was still the conservative accountant he had always been, but without the judgmental perfectionism. Deanie remained her flamboyant and fun loving self, but she too learned to trust God instead of her own resources when the going got tough.

Mark had witnessed these changes firsthand. He had been about twelve at the time, and although he had always been sent to Sunday school before that, and had been ministered to by his grandmother, he had never really experienced a living faith like what he saw in the lives of his parents and their friends. The evidence of positive change in his own family should have been proof enough of the existence of God, but sometimes he'd felt more like a spectator.

His grandmother said it was okay; that not everyone had the same emotional response to God. He was naturally reserved and reflective like his father, so he accepted his lack of emotionalism as normal.

But his scientist's mind opened up to other possibilities as he grew older and went on to study at university. Some of the things that he had witnessed as a child were just not logical. Added to that his own lack of spiritual connection with any unseen forces, and he came to the conclusion that most of what he had witnessed was human emotionalism, pure and simple. Not that there was anything bad in that; as emotional creatures, people needed an outlet of some kind, and he was glad that his parents had found something that seemed to work for them. But he'd long since dismissed any need that he might have himself for such an outlet. He had his work, and the fulfillment that he felt with each new discovery was enough to keep him going for the time being.

Or was it?

He wondered at the unsettled feelings he'd experienced when

Deanie had brought up Jack's faith. Mark had always looked up to Grandpa Jack as an imparter of wisdom. To find that he had succumbed to the same kind of blind faith as his parents was news that left him feeling strangely upset.

The journey back to the archaeological site also afforded Mark plenty of time to read the book his father had given him. It was surprisingly well documented in its attempt to undermine the pervasive theories on the origins of the planet and life on earth. It also presented some interesting alternatives a.k.a. creation, which, if not altogether convincing, were food for thought. Certainly, the concept of intelligent design, be it by a benevolent Creator or by some other form of advanced being, explained many of the discrepancies that the more accepted theory of evolution only seemed to exacerbate. It pricked enough of an interest in Mark, at any rate, to have him wanting more. He would have to do some research of his own.

Mark arrived back at the archaeological dig armed with new insight into the possibilities of creation theory, and plagued with his own resistance at believing it. He felt like a man being pulled in two directions. At some point, joints and muscle would be severed, as neatly as if he were on one of those ancient inventions of torture.

He had also stopped in Harare, and secured the remaining time they had left from the original four-month contract he'd negotiated last time. At least that was something.

"So? What news?" Rocco asked, joining him the moment he'd stepped from the jeep.

Mark took out a hanky and blew the dust from his nose. "We're back to the same time frame as before," he replied, stuffing the hanky into his back pocket. "That gives us less than six weeks."

Rocco swore in Spanish.

"I know, I know," Mark agreed. "But it's better than nothing. Your work crews still going around the clock?"

Rocco nodded. "Another day or two, maybe. That's it. We'll rescue the king, don't worry, Boss."

"I'm counting on it."

Mark strode to the tent where he knew he would find Laura. She was leaning over the microscope as usual.

She looked up, relief at seeing him obvious in her eyes. "What took you so long?" she teased.

He didn't smile back. "I want all - and I mean all - of the artefacts crated and ready for transport to the States. Only do what cataloguing is absolutely necessary. Any other analysis can be done later."

Her eyes widened. "What's going on?"

"We've only got a couple weeks to wrap this up. I'm afraid the government isn't taking too kindly to what they consider unnecessary disturbance to the temple. I've explained the magnitude of our latest discoveries, but they seem adamant in their original time frame. And I don't want to take any chances with what we've discovered here, either. I got wind that some of the more nationalistic minded in the government don't want any artefacts leaving the country. Before they come in here and start asking for access, I want everything safely on its way. We can always plead ignorance and return it later. Once it's safely at the university in New Mexico we can piece it together then."

"I had the feeling something like this would happen," she said. "I'm already on it."

"Good." He turned to leave.

"Um, Mark?" Laura asked tentatively.

He stopped in his tracks. "Yes?"

"Aren't you glad to see me?" A hopeful smile softened her lips.

He blinked. He had been so focused on the task at hand he hadn't even stopped to consider niceties. "Oh. Oh, yeah." He waved awkwardly, then turned abruptly and strode from the room.

Later that night, Laura snuck into his tent. It had been awhile and he was only human...

They lay now, on the narrow cot, his arm behind her neck, her head cradled against his chest. Mark laid there, his eyes fully awake, staring at the ceiling.

"So how was your family?" Laura asked quietly, playing with some of his chest hairs.

"Huh? Oh, okay. As good as can be expected, I guess."

"It's hard to lose someone you love," she said, her tone sympathetic.

"Yep. That it is," he agreed.

"You were close to him. Your granddad."

"Yes. I learned a lot from him."

"About what?"

Mark shrugged. "Life in general."

Jack had opened up a whole new world to Mark. He'd sat in on countless jam sessions with Jack's cronies, never realizing the musical genius to which he was so casually privy, or the celebrity status of those with whom he had been allowed to hobnob. He was simply allowed 'in', and was witness to a creative passion that in retrospect filled him with amazement. To say that Jack Burton had influenced his life would be to grossly underestimate the powerful bond that had brought them together. He was his grandfather, not merely by chance, but by choice.

"Hm. That's nice." She snuggled in further and sighed contentedly.

Mark's arm began to throb, the circulation cut off. He shifted uncomfortably.

"Sorry. Am I too heavy?" Laura asked, sitting up slightly.

"Probably just the long trip. I didn't sleep much on the plane."

"Oh. I suppose I could go back to my own tent and let you get some rest."

Mark knew she was trying to get him to ask her to stay. But he kept his mouth shut. Right now he needed some space.

Laura rose from the cot, which made a creaking noise as soon as the added weight of her body had been released, and grabbed for her clothing. Mark could see that she was hurt, but he couldn't do anything about that right now.

"Bye," he offered lamely as she lifted the tent flap. She turned and stared at him a moment, but didn't say anything. He watched her leave and heaved a great sigh of relief.

What was he doing, sleeping with a woman he didn't really have any feelings for? He knew it was not something he could admit to his father - or Jack for that matter - with comfort. Jack's commitment to passion, and his own father's unwavering adoration for his stepmother were examples that made him now feel ashamed. But he was a man, after all. It was pretty hard to say no when it was offered so casually. And Laura didn't seem to mind - she usually didn't demand a lot in return.

The thought crossed his mind that Laura would probably never fit in with his family. And she was no Amy Walters, either.

He froze for a second, his mind having a knee jerk reaction to its own meanderings.

Now where had that come from? Amy Walters was just a kid - his little sister's friend. Someone he used to babysit. And what kind of man was he anyway, to be thinking of one woman after having just made love to another?

His family would indeed be disappointed if they knew just how far he had fallen.

CHAPTER 11

Mark stepped out of the storage compound and let his eyes adjust to the brightness of the sun. The facility was being systematically emptied and its contents shipped. Anthony, a few metres away, waved and stopped his own progress to wait for Mark.

"Looks like today might be the day," Anthony said.

Mark nodded. "I was worried we'd never get that casket out in time. But it looks promising. Now I just have to make sure the final arrangements for the airlift are in place. Our mystery man is about to make his first overseas flight to Albuquerque."

"You're going with?" Anthony asked.

"You bet I am. I'm not letting it out of my sight." Mark hesitated before continuing. "Before I forget, I have a book I think you might be interested in. My father lent it to me."

"What kind of book?"

"Come on and I'll show you."

They strode with purpose to Mark's quarters and ducked under the flap. Mark found the book where he'd left it right beside his bed and handed it over to Anthony for inspection. "A pretty interesting read, if I do say so."

Anthony perused the cover and nodded. "Thanks man. I'll return it when I'm finished."

"According to the author, our find isn't so unique after all. There have been lots of dinosaur remains found with more, so called, modern species."

"Just like Rocco said."

"Right. There are all sorts of discrepancies. Human remains in layers labelled millions of years old. Fossils of modern horses alongside their ancient ancestors - all kinds of discrepancies in the geologic layer that are either ignored, hidden, or otherwise explained away by elaborate means."

The two men stepped back out into the African sun, and Mark continued, "After reading that book, I'm beginning to wonder if Rocco's conspiracy theories aren't so off base. Did you know that scores of fraudulent 'missing links' that were documented as fact and then found to be untrue are still being used in reference books?"

"Really? You don't say."

"Absolutely. Take for instance, Neanderthal man. Although the scientific world has long since dismissed that discovery as a fake, most of the general population still believes it to be a fact. And get this. Modern DNA testing has even proved the impossibility of any link between bipedal primates thus discovered and man. Yet there are some less scrupulous scientists out there, with federal backing I might add, that are willing to tweak their findings just a bit in order to fit them into acceptable theories. As a strict follower of scientific methodology myself, that really irks me! That's not even science."

"Sounds like a pretty fascinating read," Anthony noted with upraised brows. "Certainly caught your interest, anyway."

Mark allowed a smile to pierce his features. "I guess I was getting pretty excited, wasn't I? It's why I thought you might want to read it. I'd appreciate your thoughts on the subject once you're through."

They parted ways with a wave and Mark entered the lab where Laura was hard at work.

"You're looking much more chipper this morning," she noted, looking up from her computer.

"I'm feeling better, too," Mark replied. "Probably the fact that we should be able to recover that casket today."

"That is good news. What were you and Anthony having such a heated discussion about just now?"

"You heard us?"

"The walls are only made of canvas," she reminded.

"Oh, just some research I've been doing." He looked over her shoulder at the computer screen. "What are you working on?"

"I think I have a plausible explanation for the reptilian remains," she said.

"Okay," he nodded. "I'm listening."

"Well, since there is a fair bit of seismic activity in this region, that well preserved headpiece we saw in the casket could well have been buried and almost instantly freeze dried during one of the ice ages. Eons later, more seismic activity reopened the long buried remains, which the people of the region must have come across. They then used them in their ceremonial burials. It's probably how the whole legend started."

Mark raised his brows. "That's a fairly elaborate explanation. What's wrong with just accepting that there could have been a Pterodactyl like reptile alive at the same time as the humans living in the region? Scientists are discovering new life forms in the jungles of South America practically every day. Why are we so reticent to admit that there could be dinosaur like creatures that lived contemporaneously with man?"

Laura gave him a withering look. "I thought we'd been through this."

"What?" Mark crossed his arms. "Did you know that there are numerous documented cases of human remains found in geologic layers where they're not supposed to be? Take for instance, a site in Germany where a human skull was found buried in the layers of coal. Coal! You know how many millions of years old that's supposed to be? Or in Texas, remains that are clearly human were found in the same geologic layer as long extinct fossil remains. There are dozens of discrepancies. Recognizably modern birds have been found side by side with, oh... what's the name of it?" He frowned, snapping his fingers and then his face cleared. "Archaeopteryx, that's what it's called."

Laura blinked, her eyes wide. "What on earth are you talking about?"

"Archaeopteryx. The supposed link between flying reptiles and birds," Mark explained.

Laura held up her hands and shook her head. "Listen to yourself! If these finds are so well documented, why aren't they common knowledge?"

"Well -"

She interrupted him. "Just think about it. You've been doing a little reading from a book written by who? Some quack who has a questionable background in science, with degrees from some obscure university that nobody's heard of, and who obviously has a religious agenda behind it all."

Mark frowned. "How do you know what I've been reading?"

"I saw the book by your cot," Laura answered. "I have been in your quarters since you've been home, just in case you've forgotten," she added sarcastically.

"And?" Mark felt the tick in his own jaw as he waited for the rest.

"I looked the author up on the internet. His credibility is iffy, at best."

Mark felt suddenly deflated. And foolish.

"I'm worried about you, Mark." Laura put a hand on his forearm. "You've got your reputation to think about."

Mark inhaled deeply. "So what you're saying is, I should just turn a blind eye to anything that might raise a few eyebrows and pretend it never existed."

"Well, no. Not exactly," Laura replied.

"No? Then what are you saying, Laura? I'm a little confused here."

"Just don't go making any claims that you can't verify one hundred percent."

"I wouldn't do that," Mark retorted. "It's not my style and you know it. But I'm not going to make up a bunch of complicated hooey just to save face either."

"Well, don't go looking for trouble, then."

"You mean, ignore the facts, if necessary."

Laura let out another exasperated sigh. "You're impossible!" Turning, she stormed out of the lab.

With no further incident, the casket of the mysterious king was brought to the surface. It was the moment of triumph Mark had been straining toward for weeks. He thought he might burst with it.

"Okay, people," he called out to the crowd of onlookers. Every single person who was part of the archaeological team had gathered at the entrance to the tunnels. "Make way. We need to get the king, here, to the lab for some initial analysis. I want all the stats, pronto! Photos, measurements, skin and hair samples - everything within the next hour! And don't forget a sample from the reptilian headdress."

"What's the rush?" Laura asked, frowning. "I thought the chopper wasn't coming until the day after tomorrow?"

"That's what I wanted everyone to believe. It might actually arrive as early as this afternoon."

"What?" Laura practically choked on the word. "Why?"

"I told you before. I'm worried that the authorities are going to put the clamp down on removing artefacts from the country. A little innocent mix up in paperwork is my insurance that I get him back to New Mexico in one piece for some proper analysis."

"You're as paranoid as Rocco, for heaven's sake! This isn't some spy movie, Mark. We're scientists and this is an archaeological dig. Remember?"

He gave her an icy stare. "Get to work, please, Doctor Sawchuk. We might not have all day."

The team worked efficiently to get the requested statistical information and samples and the casket was resealed and readied for transport. It was first vacuum-sealed in a protective, heat, fire and moisture resistant shroud. Then it was placed in a large wooden crate, surrounded with several feet of foam. Once air lifted by helicopter to Harare, it would be placed inside a metal container and flown the rest of the way to New Mexico.

The crate was resting on the back of a flat bed truck, awaiting the arrival of the helicopter. The tension around the camp was palpable. There was still a lot of work to be done, but everyone seemed preoccupied with anticipation.

Mark was packed and ready himself. He wasn't about to let this find out of his sight. He gathered together the crew chiefs to give them some final instructions before his departure. "Laura, you'll be in charge of the final cataloguing and crating of the artefacts. Joey, you and Rocco look after getting that tunnel sealed off so no would-be raiders come and disturb the site after we're gone. Hopefully the government will do a proper refit and will make the site accessible to the public. We've already got the schematics of the site mapped out and catalogued, but there might be a few additions now that the initial tunnelling has been disturbed. If any government officials come by asking questions, plead ignorance. But I want this site ship shape, sealed off and ready to leave in their hands with no glitches by the time the deadline is up."

"Aren't you coming back?" Rocco asked.

"I'm not sure," Mark answered. "It's my intention to, but I'm just not sure what's going to happen once I get to Albuquerque. I want everything wrapped up nice and tidy just in case I don't."

"Great. So you're leaving us to deal with irate government officials," Laura said. "Once they find out we've hauled everything off to the States, they're not going to be happy."

"I'll deal with it," Mark assured. "You must see there's no other way?"

Laura just shrugged.

"So? Any other questions or concerns?" Mark asked, looking around the group. A slight smile suddenly turned up the corners of his mouth as he cocked his head to one side. "Is that a helicopter I hear in the distance?" He shielded his eyes from the sun as he scanned the sky.

The rest of them heard it, too. The distinct double chop-chop of the huge propellers on a military type helicopter used for transporting cargo to remote locations. The crowd gathered again, as the giant locust came into view, scattering just enough for safety's sake once the beast was close to touching down.

Mark waited as the whirling knives at the crown and tail of the vehicle slowed and the door was thrown open. He walked forward to greet the pilot, a trusted member of the underground opposition. Suddenly, the smile that had formed on his lips froze. Several men in green camouflage army fatigues stepped out, automatic weapons trained and ready.

They advanced forward with crouching gait, sweeping the area with their eyes, weapons never straying from the locked in position by their sides. Mark blinked nervously, raising his hands slightly for lack of a better idea. Finally, a well suited government official, a man whom Mark had dealt with quite pleasantly on several occasions, stepped down from the now immobile chopper. He surveyed his surroundings and with a raised hand gave the signal for the soldiers to lower their weapons.

With a sigh of relief, Mark lowered his own hands as well. "Mr. Sangeruka," he called out, trying for pleasant nonchalance.

"This is a rather unexpected surprise. Don't you think the armed guards are a bit much, considering this is a government sponsored archaeological dig?"

The official glared back at Mark, his eyes never wavering, his mouth never cracking a smile. "We need to talk, Dr. Graham."

"Fine. Shall we step out of the sun?" Mark suggested with a gesture.

Without warning, an engine roared to life. All eyes swung in the direction of the sound as a cloud of dust and rocks sprayed up from spinning tires. Someone had commandeered the truck that held the casket! Shouts and gunshots rang out but the truck was already swerving crazily around the side of the mountain, out of sight.

Mark sped toward another jeep and vaulted inside, searching frantically for the keys. A spurt of machine gun fire pelted the air and he looked up to see the government official with his hand in the air, gesturing for calm.

"Let him go," Mr. Sangeruka yelled. "He won't get far on these mountain roads. We'll cut him off before he gets down the side of the mountain."

"But the casket!" Mark shouted. "What if it gets damaged? What if he has an accident?"

"That is out of your hands, now," Mr. Sangeruka said point‐edly. "It is not your property. It belongs to the people."

"But..." Mark surveyed the crowd of gaping spectators. His eyes searched and catalogued every face. Who was missing? Then it came to him. Rocco. His mouth became a grim line. He unfolded himself slowly from the jeep and stepped onto the dusty ground.

"We would ask that your crew pack up their personal belong‐ings as quickly as possible. Transport trucks will be arriving tomorrow to take them from the site."

"What's going on here?" Mark asked, his eyes steel.

"The government of the people is taking over the rest of the operation of this sacred and holy site," Mr. Sangeruka explained quite calmly. "Any equipment that belongs to you or your governments will be shipped to you at a later date. We will also be launching an official requisition order. All missing artefacts must be returned immediately to their place of origin. As for you, Dr. Graham. You are under arrest."

CHAPTER 12

It was like a terrible nightmare. Soldiers watched Mark as he unpacked his personal belongings for their perusal and then repacked it all again. At one point he tried to make eye contact with Laura; to try to tell her to get the skin and hair samples out - somehow.

But he was never given the chance. Before the eyes of the rest of the team, he was handcuffed and pushed unceremoniously into the waiting helicopter. Several soldiers were dispatched to stay behind until the rest of the transportation trucks arrived. But in the meantime, Mr. Sangeruka was anxious to get his prisoner safely back to Harare. Not to mention the fact that they still had a thief to catch.

With a deafening whir of propellers, the helicopter lifted off. Mark watched out the window as the archaeological site became a tiny cluster of doll sized tents and roped off squares. The people below scurried about like ants. Soon they were out of sight all together as the chopper gained altitude and swung around to the north.

The treacherous alpine road leading to the nearest airstrip wound around the side of the mountain like a snake. Mark strained forward to see if he could catch any signs of Rocco and the flatbed truck. Where did Rocco think he was going with that casket, anyway? Didn't he know there was no way he could outrun them? And even if he managed to hide in the hills for a few days, he was still going to need to surface at some point. He'd never be able to transport a package that size anywhere without alerting the authorities somehow. Whatever his former friend and colleague's plan, it wasn't very well thought out, that's for sure.

They spotted the errant vehicle a few moments later, just up ahead, still creating a cloud of dust in its wake as it careened along the side of the mountain. The helicopter swooped down to overtake the truck. Mr. Sangeruka signalled for one of his soldiers to fire on the vehicle.

Mark protested loudly, but his voice was caught in the combination of propeller chops and gunfire that spewed from the armed man's weapon.

This was no action movie, Mark realized with sickening clarity. There would be no near misses as bullets inexplicably ricocheted off their intended target. No. With the very first ejaculation of the automatic weapon, the tires on the truck blew apart, sending the vehicle swerving uncontrollably on the narrow roadway below. Then, with the grace of a slow motion replay, the truck veered off the edge of the cliff, bouncing and bumping like a toy, end over end. Mark caught a glimpse of the crate flying gracefully through the air and disappearing into the brush below. He thought he might pass out.

"Don't worry, Dr. Graham," Mr. Sangeruka shouted above the din. "We'll send a crew to recover the remains. For now, I think we'd be better off getting you to Harare."

Idiot. Didn't he realize the priceless nature of the cargo he had just sent off the cliff?

Not to mention, another man's life. Rocco had some quirks, that was for sure, but Mark felt more certain than ever he had just been trying to protect the discovery from getting into the wrong hands. Apparently he was correct in trying to do so.

Once the helicopter touched down at the military airport on the outskirts of Harare, Mark was practically thrown from the aircraft and pushed, headfirst, into a waiting dark blue Escalade. His duffel bag of belongings, along with the saxophone case, were thrown in beside him on the back seat.

Didn't people learn how to drive in Africa, he wondered? The government official in the front seat seemed unfazed by the way the driver careened through the streets of the city, nearly missing pedestrians and other vehicles alike.

"So what am I being charged with?" Mark asked flatly. He was still reeling from the knowledge that Rocco was dead and the casket probably lost forever.

"Malpractice, substandard working conditions, breach of trust," Sangeruka replied.

"Although I object to all of those accusations, they are hardly grounds for arrest," Mark stated.

"How about theft of public property?" Mr. Sangeruka suggested, never changing his expression from one of stony coolness.

"That's ridiculous," Mark said quietly. "I did nothing that wasn't specifically laid out in the agreed upon contract with your government."

"Really, Dr. Graham? What about the secret shipment of artefacts to the United States without the express permission of the proper authorities?"

"Sending artefacts out for analysis is standard procedure on most archaeological sites."

"Without proper paperwork documenting their departure?" Mr. Sangeruka asked.

"Your government was placing such unrealistic time constraints on us that we couldn't take the time. Besides, a general release waver was signed at the beginning of the project.

It covers any odds and ends that might get missed in the initial shuffle."

"Artefacts of such importance could hardly be classed as 'odds and ends'," Sangeruka replied.

Mark frowned but remained silent.

"As I suspected. That type of unethical procedure constitutes a definite breech of contract."

"I wasn't going to steal anything," Mark countered. "A find of that - delicacy - requires specialized care and attention during analysis. There's always a danger of deterioration when dealing with something that ancient."

"Or that valuable," Sangeruka stated.

"Are you suggesting that I was out for personal gain from this find?" Mark asked. "My track record speaks for itself. I'm interested in scientific discovery, pure and simple."

Sangeruka shrugged. "You wouldn't be the first. The promise of wealth has turned more than one head."

"And what have you gained, Sangeruka? Not only have you lost - or at least irreparably damaged - possibly the greatest archaeological find of this century, but you wasted an innocent life doing it."

"Innocent?" Sangeruka laughed humourlessly. "I hardly think so."

"What do you mean?"

"Rocco Cortez had connections to an underground smuggling operation which dealt in rare artefacts. All old, priceless - and stolen."

This information shook Mark to the core. He had known Rocco for years; considered him a personal friend.

"I can see that this information shocks you," Sangeruka noted. "That will probably bode well for you. Perhaps you will be given a lighter sentence. In any case, shed no tears for Mr. Cortez. He was a 'bad apple', as they say, and needed to be discarded before he tainted the entire barrel."

They rode the rest of the way to the police station in down-town Harare without any more conversation. Mark was still trying to wrap his mind around this new piece of information. If Rocco was involved in an illegal smuggling operation, there may be others. If he couldn't trust Rocco, whom could he trust? Joey, Anthony... Laura?

Maybe nothing and nobody was safe anymore.

"We have arrived at your hotel," Sangeruka said as they pulled up to the police station. It was a large stone building, several stories high with reddish streaks of rust bleeding down onto the stone from the iron bars on every window. Sangeruka disem-barked and allowed two armed guards, heavy artillery still intact, to escort Mark into the building. It was muggy, close and dusty grey on the inside.

Apparently they were expecting him. The uniformed officer at the front counter waved them forward without even a greeting. Another officer joined them, a jangling ring of keys at his waist and with a brisk nod at Sangeruka, he led the way through a door, down a dark hallway, and into a section of the building that housed the jail cells. The man swung one of the iron doors open with a creak and gestured for Mark to enter. He had little choice but to comply.

"I'm a Canadian citizen," Mark offered. "You can't just lock me up without specifying the charges against me." The door to the cell had already been firmly shut. "What about legal counsel?" he asked, grasping the cold steel of the bars.

"All in due time," Sangeruka said, smiling for the first time since the horrific trip had begun.

"I also have working visas from the US government that provide protection," Mark added for good measure.

"Need I remind you you're not in the US or Canada at the moment, Dr. Graham? While in this country you are subject to our law."

"I have special protection under the International Archaeological Agreement," Mark said desperately. "I stuck to the letter of the law in fulfilling my end of the contract, and I've got documentation to back me up."

Sangeruka waved dismissively. He turned and was about to leave when Mark called out one last time. "Sangeruka! Who's breaking faith, now? I demand to know who is behind this and what I'm being charged with."

"You will demand nothing," Sangeruka said calmly. "Enjoy your stay, Dr. Graham. Oh, and dinner is served at... " He consulted his watch and then looked up pleasantly. "I'm sorry. I guess you've missed dinner." With that he turned and retreated down the dark hallway, the click of his shoes resonating on the cement floor.

Mark rested his head against the bars for a moment, utter dejection seeping through him like poison injected into a vein. With a sigh he turned and surveyed the small cell in the dim light coming from the single bulb in the hallway. It consisted of crumbling concrete walls, ceiling and floor and sported a stainless steel toilet, a sink and a wooden bench with no mattress. So much for five-star amenities. How long he would have to endure it, he did not know.

Another thought struck him with sickening clarity. His personal belongings had not been deposited with him. There was nothing of great value in the duffel bag, but Jack's saxophone... It was the only remaining tie he had to his grandfather. He just hoped he'd get it back when all this got straightened out.

———

Dreams of Pterodactyls swooping down to capture unsuspecting men, women and children, plagued Marks sleep. Among the victims were various family members including his sister Harmony, his parents, and family friends like Amy Walters. Presiding over the crazed mob was the grizzled face of the ancient king, smiling with the toothy grin of the dead, yet very much alive in his gestures and mannerisms. Hovering over everything was Grandpa Jack, glibly playing his saxophone for all he was worth, oblivious to all the grisly mayhem below.

What could one expect, sleeping on a hard wooden bench in a musty jail cell? Especially when the only other occupant in another cell, groaned all night long. Mark got to his feet slowly and stretched his aching body. His stomach protested with a loud growl. It had been a long time since he'd eaten and his gut was crying out for some sustenance. Not to mention the fact that he was parched with thirst. He was afraid to drink the tap water for fear of contaminants, but was getting close to taking just a sip anyway.

A clanging noise brought his attention to the door at the end of the hallway. Someone was opening it. Hopefully it was breakfast. He rubbed his chin absently, a night's growth of stubble shadowing his face.

It wasn't breakfast. "Come with me," the uniformed officer said, opening the cell door.

"Where are we going?" Mark asked. The officer didn't answer.

Mark followed the man down the narrow hallway. At least he was out of the confines of that cell. He squinted slightly when they emerged into the main part of the building.

They continued through a maze of desks until they reached an office door. Two armed guards, vaguely familiar in appearance, stood guard. The police officer rapped on the door with his knuckles and was answered by a sharp "Enter!" from within. The officer opened the door and held it ajar for Mark's admittance.

"Sangeruka," Mark said, nodding to the government official who was sitting in the room, along with a man Mark assumed was the chief of police.

"I trust you slept well," Sangeruka said.

Mark grunted a noncommittal reply.

"You may take a seat," the police chief said, gesturing to an empty chair on the other side of his desk. Mark complied just as his stomach growled loudly.

Sangeruka raised an eyebrow, but said nothing.

"So? Have you figured out that you've made a big mistake yet?" Mark asked.

Sangeruka's reply was cool. "Don't press me," he said, his look one of steel. He stood lazily, sauntering to where Mark sat across from the chief. "You are in no position to negotiate."

Mark took that statement for what it was worth. There was no arguing one's rights in this situation. He rubbed the stubble on his chin thoughtfully, waiting for Sangeruka to make the next move.

"Chief Ganges, here, has offered you police protection during your transport to the State Penitentiary," Sangeruka said, gesturing to his stern and silent cohort. The chief's expression never changed.

Mark's eyebrows rose. "The State Penitentiary?"

"I'm not finished, Dr. Graham," Sangeruka said patiently, much as one would speak to an unruly child. "We believe it necessary - for security reasons - to move you to a more secure facility."

"You've got to be kidding," Mark shook his head in disbelief. "If I only knew what the charges against me were, I could -"

Sangeruka silenced him with a raised hand. "I think I must warn you, however. The accommodations at the State Penitentiary are far less... comfortable than here."

Mark's eyes narrowed. "Oh?"

"Of course, I might be able to find a way to alleviate that situation... shorten your stay, so to speak."

"What are you getting at, exactly?" Mark studied the other man warily.

"Absolute silence about your discoveries," Sangeruka replied.

Mark frowned. "I don't see how that's possible."

"Anything is possible if you choose it to be so," Sangeruka stated.

"But why? This could be the biggest scientific discovery of -"

"I know," Sangeruka cut him off. "Of the century. So you said."

"You can't expect me to just pretend nothing was discovered. What about all the samples, the artefacts already sent away for analysis? The rest of the crew? You've got up to fifty people who have in one way or another been exposed to that information already. You can't expect to arrest and threaten each one in order to keep them quiet."

"You are the head of the operation. People will listen to you. Follow your lead." Sangeruka leaned back against the desk, folding his arms.

"No. It's unethical. It's -"

"It's a potential disaster." Sangeruka's mouth twisted upward. "Come, come, Doctor. We both know what a devastating career move this could turn out to be. You'll be the laughing stock of the scientific community. Everyone on that crew is probably looking for a way out. You should be thanking me."

"Hardly."

"You can do things the easy way or the hard way." Sangeruka shrugged, turning away from Mark momentarily as he pushed away from the desk. Suddenly, without warning, he swung around and landed a crashing backhand to the side of Mark's head.

Mark reeled sideways, almost falling out of his seat. It took a minute for him to regain his equilibrium, and as he did so he caught a glimpse of the police chief. His expression of cold hard steel had not changed. Mark focused instead on Sangeruka, who was continuing his discourse, almost pleasantly.

"Either way, the site will be shut down and all the evidence confiscated or destroyed. It will be up to you whether your crew - as well as your own name - are discredited."

"And if I refuse?" Mark tenderly touched his jaw, noting the taste of blood in his mouth.

"I don't see that you have much choice. Chief Ganges has men waiting to take you right now to the State Penitentiary." At a nod from Sangeruka, the chief stood up, crossing his arms.

Mark surveyed the lawman. Sangeruka could throw a punch, no doubt about that, but the police chief was truly gorilla like in proportions, and Mark had no doubt that a blow from him could put him to sleep permanently.

"This is blackmail," Mark muttered. "Isn't that against the law or something?"

The chief was silent. Unwavering.

"I am the law," Sangeruka said in no uncertain terms.

Mark sighed heavily, torn between what he knew was right and the possibility of rotting in a prison where they might throw away the key. "But, why?" he asked. "Why cover it up? This is a great find for your country. For all mankind."

"I don't expect you to understand," Sangeruka replied.

"Try me."

"Those burial grounds are sacred. Tampering with the dead is taboo among my people."

"So this is about superstition?" Mark asked, trying to understand.

"Our religious practices are more than just superstition."

"If that was the case, why did your government agree to the excavation in the first place?" Mark asked. "You knew right from the get go that we would be digging through a potential burial site."

"There are some politicians who are not as vigilant at keeping the old ways," Sangeruka said.

Mark's eyes narrowed. "Like the president, maybe?"

Sangeruka just shrugged.

"So, you're not really acting on behalf of the government at all. This is elected official Sangeruka acting as solo vigilante."

"I would watch my mouth, Doctor," Sangeruka warned, raising his hand again as if to strike. Mark tried not to shrink back, waiting, but the second blow never came. "There are many in the government - and out of it - that see things the same way."

Mark looked at the ceiling, talking more to himself than anyone else. "So, if I took my chances with the truth, I might get an audience with the president himself. I'm sure he'd be interested to know that one of his trusted advisors has resorted to kidnapping, bribery, even murder. Not to mention undermining a very specific directive coming right from his own desk…"

"Don't worry," Sangeruka laughed mirthlessly. "You would never get that chance. Many unfortunate things can happen in prison. Especially to a white foreigner seen as a power hungry oppressor. Besides, there is enough evidence of malpractice on your part, that I'm surprised the president didn't give the order to shut you down himself, long ago. Let's see… cave-ins, dangerous working conditions, disappearing artefacts, discrepancies left and right. What kind of operation were you running out there, Doctor?"

"Perhaps the site is cursed," Mark suggested with a shrug. He thought for a minute. "What about the media? They're sure to get a hold of this and make something out of it."

"It's up to you to make sure they don't."

"And if I don't?" Mark asked.

"Believe me when I say that would not be wise," Sangeruka responded. "Remember, the rest of your crew are still packing up at the site. It would be extremely unfortunate if one or more of them met with an accident similar to your renegade friend, Rocco Cortez, now wouldn't it?"

"You wouldn't dare," Mark breathed, his eyes narrowing.

Sangeruka laughed, a sharp, mirthless sound. "As I suspected. You have no regard for your own personal safety, but your crew… now that's another thing, isn't it?"

"How would you explain the deaths of innocent scientists who were entrusted to your country's care?"

Sangeruka shrugged. "The mountain roads can be treacherous, as you well know."

"What if the findings get published anyway?" Mark countered. "Is murder really worth that chance? This discovery can't be kept secret forever."

"North America is not that far away. I'm sure your family means as much to you as your friends?"

Mark let out a sharp gust of air. "That was definitely a threat," he observed tightly, more to himself than to Sangeruka.

"A friendly warning," Sangeruka corrected. He refused to remove his icy stare from the hold it had over Mark.

Finally Mark lowered his gaze and sighed. "This is a tough one. You know you've got me between a rock and a hard place. But the only way you'll keep me quiet is to lock me up." He turned to the chief. "I guess I'll need that ride after all."

"A very foolish decision, Doctor," Sangeruka said. "Although, I could have predicted as much. Perhaps you'll change your mind in a few weeks once you've had the benefit of, shall we say, reflection." He smiled cruelly.

"What about my personal effects?" Mark asked, rising warily. "A duffel bag and a small black case?"

"Ah, yes," Sangeruka nodded, surprisingly congenial. "They have been thoroughly searched, so I see no reason to retain them. Chief Ganges will see to it that you receive them on your way out. There's nothing like lost luggage to sour one's memories of a trip abroad." He walked to the door and opened it.

Mark took a step forward, but quickly realized his way was blocked by the two guards who had entered the office. Before he could do anything to prevent it, the men had grabbed his arms, holding them back behind him in a vice like grip. He tried to stiffen himself for the blow that he knew was soon to follow, tightening his stomach muscles.

Instead, a blinding light of pain shot through his core as Sangeruka jerked his knee upward to the groin.

Mark doubled over, gasping in agony. "I'm not afraid of you," he was finally able to grind out between clenched teeth. "Beat me all you like, but the truth will be told."

"We'll see about that," Sangeruka replied. This time his fist connected with the side of Mark's head. Everything else went black.

CHAPTER 13

Mark opened his eyes slowly and allowed the room to come into focus. He was back in his cell - at least he was pretty sure it was the same cell - but had no idea how long he'd been there. It could have been minutes, it could have been hours. He had no clue. All he knew was, he had a splitting headache, every muscle ached, and his mouth tasted like crap.

You've really done it this time, he chided himself. The excavation was probably already in ruins. And the crew... he didn't even want to think about what might have happened to them out there.

The image of the flatbed truck careening over the cliff edge, Rocco inside, flashed across his mind. He could see the casket - so carefully wrapped for transport - catapulting into the air and down out of sight. There was no way it could have survived intact. He felt suddenly sick and jerked upright in an attempt to get to the open toilet. He didn't make it, his brain screaming out in pain as a blinding light overtook his senses for a split second.

Good thing he hadn't had much to eat recently, he observed wryly. The acrid stench of bile assaulted his nose, but he didn't even bother trying to wipe it off his shirt. He lay back down instead, slowly this time, hoping that the nausea - and the images plaguing his brain - would dissipate.

Sangeruka couldn't be trusted, that was for certain. All that talk about superstition and religious beliefs was probably a load of crap. But that didn't change the fact that the man had threatened his family. He just hoped he hadn't put his parents in any jeopardy. He'd been secretly sending his father shipments of artefacts with strict instructions to keep them in a safe location out of the elements. An insurance policy should things go south, which they appeared to be doing. Not that it was likely he'd get out of this mess in one piece...

He heard the rattling of keys and the creak of squeaky hinges somewhere down the hall. Heavy footsteps advanced and Mark carefully propped himself up on one elbow.

He recognized the same guard who had let him into the cell yesterday. A lifetime ago. The guard jerked his head, signalling for Mark to exit the cell.

They walked down the dark corridor, shoes clacking hollowly on the concrete floor; Mark in front, his hands secured behind his back with handcuffs, while the guard brought up the rear. Mark readied himself for the bright assault on the eyes that was sure to come once they entered the front of the building. However, they made a quick detour to the left, through an unfamiliar doorway. Several more security doors later, they emerged onto a darkened parking lot. Two more armed guards were waiting, along with Chief of Police Ganges. It was a lot later in the day than Mark had suspected and he glanced questioningly toward the Chief.

"Whisking me away under the cover of darkness?" he asked, just a tinge of sarcasm in his voice. The chief did not answer, but just looked at him long and hard with his penetrating stare. Mark's mouth felt even drier. He swallowed with great difficulty. Better watch it, he thought to himself. They could do away with me right here and no one would be the wiser.

The guards marched him to a waiting police van, and before

shoving him roughly into the back seat, a blindfold was tied securely over his eyes.

"There's really no need," Mark protested, a new and more intense wash of fear spreading through him.

"Quiet," was all someone said. Mark couldn't tell if it was the chief or one of the guards, but he did as he was bid.

The vehicle sped away and Mark could do nothing but allow his body to sway with each curve. The handcuffs were still in place, making it very uncomfortable to sit properly.

The horrible ride seemed to take hours - whether it really did or not was another question. At one point he dozed off, utter exhaustion overtaking his tensed up nerves.

Suddenly the vehicle came to a stop and Mark almost pitched forward into the seat in front. He could hear the familiar whine of a small plane engine - probably a Cessna - as he was hauled unceremoniously from the car.

"Can I get the blindfold off now?" he asked hopefully. There was no reply as he was half pushed, half pulled closer to the sound, tripping a couple of times along the way. Good thing the guards had a strong grip on his arms, or he would have pitched headlong into the gravel. Up the stairs, bumping down the narrow isle, shoved into a seat... The blindfold was retightened for good measure and before he knew it, he could feel the small craft moving forward, the engine revving up to a near scream. Soon he felt the sensation of take off and the plane was air born.

There were other passengers on this flight. Two that he could make out besides the pilot. He strained his ears, listening for any clues as to who they were or where they were headed. The voices were deep, ribald laughter cutting into their words sporadically.

Except for the odd word in English they were speaking a language he did not understand and he could not make any guesses about their identity. Other prisoners? Probably not. They seemed too jovial for that. Government officials? Probably not that either. He knew he was not merely being transported to the

State Pen. They must be miles from Harare by now, and he doubted that the rebels - even Sangeruka - would go to this kind of trouble or expense on his account.

The plane touched down and much to Mark's surprise, the blindfold was taken off and he was allowed to descend from the plane unaided. A feeling of disorientation washed over him and he stood still for a moment, steadying himself. It was pitch black out now, but he could see that they must have landed on some deserted landing strip - if it could even be called that - out in the middle of nowhere. The men, presumably those from the airplane, were unloading cargo from the plane into a square, canvas covered army truck. The pilot didn't seem to be inclined to lift a finger, and the driver of the truck stood guard with an automatic rifle. Who were these people and why had he been sent with them?

As if in answer to his unspoken question, one of the men looked at him and laughed, a toothy grin spreading across his pock marked face. He was tall, but lean and wiry. The other man was broader and less friendly. Arms dealers? Drug smugglers? Some other type of contraband?

They were finished now. The pilot was closing the cargo doors and one of the men - the lean one - was climbing back into the plane.

"Uh... what do I do now?" Mark asked no one in particular.

"Town's that way," the lean one said, pointing with his finger into the blackness of the night. "About forty miles." He laughed. "Of course, the lions are out so it's doubtful you'll get there in one piece."

Mark blinked, his stomach tightening. Was that the game? Leave him out in the wilderness to be attacked and eaten by wild animals? That would be one way of disposing of him without a trace.

"Or, you could catch a ride," the man continued, still grinning. "I'd hurry, though. I think they're ready to leave."

Mark looked toward the frowning burly man, who had just finished securing the flaps on the back of the truck. He scurried toward the passenger side and awkwardly climbed in ahead of the other man. It was a tight fit with the driver on one side and his flight comrade on the other.

"The cuffs? Can I get them off now?" he tried.

"No." The answer was brisk and to the point. There really was little use in arguing, Mark decided. It was better than taking his chances out there with the wild life.

They bumped along the track for about an hour, every movement jarring Mark's already aching body. Finally he saw lights in the distance. Civilization.

Sticking to the outskirts, they wound their way past ramshackle evidence of industrialization. Soon they were immersed in the tangle of streets - narrow and dirty - obviously not the best area of town, Mark noted. Much to his dismay, the truck pulled over on one particularly seedy looking street and came to a halt.

"This is where you get out," the driver said.

Mark blinked. "Here?" His other traveling companion slid from the truck and waited while he scrambled out.

"Wait," the big man spoke. Now what? Was he going to be shot after all? After all he had endured already?

"The cuffs," the man stated, gesturing toward Mark's back.

Mark felt his hands being released as a wave of numbness coursed through his arms all the way from the elbows down. He was sure that the circulation had been totally cut off for quite some time and the sensation was almost surreal, like he had huge stumps for hands that were not really connected in any way to the rest of his body.

"Thanks," Mark said, circling his wrists and trying to rub the feeling back into them. The other man went around to the back of the vehicle and a few minutes later, threw a couple of bags at

Mark's feet. Mark blinked in surprise. It was his duffel bag and saxophone case.

The big man caught Mark's eye for a moment, sending some kind of unspoken message, which Mark could not quite interpret. Then he turned and got back into the vehicle.

"Um, is that it? Are you just going to leave me here?" Mark asked, frowning.

"Good luck," was all the other said as the vehicle rolled forward. Mark watched it turn the corner and trundle out of sight. Okay. So maybe this was Sangeruka's next best tactic. Abandon him in some ghetto where he would get mugged or stabbed to death. But then why give him back his luggage?

He looked around uncertainly. It was pretty deserted, and for that he was thankful. He spotted a narrow doorway with an alcove off to one side. Just big enough to curl up in for the night. He headed that way, clutching the duffel bag and saxophone case close.

Noise. Honking. Shouting. Mark opened his eyes, squinting at the brightness of a new day. He groaned as he struggled into an upright position. Every bone ached; every muscle cried out in pain. And the sandpaper in his mouth was enough to make him want to gag. Not to mention the gnawing hunger in his belly.

Okay. What to do first. Find out where in the heck he was, that's what.

"Excuse me," he tried, greeting a rather large black woman dressed in a brightly printed dress. "I was wondering -" The woman glared at him as she made a wide berth around him.

Mark threw up his hands and turned to another passer-by, this time approaching a man in a loose fitting cotton shirt. Again, no response as the man hurried past.

Mark frowned. What was up? Did he look like an escaped convict who hadn't eaten in two days?

"Ma'am? Ma'am!" he cried, sounding desperate to his own ears as he stepped in front of the next person on the street. "I just - what city is this?" She stopped momentarily, surveying him as if he were deranged. "What city is this?" he repeated.

She stepped back and then shook her head condescendingly before continuing briskly on her way.

Mark sighed. He'd just have to find his way to a hotel or hostel and get cleaned up; get some food and water in his system.

He squatted down on the sidewalk and opened his duffel bag. He dug around, taking mental inventory of the contents. Change of clothes, deodorant... His heart sank. Naturally. No wallet, no passport, no cell phone. He should have expected as much. Whoever helped him escape was obviously not that altruistic.

He needed some cash, but there was really nothing of value that he could pawn. He stopped short. Well, there was one thing. He looked at the battered black case that held Jack's saxophone. He couldn't part with it. He just couldn't. It was out of the question.

But what else was he supposed to do? Beg? Starve to death? Die of thirst? With resolve he stood erect, clutching the case firmly in one hand. Jack had told him the story of how the saxophone had saved a life once. His stepmother Deanie's life. A former boyfriend had attacked her and another one of her friends used the sax to hit the guy over the head. Jack had the instrument repaired, but you could still see the traces of dents on its gleaming surface. Well, it looked like the instrument was going to have to pull double duty. This time, his was the life on the line.

Twenty minutes later, Mark emerged from a pawnshop, burden lighter, but definitely with a heavy heart. Another half hour passed and he'd satisfied his thirst and wolfed down some food from a local market. Next on the list was finding a decent washroom where he could clean up a bit, and then it was off to find the Canadian Consulate. With any luck, he'd be able to get some temporary documents and access his bank account. Then it would be straight back to the pawnshop to retrieve his beloved sax.

He knew better than to even consider trying to make it back to the dig. That was just asking for trouble. He had no idea who had arranged for his escape, or if it was all part of some elaborate plot arranged by Sangeruka himself. In any case, he'd be watching his back for the next little while, that's for sure.

In the mean time, he needed to find out what had gone down back at the site. He needed to get a hold of Laura somehow. And he needed to get back to New Mexico asap. There was just too much valuable information floating around out there.

CHAPTER 14

Mark sat at his workstation, microscope in front of him, as he contemplated his next course of action. He had been back in New Mexico for exactly a week. He debated long and hard about what his next move should be. With the artefacts he had sent to his father and the lab in Albuquerque, as well as the correspondence he had continued with his friend and colleague, John Bergman, he should have more than enough evidence to present his findings. But Sangeruka's threats continued to haunt him. It wasn't his own personal safety that he was worried about, but until he was sure the rest of the crew were safely out of Africa, he wouldn't - he couldn't - do anything. And his family... the possibility of harm coming to them was so preposterous, and yet so frightening, that he couldn't even allow his mind to travel down that road.

He could not believe what he had gone through in the last week. It almost seemed like a dream, now that he was back in familiar surroundings. After visiting the Canadian Consulate, he had stayed in Messina, South Africa - which is where he'd ended up he found out - for the next several days, trying to make contact with Laura or anyone else who might have any information about what had happened after he'd been removed from the archaeological site. He had also left a short message - very short - with his father. He skipped the part about abduction and jail, simply informing them that he was on his way to New Mexico to continue with the next phase of his work there.

His friend and colleague John Bergman was at the airport to meet him when he arrived in Albuquerque and they had set to work on analyzing all the data that he had gathered.

"Graham! Still hard at it, I see," John said as he strolled into the lab where Mark was presently working. John was about Mark's age, smaller in build, but with a wiry, athletic frame. He had sandy brown hair which he kept closely cropped and wore thick rimmed glasses. He was wearing his usual white lab coat, which flowed out behind him when he walked.

"Hi, John," Mark answered, only looking up briefly from his microscope.

"When are the rest of your team coming, again?" John asked, propping himself on the edge of the worktable. "You've an awful lot of samples to scour, yet."

"I told you. Laura and the rest need to finish closing out the site."

"Any timeline on that?" John asked, examining a pencil he had picked up off the desk.

Mark frowned slightly. What was up with John, anyway? Why was he being so inquisitive when he already knew the answers to his questions? "Not exactly. But should be soon. Any reason?"

"I know I told you I didn't mind helping until the rest of your crew arrived, but I've got some other research I need to finish up myself," John said, putting the pencil down.

"Thanks for all your help. I appreciate it," Mark said, surveying his friend. So far he hadn't shared Sangeruka's directives with anyone. He wanted to wait and see just what kind of final analysis they came up with first before alerting anyone else to any potential threats. And of course, he wouldn't do anything until he knew Laura and the others were safe.

"Man-oh-man, you've got some pretty interesting stuff here, Graham." John whistled. "Kind of all over the map in terms of geologic dating, but interesting none the less. You think seismic activity accounts for some of the discrepancies in age?"

"Could be," Mark answered noncommittally.

"Must be something," John said, shaking his head. "I've never seen a more perfectly intact Pterodactyl wing before. When you sent me the first sample I was impressed, but what you've sent since... " He whistled again. "Beautiful."

"You should have seen the headpiece," Mark offered. "The one I sent pictures of?"

"Too bad you weren't able to send one over as well. I would have liked to take a look at that baby first hand."

"The first ones we found were pretty fragile, although I think Laura was packing some fragments. At least I hope."

"And that last one? The one on the mummified specimen. That's still on its way, right?" John asked.

"We ran into some glitches with the government. It was considered sacred and not to be removed from the country." It wasn't really a lie. Just a bit of spin on the truth.

"Too bad," John said, shaking his head again. "I suppose you'll be going back to do your analysis on it there."

"Uh, I'm not sure about that yet," Mark hedged.

John raised his eyebrows in surprise. "Why not?"

Mark sighed. Maybe it was time to confide in John about the actual events that took place before he arrived back in New Mexico. So far John had proven to be a helpful and enthusiastic ally. If there was a conspiracy, he doubted that John would be part of it.

"Listen, John. There were some pretty - strange - things taking place out at that site and afterwards. I wasn't going to say anything, but I guess it's time I was straight with you about it, especially since you're putting so much time and effort into helping me."

John looked at his friend with a sideways frown. "What is it, buddy?"

"I was arrested and forcibly removed from the site," Mark said.

"What?"

Mark nodded. "The last I heard, the army was coming in to move everyone else off site as well. I haven't heard from any of them since. Not Anthony, not Laura. I don't even know if they're okay."

"But why? How? I don't get it, man. What else did you find out there?"

"You've seen it," Mark replied. "But apparently somebody doesn't want the information to go public."

"Why not?"

"I'm not quite sure. Could be political. Somehow I think there's more to it than that."

"Yeah? Like what?"

"Well," Mark said hesitantly. "Just some theories. Kind of way out there. Never mind."

John laughed. "No way, Graham. You can't feed me a lead like that and just leave me hangin'!"

"Remember you mentioned something about the discrepancies in geologic dating?" Mark began tentatively.

"Yeah." John nodded.

"There's a theory out there that suggests those aren't discrepancies at all. That dinosaurs and man lived contemporaneously and the world was subsequently exposed to a catastrophic flood that wiped out the dinosaurs."

"You're kidding, right?" John said with half a grin.

"No. We found evidence of massive sedimentation that corroborates that theory. It cemented off the burial tombs and created almost a vacuum-sealed environment to preserve the artefacts within. That, and the advanced technology used to bury the king himself, preserved the specimens - both man and reptile.

And remember that antechamber and the plaster chip I sent you for analysis?"

"Mmhm."

"Very advanced technology. The Bible speaks about just such a time before the flood -"

"Whoa! Wait a minute." John held up a hand in a stop motion. "So we've suddenly made this quantum leap to the Bible?"

"I told you it was just a theory," Mark defended. "Anthony and I have both been doing some research and it is a plausible explanation."

"Okay, okay. Back up here for a minute. Let's just leave the religion out of it and get back to the site itself. So you found all this evidence of dinosaurs and man and an advanced civilization, but you still haven't told me how this ties in with why you got shut down and arrested."

"The theory goes that there is this international conspiracy to discredit all finds that could possibly back up the creationist model. The first I heard of it was from Rocco, but I've been doing my homework, and it appears to be true. There's all kinds of unpublished, slanderized evidence out there that is just not making it into scientific journals, while at the same time people are bending over backwards to make the evolutionary model fit the evidence."

"Rocco..." John furrowed his brow. "Rocco Cortez?"

Mark nodded.

"I remember hearing something about that guy from another dig I was doing some lab work for. From all accounts, most people thought the guy was a bit nuts."

"Exactly my point," Mark responded. "Nobody wanted to believe him. He's dead, by the way," he added quietly.

John looked over at Mark in surprise.

Mark nodded. "The day I got arrested and taken off site - at gun point, I might add - we had the casket all crated and ready for transport. It was sitting on the flatbed waiting for the transport helicopter when all of a sudden the government official stepped off the chopper. Rocco high jacked the truck and the chopper took off in pursuit, with me on board. I saw it happen, John. These guys mean business. They shot him down and the truck went flying off the road into a steep ravine, casket and all. There's no way Rocco could have survived that crash, and I doubt that they'll be able to recover the casket either." Mark paused for a moment in reflection. Rocco had been his friend, despite what John - or Sangeruka - said about him.

John shook his head. "So you think this conspiracy is so deep that they'd resort to killing for it?"

"Maybe." Mark shrugged. "Look, there was lots of other stuff going on at the site as well, before that. Stuff going missing, cave-ins, deletions on the computers, analysis getting lost in the mail. You name it, it happened. It was just too much to be a coincidence."

"You know what it's like working in these backwoods locations," John said.

"I know. But this was way above and beyond that."

"And that's why they arrested you?" John asked.

"They tried to make it sound like they were shutting down the site for safety reasons, but my arrest was completely bogus. Mr. Sangeruka, one of the president's advisors and a member of the government assembly, apparently had his own agenda for scaring me off the job."

"And that was?" John asked.

"He says that tampering with the dead is taboo in his culture." Mark let out a small scoffing huff.

"Maybe it is."

"Sangeruka doesn't strike me as a man who cares much for culture if it doesn't benefit him personally. I think there's more to it than that."

"Your conspiracy theory," John stated.

"He warned me not to publish my findings. Not to pursue it in any way, in fact. If I didn't agree, they were going to slam me in jail indefinitely - not a fun prospect, I can tell you. He also warned me that if I did try to make any of the discoveries public he would see to it that my entire career and credibility would be ruined. He even threatened me personally, as well as the crew. It's why I'm a bit concerned that I haven't heard from any of them yet, and also why I haven't mentioned any of this to you earlier. I need to make sure everyone is safe before I can go ahead and publish my findings."

"What kind of threats?" John asked.

"The worst kind," Mark answered simply. "I don't think Sangeruka's arm is really as long as he tries to make out, though. At least I hope not. However, if he is involved in some kind of international conspiracy, I could be wrong."

"And you think he might be?"

"It seems to me he was going to awfully great lengths if it was just a matter of preserving cultural taboos. I mean, I hope that's all it is, because then I think we're pretty safe in pursuing this thing. But if it's something bigger..." He trailed off.

"Looks like you may have dug yourself a pretty deep hole this time, my friend," John said.

Two days later Mark was back at his usual station analyzing more samples, when John breezed into the lab.

"Look what the cat dragged in," John called.

Mark looked up and his eyes widened in surprise when he saw who accompanied John.

"Laura, Anthony!" Mark stood and grabbed Anthony, slapping him soundly on the back a few times.

"Got something for you," Anthony whispered before Mark let him go.

Mark's eyebrows shot up in question, but Anthony shook his head, almost imperceptibly.

Okay, whatever it was, it would have to wait for later. He turned to Laura. Their embrace was more like a gentle, lingering squeeze. "But you didn't call. You didn't even email me!"

"Sorry about that," Laura apologized, pulling back from Mark's arms. "I was having some trouble sending messages while on site. They kept coming back to me." She looked down sheepishly.

"We knew you'd love the surprise," Anthony added with a wink.

"I'm just glad to see that you're safe." Mark gestured for the group to find a seat somewhere. "So, tell me everything."

"You first," Laura countered. "Believe me, we were worried sick for quite a few days until we actually got back to Harare ourselves. Then we were told you had already flown back to the States."

Mark shook his head. "It wasn't good." He looked over at his colleagues, calculating just how much he should tell them. "The casket got destroyed," he informed bluntly.

A look of utter shock crossed both Anthony's and Laura's faces. "How?" Anthony asked.

"The truck went over the side of the mountain," Mark replied.

"And Rocco?" Laura asked sharply.

"Dead."

Anthony let out a gasp. "Oh God."

"Sangeruka said everything was looked after," Laura said quietly. "He never mentioned this. "

"Figures," Mark said under his breath.

"I don't understand." Laura frowned.

"So what happened?" Anthony asked. "We thought you were under arrest. Then, when we got to Harare, Sangeruka said it was all a mistake and that you had left the country already."

"Is that all he said?" Mark asked.

"He had a little chat with most of the crew members. Individually," Anthony replied.

Laura's eyes flickered momentarily toward John before squarely focusing on Mark. "Maybe we should talk about it later," she said.

"I can leave you folks alone, if you'd like," John offered, rising from the stool that he was occupying.

"It's okay," Mark said, gesturing for John to take his seat. "I've already filled John in on everything, as far as I know it, anyway. He's been helping me with this thing all along. He deserves to know the truth." Laura frowned, looking uncomfortable. Mark persisted. "Did he threaten either of you?"

"He made some insinuations about my future employment opportunities, so to speak," Anthony said with a laugh. "But I wasn't too worried. Everyone pretty much thinks I'm a screw ball, anyway."

"Laura?" Mark directed at her.

"Um, the same as Anthony, I guess," she said lightly. "Let's get to what happened to you."

"Not yet." Mark shook his head decisively. "I need to know what else happened at the site."

"Well, we started packing up the minute you took off," Anthony explained. "But I think it took a lot longer than they were expecting. Obviously they didn't realize the extent of the equipment and artefacts we had to deal with, not to mention the dig site itself. Anyway, a whole battalion of army trucks showed up the next day. They were actually pretty friendly. Helpful even. Wouldn't you say, Laura?" He looked over at her for confirmation. "Anyway, the guy in charge, I forget his name, seemed genuinely interested in preserving what was already discovered, so I wasn't as worried as I had been about leaving things in their hands. Unfortunately, there was no more shipping of the rest of the arte-facts. They are now the sole property of the 'people'. It took quite awhile to pack up all the equipment, though, as well as finish cataloguing what was there. They took copies of our records, so the government will be expecting the return of all missing artefacts that are documented as going overseas for analysis."

Mark nodded thoughtfully. "At least that is something. There is enough documentation to prove where each and every artefact was found. Nobody can deny their existence."

"Who would want to do that?" Laura laughed. The sound was stilted; nervous.

Mark scowled, looking at Laura speculatively. "After all we've been through, I'm surprised you even have to ask that question."

She turned to John and smiled. "He's become a bit paranoid over the last few months."

"With good reason," Anthony piped up.

"Don't worry. He's filled me in on his latest theory," John responded with a grin. "A bit too much time in the African sun, I'd say."

"Exactly." Laura nodded.

"Although," John continued, "In the good Doctor's defence, the lab results are pretty darn intriguing."

"I can hardly wait to see what's come out of that." Anthony rubbed his hands together.

"Um, guys," Laura said hesitantly, looking from John to Anthony. "Do you think Mark and I could spend just a couple of minutes together? Privately?"

John glanced over at Mark, brows raised in question. "Oh, right. I forgot that you two are an item now."

Mark scowled. Anthony rose from his seat. "Come on, John. You can show me some of those lab results."

John led the way from the room and shut the door behind them with a click. There were a few moments of awkward silence before Laura spoke up. "Mark, what really happened after you got taken away in that helicopter? I know there's more to it. I can always tell when you're hiding something."

Mark surveyed her for a second or two. "Same here. I don't

think you've been completely forthright about your conversation with Sangeruka, either."

Laura sighed. "He said you had decided there was nothing worth pursuing at the site. That you had just taken off for the States and left it all behind because you didn't want to ruin your reputation. I knew it wasn't the truth. I know you better than that and it just didn't sound like you. What really happened?"

"He threatened me if I told the truth," Mark said simply.

"Truth as in...?" she trailed doff.

"You know exactly what I mean, Laura. Why do you insist on denying the facts when they're staring you right in the face?"

"I'm not denying the facts," Laura defended. "You know as well as I do that there is a plausible - and scientific - explanation for everything we've discovered."

"So how do you explain the shut down? Sangeruka? The army?"

"Obviously there's something going on, but I don't see that the two are related. Shutting the site down because of some kind of plot to stop the advancement of creationists - well, it sounds as lunatic as it is."

"Now I'm a lunatic."

"I didn't say that." Laura stopped for a moment, watching Mark as a muscle moved rhythmically in his jaw. "Mark, come on. You're entirely too tense. You're paranoid."

"Who wouldn't be after what I've been through?" he countered.

"Exactly. Which brings me back to my original question," Laura said more gently. "Just what did happen?"

"Let's see," Mark began cryptically. "After I witnessed Sangeruka kill Rocco in cold blood, and completely destroy the most valuable archaeological find of the century, I endured a night in a dark prison cell with no food or water. Then I was interrogated, threatened, beaten up, and finally blindfolded, handcuffed and transported to South Africa, where I was dumped and left to fend for myself. Let's see. Did I miss anything?"

"Oh Mark, I'm so sorry! They beat you and threatened you and then let you go? But Sangeruka said -"

"Sangeruka is a lying S.O.B," Mark interrupted. "He can't be trusted. I have no idea if it was him who arranged for my release and if so, if it was done just to solidify his threats. Or it could be somebody else working against him for who knows what purpose. All I know is, this is no game, Laura. We're dealing with something bigger than any of us thought. And for some reason, they don't want us to share the information."

"What kind of threats did he make?" Laura asked.

"Against me, my family, the crew," Mark listed. "He said not to publish the findings from the dig or else."

"Or else what?"

"What do you think? After what he did to Rocco, I don't think he meant a slap on the wrist."

"Did he really - kill Rocco? You said before Rocco's truck went off the cliff."

"After Sangeruka purposely blew all four tires."

"Oh," she said softly.

"And what exactly did he say to you?" Mark demanded. "You never did say."

"Nothing quite so lethal," Laura offered.

"Meaning?"

"He said he'd ruin you. All of us. Our reputations, I mean."

"Bastard," Mark breathed. "Who does he think he is? The public has a right to know."

"What? You're not thinking of doing it, are you? Going public with this?"

"What do you propose I do?" Mark asked. "Lie? Make something up? People know I've been working on that dig for quite some time. Not just the actual fieldwork, but I've got a couple of years of research into it as well. Now all of a sudden, I'm not interested anymore?"

"It's not worth that much. This is your entire life's work we're talking about. Not to mention the rest of us. Have you thought about that?"

"When we start bowing to terrorists like Sangeruka we're really in trouble."

"You used to be so solid. Logical. Now you're ready to throw away your career -"

"What about the evidence," Mark cut in. "Huh? You can't deny what we all saw."

"The evidence was very sketchy. Almost like it had been contaminated; tampered with. And with all the mishaps on site it's probably best just to shut down quietly and say it wasn't worth the effort," Laura said reasonably.

"Why, Laura? Why so reluctant to face the facts?"

"Facts? The fact is we're in possible danger, here, Mark. Not to mention the fact that we could all become the laughing stock of the scientific community."

"So we're back to that."

Laura sighed heavily. "Mark, I care about you. I know we haven't been getting along that well lately, but once this is behind us things will go back to the way they should be."

"And how's that?"

"You know. Us. Together."

"I don't think I want any 'us together' if it means lying about what we've found." He rubbed a hand over his hair.

"I didn't say lie."

"Oh right, you just said pretend it didn't happen. In my books that's a lie. I know what I saw, Laura."

"Your seeing and other people believing are two different things. You need evidence. And what kind of credible evidence do you have left to back it up, huh? Think about it Mark. Sangeruka's already been busy tampering with the documentation. You can bet on that. All the records in the world mean nothing without the specimens themselves."

"I've still got specimens," Mark said irritably.

"Fine. We have a few bones and other samples here, but nothing compared to what was left behind. And the most important piece of evidence is destroyed."

"I've got some other evidence tucked away in a safe place. Remember I told you I was taking precautions."

She closed her eyes for a moment and shook her head. "You're just not getting it, are you?" she breathed.

"I'm not going to roll over and play dead, Laura," he stated firmly. "You know me better than that."

"No?" she asked. "Maybe you won't be playing." She looked at him with candour. "Okay, Mark. Listen. I wasn't completely truthful just a few minutes ago. He threatened me, too. He said it was up to me to make sure you didn't publish any of your work from the temple site. If you did, he said he'd kill you. And if I told anyone else about it, he'd kill them, too."

Mark let out a gust of breath. "I… I just don't know what to do."

"Don't you?" Laura asked.

"I can't just back down. Surely you must understand -"

There was a light rapping on the closed door and John stuck his head in. "Excuse me, you two, but I forgot something in here. Anthony's waiting out in the hall. I've got another appointment I need to make." He slipped inside and headed to one of the cupboards.

"It's okay," Mark said. "We were through anyway."

"This conversation is by no means over," Laura said under her breath as John left the room.

Anthony peered around the doorframe. "Safe to come in?" he asked.

"Of course," Mark replied with a slight edge to his voice. "What did you think we were doing in here?"

Anthony raised his hands in a sign of surrender. "Hey, that's not up to me to speculate."

Laura rolled her eyes.

Anthony continued. "Laura, you'll want to take a look at some of the stuff John's been working on. I think even you will be impressed."

"No thanks," Laura said in a clipped voice. "I think I've seen and heard enough for one day." She turned to Mark. "Just remember what I said and don't do anything stupid. At least not for awhile anyway, until the rest of us have had time to distance ourselves."

"Thanks for being so compassionate," Mark quipped.

"It's your life," she countered angrily, tears in her voice. "If you're set on throwing it away, I can't stop you. Just don't expect me to follow along."

She turned and strode from the room.

"What was that all about?" Anthony asked, his eyebrows raised. "Lover's quarrel?"

"Hardly," Mark said under his breath.

"So, uh, Mark... " Anthony asked tentatively. "Is it true that you're not going to publish your findings?"

"Who wants to know?"

"Whoa! Buddy! This is me, remember? It's what Sangeruka claimed. I told you that already. I asked John, but he seemed pretty uninformed."

"I haven't decided for sure yet," Mark replied.

"By the look of what you're sitting on, I'd say you'd be hard pressed not to. I mean, we all saw what was in the burial chamber with our own eyes. Now that you and John have been crunching the numbers, I'd say it's your duty to tell the truth just the way we found it."

Mark surveyed the other man closely. "You finish reading that book I lent you?"

Anthony nodded. "My feelings on the subject are - mixed. It

all makes perfect sense and what we've seen in the last few months certainly seems to verify that an international cover up against creationist theory is definitely at work. I'm just not sure I'm ready to believe in all that Bible stuff again. It would mean eating some humble pie with my folks and I'm not much for the taste of that."

"I see. But you do think it's part of the conspiracy?" Mark asked. "All of the glitches, the mishaps, getting run out of the country. Everything?"

Anthony nodded. "It's got to be. What else could it be?"

"And Sangeruka? What do you make of his involvement?"

"Now that's one I haven't quite figured out yet, although I'm sure he is involved somehow. I just didn't buy his whole story about wanting to preserve the traditions of his countrymen."

"Me neither," Mark agreed. "He blackmailed you, too?"

"What do you mean, 'too'?" Anthony asked.

"He threatened the lives of the crew if I didn't promise to keep quiet. Not to mention my own life as well as my reputation."

"Hm. He didn't go that far with me," Anthony said. "He just tried to appeal to my intellectual side. My training as an expert in folklore and the importance of keeping the sacred trust of the local people. He said their rituals demanded that the ancient dead be left undisturbed and that it was also taboo to even talk about it. He made me swear to secrecy. As a scholar, I guess he figured he could safely take that route without going any further."

"But you didn't buy it," Mark observed.

"Are you kidding?" Anthony scoffed. "He was obviously forgetting that as an expert I do have some background knowledge about these things. I've never heard any such references to such things in that area of the world at all."

Mark nodded in understanding.

"So?" Anthony asked again. "Are you going public or not?"

Mark let out a heavy sigh. "I'm leaning in that direction."

"That's the spirit," Anthony said enthusiastically. "I'd hate to see the bad guys win, you know what I mean?"

"What makes you think they won't?" Mark asked soberly.

"Well, I suppose that is a possibility," Anthony conceded. "But we can't let them win without at least putting up a fight. Say, you want to know what I got you?"

Mark raised his eyebrows. He had almost forgotten. "Sure."

Anthony put up one finger as a signal to wait for a minute. He went to his backpack, which he had deposited on the counter by the door. After a few seconds of rummaging, he pulled out a slim, silver cylinder.

"What is it?" Mark asked with curiosity.

Anthony brought the container over to where Mark sat and popped off the lid. Inside were several small plastic bags. "I got those skin and hair samples, just like you asked," he said with a grin.

Mark blinked in disbelief. "You what?"

"The skin and hair samples," Anthony repeated. "To be more specific, skin, hair and a nail sample from the king himself, and some scales and leather from the Pterodactyl headdress as well as a fragment from the beak."

"But how did you..." Mark trailed off as the probable method of smuggling the evidence dawned on him. "You didn't, did you?"

"Don't worry," Anthony replied with a smile. "I had the cylinder itself wrapped in plastic with a coating of Vaseline. Absolutely no contaminants reached the samples themselves."

Mark squeezed his eyes tight, trying not to let a picture form in his head. He couldn't help the smile that crept across his face until he suddenly burst out in full-fledged laughter. Anthony joined him good-naturedly. "I can't believe you actually did that."

"Anything for the cause, right?" Anthony grinned.

"What if you'd been caught?"

"I didn't plan on it." Anthony shrugged. "In any case, I wasn't, now was I? I know it can never replace the real thing, but at least it's something."

Mark shook his head. "You're a real trooper, you know that? Now how can I not go forward?"

"I was hoping I'd convince you."

Mark slapped Anthony across the back. At least he knew he had one solid ally.

CHAPTER 15

Now that Anthony was back, new hope seemed to rise to the surface for Mark. Any threats from Sangeruka, any warnings from Laura - even his own doubts - seemed minuscule and he dismissed them in order to single-mindedly pursue the publication of his findings.

John was unable to help as much now, since he had projects of his own to work on. But Mark had known this was the case from the beginning and was not dampened in spirit. Anthony was making valuable contributions to the project, adding his knowledge of the connections with ancient legends, including the Biblical accounts, and it was now up to Mark to put it all together in some kind of format that would explain all the data and be acceptable for publication in a scientific journal.

"Anthony, how are those specs coming?" Mark looked up from his laptop as Anthony entered the room. His smile faded when Anthony didn't answer. The look on the other man's face was grim and sounded an alarm bell in Mark's brain. "What is it?"

"I just heard a rumour," Anthony replied. "The specimens are already packed for shipment back to Africa."

"What?" Mark asked, eyeing Anthony sharply. "So soon? Who told you?"

"The lab receptionist," Anthony answered.

"That can't be," Mark said, rising from his chair. "I was just in the vault yesterday. All the arrangements have been made so that we can wait to ship after my presentation. The date has already been set. It's a done deal."

"Well, if I were you, I'd check again," Anthony advised.

Mark did just that. He strode with purpose down the hall and stopped at the reception desk. "What's this I hear about artefacts - my artefacts - being shipped back to Africa without my knowledge?"

The woman at the counter raised her eyebrows defensively. "You can check with the Dean of Archaeological Studies yourself, if you like."

Without any further acknowledgement, Mark swung his body down the hallway to his right, Anthony scuttling after him. He bypassed the Dean's receptionist with a dismissive wave and rapped briskly on the wooden door leading into the office. As soon as the muffled 'Yes?' was heard from within, Mark barged into the room.

"Are the African artefacts getting shipped back?" he asked without preamble.

The other man took off his glasses with deliberate calmness and gestured to the available chair in front of his desk. "Doctor Graham, have a seat, won't you?"

"Just answer the question, Taylor," Mark replied, not budging.

Dean Taylor was a man of about fifty, with steel grey hair and a neatly trimmed goatee. The Doctor of Archaeology and Anthropology, with honorary degrees from several of the most prestigious institutions in Europe and North America, matched Mark's gaze with unwavering determination. "An agreement was signed. You know that."

"Yes, I know, but I thought we had agreed to wait until after my presentation," Mark countered. "Institutions like this one have an overriding responsibility to make sure that the world's priceless artefacts are properly preserved and cared for. You can't just turn them over to some other entity whose reputation is questionable at best. Not until we're sure they'll be properly preserved and housed. Those artefacts are priceless. Once they're presented publicly we'll have a better bargaining tool to make the government see that. Keeping them here at least until then could buy us the time we need to -"

"Um, about your presentation..." Taylor cut in.

Mark narrowed his eyes. "What about it?"

"It seems we may have to postpone that for awhile," Taylor hedged. "Strictly a scheduling issue."

"Oh really," Mark snorted sceptically. "Why doesn't that surprise me?"

"You know that we're sitting on a bit of a hot bed, Dr. Graham. The last thing this institution needs is the kind of controversy that could lead to funding cuts. As it is, we're just holding on to many of our corporate sponsorships."

"So this is about money?" Mark asked. "Whatever happened to scholarly excellence?"

"I don't think you realize the gravity of this situation," Taylor said. "Dealing with foreign governments can be very tricky."

"Nothing you haven't handled before," Mark said with exasperation.

"This is a matter of legality. They have a legal right -"

"Legal right!" Mark exploded. "This institution has an obligation to preserve history!"

"Governments can be fickle. We can't take the chance of a law suit," Taylor continued reasonably.

"I was there, remember? Those government officials are steeped in bribery and all kinds of questionable practices. We have an obligation to do what's right, not just on moral grounds, but on scientific grounds."

"Sometimes it's best just to back down rather than push an issue that could end up bringing bad publicity."

"Oh, so this is about publicity," Mark stated flatly. "You don't want any bad press."

"That is part of my job," Taylor reminded.

"How can you be so nonchalant about this?" Mark asked. "You do realize what we're sitting on here?"

Taylor hesitated for a moment and looked down at his fingers, steepled in front of him. "I've been meaning to have a discussion about that."

Mark surveyed Taylor suspiciously. "What do you mean?"

Taylor cleared his throat and sat up straighter before meeting Mark's gaze. "I've been hearing some rather... alarming things about the way you are presenting your findings, Dr. Graham."

Mark's eyes narrowed. "Yeah? From whom?"

"That's not the point. The point is, this institution is not interested in any bad publicity over a questionable archaeological dig. The fact that we are already running into difficulty with the local governing body is bad enough and now, to find out that our premier archaeologist on site is twisting the data for some kind of personal agenda... Well, I don't need to spell out for you how bad that makes us all look."

Mark was stunned. He couldn't even formulate an immediate reply. Twisting the data for his own personal agenda? What in the world was Taylor talking about? And who was feeding him this information? Laura? He knew she was angry with him, but he would never have expected that kind of retaliation.

"Actually," Taylor continued, "what I was going to suggest to you was a brief leave of absence."

"A leave of absence," Mark repeated flatly. "What does that mean, exactly, Dean? Am I being dismissed?"

"Only temporarily. Until this unfortunate situation blows over," Taylor said with a placating smile. "You're a world class scientist, Doctor Graham, known in your field. You wouldn't want to taint your reputation with the type of questionable speculation I'm afraid you've fallen into."

"So you're telling me to drop everything I've been working on for all these months. Just abandon the evidence because you're afraid it might bring some bad press to this institution?" Mark shook his head in disbelief.

"You've obviously gotten way too personally involved."

"Personally involved? Of course, I'm personally involved! It's my life's work. My passion. You know that. It's what makes me good at what I do and one of the reasons you wanted me on board at this institution in the first place, in case you don't remember. You can't expect me to just abandon everything I've been working on."

"You can work on your dissertation all you like, but just not under the auspices of this institution," Taylor stated.

"Meaning, if I publish anything, you won't verify or back up any of my findings."

Taylor just shrugged in agreement.

"Tell me something," Mark asked, leaning forward. "Your contact from Africa wouldn't happen to be a guy named Sangeruka?"

"I am not obliged to share that information with you, Doctor," Taylor stated, pressing his lips together.

Mark nodded. "Yep. I should have known. So it probably didn't take much convincing for you to pack up all the artefacts. The farther they are away, the easier it will be to distance your-self." He laughed mirthlessly. "People are going to wonder, you know. There was enough sharing of information that it won't just disappear."

"I know that. That's why I'm going to get someone else to compile the findings."

"Who?"

Taylor hesitated, as if he was debating with himself whether to reveal that information to Mark or not. "I've got Doctors

Sawchuk and Bergman already working on it."

Mark felt numb. Laura and John. Laura he could understand. She had been threatened herself and probably thought she was saving him somehow. But John? He had been so helpful, so supportive... so interested in every detail. Now he knew why. The betrayal was almost too much to swallow.

"And what if I publish my own findings, separate from theirs?" Mark asked.

"I can't stop you," Taylor replied. "It's a free country. But don't expect to be welcomed back under the umbrella of this institution ever again, or any other reputable institute of higher learning, for that matter."

Mark was silent for a moment. To sever himself from the university was more than just an act based on moral principle. It could mean the end of his career. But the thought of out and out lying - pretending none of it had ever happened and that he had not seen with his own eyes what he knew he had...

What would Jack do? He'd always had an answer. Mark wished now that he had spent more time with him in these last years. With all of them, really. He had been so preoccupied with making his own discoveries that he had neglected the one thing that was most important. Family.

And now it was too late - for Jack, at least. He would never see him again.

A small voice inside whispered. That's not what Jack believed.

Mark blinked. That's right. Jack had given his life to Christ. If there really was a God, and Jesus was it, Jack was safely in heaven, waiting for the rest of them. It was the hope of his entire family - his father, Deanie, Harmony, his Grandmother...

If he had ever wished he believed like the rest of them, now would be the time. He needed all the help he could get with this situation.

"Well, Dean Taylor, it's been good working with you," Mark said calmly, stretching out his hand to shake the other man's.

Taylor looked surprised and didn't reciprocate the gesture immediately. Finally, he grasped Mark's hand tentatively.

"I'm not sure I understand," Taylor said.

"I doubt we'll be seeing one another again," Mark replied. "Even if I do lay low for awhile - drop this whole project - I don't think I could remain under the directorship of a man who would exchange undeniable evidence for the easy popularity of a lie."

Taylor's eyes narrowed. "I'll expect all of your personal belongings off the property by the end of the day. And don't even think about going near the storage vault - you or your sidekick."

Mark's jaw worked angrily, but he dared not open his mouth again. He swung from the room, almost bumping into Anthony on the way, who had been loitering near the door.

"You don't have to ruin your own career, Anthony. I would totally understand if you just jump ship right now. It would be the smart thing to do," Mark said as they manoeuvred their way back to the lab.

Anthony waited until they were inside and the door was shut before replying. "I suspect the damage has already been done."

"Guilty by association."

"I was thinking, though." Anthony stopped and looked over his shoulder before continuing. "Maybe you could use a man on the inside."

Mark had already started gathering books off the shelf and piling them in a haphazard stack on one of the work counters. "Why would anyone trust you?"

"I could convince them, no problem," Anthony assured. "Say I just got caught up in the excitement of the legendary aspects of the dig, but now I realize how foolish it is. Something like that."

"And what good would that do?" Mark asked.

"I could let you know what angle they're taking as they write up their findings. You could counter attack, maybe even publish simultaneously. I also might be able to track the artefacts. Even though they're supposedly packed for shipment, there is a chance they might not get shipped right away. I'm pretty good at smuggling, as you already know." He smiled.

Mark considered this then asked the obvious question. "How do I know you're not part of the whole conspiracy?"

Anthony blinked and then frowned with a hurt expression on his face. "Hey, that's not the response I was expecting."

"Sorry." Mark rubbed the back of his neck wearily. "But you've got to admit I have reason to be suspicious. Everyone else I trusted has turned against me."

"You do have a point. There's probably not much I can do to convince you otherwise, although you ought to know I feel as strongly about making sure the truth comes out as you do. If I do stick around here, I'll be trying to see that it happens, one way or another."

"You go ahead and do whatever you think you have to do," Mark said. "I think it's best if I just make a clean break and decide what to do from there. Not drag anyone else into the quagmire I seem to have created for myself."

"You never know. Our paths might cross again over this thing before it's all said and done. But maybe you're right about distancing ourselves for awhile. We can come at this thing from more than one front; maybe take them by surprise."

"You make it sound like a military operation."

"It is. It's a war, man, don't you know? A spiritual battle."

Mark surveyed Anthony with a slight frown, but didn't say anything.

Anthony smiled sheepishly and explained. "You can't be raised by a Baptist preacher and not know something about spiritual warfare."

"Right," Mark replied. "Anyway, I better get my stuff packed. Taylor gave me till the end of the day and I don't think he was kidding."

"I'll help you," Anthony offered.

"It might blow your cover," Mark warned with a grin. "You wouldn't want to appear too sympathetic."

"I'll take my chances," Anthony replied and slapped Mark on the back before turning to survey the room. "Okay, I'll scare up some packing boxes and then you can just order me around from there."

Once again, Mark found himself in his home city of Winnipeg, Manitoba. Where else would a potentially discredited archaeologist find refuge except back where it all began?

The first thing he did was find his own apartment - an older three-story house that had been converted into separate dwellings right downtown.

Although he loved his parents, just a few days in their home convinced him that his own accommodation was a necessity if he wanted to preserve their strong relationship. He had a considerable savings from which to draw and had also made some good investments over the years, so he wasn't too worried - yet. But there was no use being foolish.

As Mark climbed the creaking staircase up to his new digs, his cell phone bleeped in his pocket.

"Hello?" He propped the phone between his ear and shoulder. One hand was occupied with a plastic grocery bag, the other he was using to undo the somewhat stubborn lock.

"Hi, Mark. Can you come over for dinner tonight?" Deane asked on the other end.

Mark hesitated, manoeuvring into the dim interior and shutting the door with his foot. "I just came home with some groceries. I was going to work a bit on that dissertation I was telling you about." He hadn't told them everything about it - like the fact that he was no longer working for the university in New

Mexico. As far as they knew, he was just choosing to work in Winnipeg so that he could have some solitude.

"Oh. That's too bad," Deanie replied. "I invited the Walters over. You remember Brent and Holly?"

"Yes, yes of course. I saw them at Jack's funeral a couple months back."

"I invited Amy and Bryan, too, but I'm not sure if they're coming, Maybe Amy, since Harmony is here, but Bryan might have other things to do. He'll be starting his first year of college next week, you know."

"That's nice," Mark answered absently.

"Oh well, maybe next time," Deanie said.

"What time did you say, again?" Mark asked suddenly.

"I didn't." Deanie laughed. "You changing your mind?"

"Maybe. Depending on what you're making, that is."

"Now that will be a surprise for both of us. Your Dad is barbequing, and said he'd handle everything. So I've taken him at his word. We'll be ready to eat around six. That suit you?"

"Sure. Sounds fine." For some reason, the prospect of a quiet evening alone wasn't as appealing as it was earlier.

CHAPTER 16

Mark arrived at his parents' home around five-thirty that evening. Deanie greeted him at the door with a hug and directed him to the kitchen where his father was busy preparing salad and garlic toast to go with the steaks that were marinating.

"Hi, Son," Russ greeted. "Settling in to your new place?"

Mark nodded. "Yep. It's small but I don't need much room. As long as I've got room for my computer, I'm set."

"You'll have to tell me some more about that paper you're writing," Russ said. "So far you've been fairly tight lipped."

Mark shrugged. "It's kind of complicated. You'll get to read it soon enough."

"I'll be very interested to do that. It's fascinating that so many of your findings support the Biblical record. It's about time the scientific community started taking the idea of intelligent design seriously."

Mark didn't say anything but occupied himself with a celery stick instead. If his father only knew the truth he wouldn't be so quick with his enthusiasm.

"You're awfully quiet," Russ observed. "What's up?"

"Nothing you need to worry about," Mark assured with a slight shrug.

"You're too much like me to hide things very well."

"Well, to be honest, things aren't going as smoothly as I had hoped."

"No?" Russ sliced a celery stick down the centre and started chopping it into smaller pieces.

Mark debated whether he should tell his father more. "You know those artefacts I asked you to keep safe for me?" he asked.

Russ nodded.

"I might be moving them to a different location soon."

"Oh?" Russ's eyebrows rose in question.

"Actually I've run into more than just a bit of opposition over this project, Dad, and quite frankly I'm not sure where to turn next."

Russ set the knife down on the counter and turned his full attention to his son. "You want to talk about it?"

Mark sighed. It was killing him, not being able to verbalize his doubts and frustrations to anyone. "Let's just say I'm wrestling with the evidence I've found and it's got me questioning some things that I thought were already settled in my own mind. Not just on a scientific level, either, but here." He stabbed at his chest. "And I don't mind admitting I'm not comfortable with some of my own conclusions."

"God's truth hasn't changed," Russ stated. "It's our own way of seeing it that changes."

Before Mark could say any more, Harmony came bouncing into the room. She embraced her brother enthusiastically. "Mark! I'm so glad you decided to come over for dinner. I like having you in the city again. It feels just like old times."

"Except you're about two feet taller." He laughed.

"But just as spoiled," Russ observed affectionately.

"Oh, whatever, Daddy! You're the one who spoiled me if that's the case. Anyway, I'm especially glad you've come, Mark, because I have someone special I want you to meet."

"Oh? Your latest flame?" Mark asked with a grin.

"You could say that," Harmony replied with a coy smile.

"Anyone I know?"

"One of Toby Rantt's grandsons," Deanie informed, coming into the room.

Mark nodded. "Keeping it all in the club, eh? So when did this take place? I don't recall you having anyone particularly special the last time I was here."

"You were hardly here long enough to notice," Harmony said.

"Cory is a very nice young man. Isn't he, Honey?" Deanie directed at her husband.

Russ nodded his assent and went back to chopping the celery.

"We've always been friends, but we kind of started going together shortly after Grandpa Jack's funeral," Harmony explained. "Cory was very good at listening."

"And he is a believer," Deanie added with approval.

The doorbell rang.

"That's probably him now," Harmony said, scurrying into the hallway on her way to answer the front door.

Deanie's eyes followed her daughter's retreating figure with affection. "Now if we could only find you a nice girl, Mark."

"You make it sound like Harmony and Cory are getting married," Russ said. "They've only been going together a few months. Besides, I'm sure Mark is more than capable of looking after his own love life."

"Thanks, Dad."

"So do you have any one special, Mark?" Deanie asked.

"Um, actually I was seeing a fellow archaeologist for awhile, but we've decided to go our separate ways," Mark explained uncomfortably.

"Mom, Dad!" Harmony called from the entryway. "It's the Walters."

Deanie went to greet her guests, leaving Mark and Russ alone in the kitchen.

"Don't mind Deanie. She just wants the best for you," Russ said.

"I know," Mark replied with a smile. "She's been asking the same question since high school. You need any help in here?"

Russ shook his head. "No. I'm almost ready to throw these steaks on the grill. Why don't you go and say hi to the Walters instead and tell them I'll be right with them. Maybe everyone can go out on the back deck. See if they want a soda or something."

"Okay," Mark agreed, turning to exit the kitchen.

"Oh, and Mark?"

Mark turned back to face his father.

"Whenever you're ready to talk about that other situation - you know, your own spiritual journey - I'm more than willing to listen."

"I know, Dad. Believe me, I think we'll be having a talk about quite a few things really soon."

He turned and walked down the hall to the living room where Harmony, Deanie and the rest of the guests had gathered. Mark's insides clenched unexpectedly when he saw Amy Walters among the group "Hi," he said with a general wave. "Good to see you again."

"Likewise," Brent said, standing to shake Mark's hand vigorously. "And under better circumstances."

"True," Mark agreed. "I guess Bryan decided not to come?"

"He already made plans to go out with some of his friends," Holly explained.

"Mark, you remember Cory Rantt?" Harmony stepped up, pulling a somewhat shy Cory with her.

"Of course." Mark nodded, not really remembering too well, but faking it none the less for Harmony's sake. He shook the younger black man's hand. "Good to see you, Cory. Dad said we should go out onto the deck, if that's okay? Can I get anybody a drink?"

"I'll get the drinks," Deanie offered. "There's iced tea and lots of pop." She took everyone's request and headed back into the kitchen while Harmony led the way through the family room and out the patio doors onto the back deck, Cory in tow. Mark found himself bringing up the rear.

Russ was already out on the patio lighting the barbeque. He waved a greeting to all the guests and proceeded to place eight large steaks on the grill. "Mark, there are a few of those stacking lawn chairs in the corner. You might need to grab a couple."

Mark nodded and went to the side of the house where he found the moulded plastic seats.

Harmony had already claimed the one padded lounge chair, and the others had pulled up the other deck chairs that went with the table and umbrella. He took three chairs and placed them near the table.

"So, Mark," Brent Walters began conversationally. "Your folks say you made quite a find in Africa. I'm looking forward to hearing all about it."

Mark lowered himself onto the moulded seat. "Um... right."

"So what exactly did you find, Mark?" Holly asked. "Deanie said something about dinosaur remains and human remains found together."

"Isn't that cool?" Harmony interjected. "I mean, we all know the flood is a fact anyway and of course it makes sense that God created dinosaurs along with everything else, but to actually find real, undeniable evidence! And by my own big brother, the sceptic! Bet you're not so quick to deny the Bible now, eh Mark?" she teased.

Mark frowned slightly, trying hard not to show his own discomfiture. "It's definitely quite a find, that's for sure." He cleared his throat. "I wonder what's taking Deanie so long with those drinks? Maybe I should go and see if I can help." He rose swiftly and headed back into the house via the patio doors.

A few minutes later he and Deanie re-emerged with a tray laden with soda cans and glasses filled with ice. Mark set the tray on the table and started handing out drinks while Deanie took a seat.

The conversation switched to the relative safety of the weather. "Iced tea, right?" he asked Amy, ignoring the general chatter going on around him. She nodded. He opened the can with a spurt and poured its contents into the waiting tumbler of ice cubes. When he handed it to her their hands touched briefly.

"Thanks," Amy said, taking the glass. Their eyes locked momentarily over the rim of the glass as she went to take a sip of the sweet tea, then her eyelashes fluttered downward.

Mark took the last remaining can of soda from the tray and snapped it open as he took his own seat, right next to Amy.

"You heading back to school soon?" he asked after taking a long swig of his drink.

She nodded. "Mmhm."

"As I recall, you weren't that enthusiastic about it last time we talked."

"I'm getting more used to the idea. Especially when I think about the opportunities I'll have on the mission field if I have my degree in nursing. It will open up so many more doors."

There it was again, Mark thought irritably. Always some reference to God.

"And you?" Amy continued. "After you finish writing up your latest report, what's next? Some other exciting adventure in a far off country, no doubt."

"Time will tell. Sometimes I think it might be nice to give up the fieldwork for awhile and settle down - at least for a year or two. It gets tiring, living on site all the time."

"But what would you do?" Amy asked.

"I'm not sure. Research, write, teach, I suppose. There might be some small university somewhere willing to take me," Mark said with half a smile.

"What about New Mexico?" Harmony asked, over hearing their conversation. "I thought you already worked for them?"

"I might be looking for a change of scenery," Mark hedged, not really wanting to get into the details in front of guests.

"Really? Why?" Harmony persisted. "I thought you liked it there. And besides, you've had pretty much your choice of digs to work on since being associated with them. Why not just teach there if that's what you want to do?"

"Steaks are almost done," Russ called from the barbecue. "Mark, you want to come inside and help me get the rest of the fixings?"

Mark rose from his chair, again glad for the reprieve.

Once inside the kitchen, Russ came right out and asked the question. "Are you in some kind of falling out with the university?"

Mark sighed heavily, knowing he couldn't hide things very well from his father. "You could say that. I was going to tell you all about it at a more opportune time."

"Does this have anything to do with your discoveries in Africa?"

Mark nodded. "It has everything to do with it."

"Exactly what's happened?"

"Let's just say, the scientific community isn't always interested in new discoveries - especially if they don't fit into their preconceived notions of how things are supposed to work."

"Meaning the theory of evolution," Russ supplied.

"Exactly," Mark affirmed.

"And how do you feel about all of this?" Russ asked.

"I'm still feeling my way," Mark admitted. "Don't expect an instant conversion, if that's what you're hoping for."

"Fair enough," Russ replied. "But...?" he prompted.

"I can't ignore the evidence, Dad. It's all there."

"And that institution wants you to do that? Ignore the evidence?"

Mark nodded. "Or get black listed."

"And what did you decide?" Russ asked.

"I can't ignore the truth," Mark stated simply.

"That's my boy." Russ smiled.

"Oh yeah?" Mark grinned sheepishly. "Except now I'm out of a job, with no backing whatsoever from the institution that commissioned me in the first place."

"What are you going to do?"

"Write that dissertation," Mark stated firmly. "What else can I do? People deserve to know the truth."

Russ nodded in agreement.

"Except, now that my credibility is shot, I might find it diffi-cult convincing anyone to believe me. But I've got to try. Which is why it's so important that I keep those artefacts that I sent you safe. I need some real, credible evidence to back me up. I can't let anything happen to those items. I just don't want to put you and Deanie in any danger."

"And you think something could happen?" Russ asked. "That we could be at risk?"

Mark sighed and rubbed the back of his neck wearily. "This is a lot messier than you know. Not only is my career in jeopardy, but there have been threats as well. I don't want to drag you into this, but I have to do what I know is right."

"However we can help…" Russ offered. "You know we back you one hundred percent. Just tell us what to do."

"Don't do anything for now," Mark advised. "I've been trying to lay low, so to speak, but soon, when I'm finished writing my dissertation, I'm going to have to make quite a bit of noise. I just hope there will be somebody out there listening."

"Too bad I hadn't known about this sooner," Russ mused.
"Why?"

"I heard about a temporary position here in Winnipeg," Russ

replied. "They're looking for a professor in the archaeology department to fill in for someone who is on temporary leave due to an accident."

"You don't say," Mark said, raising his eyebrows with interest.

"Maybe it's not too late," Russ suggested. "It wouldn't hurt to stop by and ask."

"Maybe I'll do that tomorrow. I could use the credibility," Mark mused. "I just won't tell them what I'm working on."

"In any case, we better get this food out on the table before those steaks get burnt to a crisp," Russ said.

"Right. I hope everyone likes well done," Mark answered with a grin.

CHAPTER 17

The office was small, tucked in the back corner of the building, but it was his. At least for the time being, anyway. The university had been more than happy to welcome back one of their own for a short-term position on staff. He'd be lecturing twice a week, have a few papers to mark and have plenty of time for his own research. Perfect. And he'd be getting paid besides. Mark couldn't ask for a better arrangement.

He'd been looking into his Bible a lot lately, trying to line up some of the questions he had with the scientific evidence. Naturally, he had begun to research the whole creation theory quite extensively. There was a lot of information out there that was not making it into regular scientific journals.

Questions about astrophysics and time travel were just some of the latest items to cross his path. The theory that time sped up when traveling at the speed of light was nothing new - it had been estimated that a person traveling at the speed of light for only a few weeks would actually arrive back to earth hundreds of years later. So it made sense that the stars could be a lot younger than most scientists were willing to admit. Then there was the problem with current radiometric dating techniques. A scientist from the states had been studying microscopic halos left from radioactive material in granite. In order for the halos to form, it had to be crystallized within three minutes of formation, not the millions of years assumed by most scientists.

Mark sat pouring over this most recent batch of information he had unearthed. How could the scientific community choose to overlook such a large volume of documented evidence? He was astounded that someone, somewhere, didn't blow the whistle on this tightly guarded club. Well, maybe he was the man to do it.

There was a knock on his office door. He looked up as the receptionist popped her head inside. "Excuse me, Dr. Graham, but there's a woman outside who seems especially insistent on seeing you."

"Who is she?" he asked absently, still perusing the documents before him.

"She says she's your sister."

Mark smiled and nodded. "Send her in." It was just like Harmony to interrupt whenever the whim overtook her. Oh well. He had some things to share he was sure she'd be interested in. This stuff was right up her alley.

He carefully marked his place with a sticky note as he heard the door opening and looked up. The ready greeting that was on his lips stayed right where it was.

"Uh... hello," he offered tentatively. "Maybe you have the wrong office. The receptionist told me my sister was here to see me."

"Oh." The young woman laughed nervously. "Dr. Mark Graham, right?"

"Yes," he replied, waiting.

She stepped further into the room and shut the door behind her. She reached forward and stretched out her hand. "Hi. Sorry to just barge in on you, like this. My name is Charlene Howard."

He half stood and barely touched her finger tips in a pseudo handshake before sitting back down.

"May I?" she asked, gesturing to a chair on the opposite side of his desk.

"Go ahead."

She perched on the edge of the seat, obviously nervous about something. She looked to be in her mid to late twenties; pretty and blonde, and was wearing a trendy yet tasteful outfit. Probably a student wanting advice about something but afraid she wouldn't gain admittance without an excuse.

"Can I help you with something?" he prompted.

She looked down at her hands, which she was twisting in her lap. "I'm a lot more nervous than I expected," she admitted with a little laugh.

"Um, okay..."

"I mean it's not every day I get to meet thee Dr. Mark Graham."

He frowned, suspicion birthed after so many weeks of tension, now rising to the forefront. "Oh?"

"Oh dear," she muttered to herself. She looked up with pleading in her eyes. "You see, you are... or rather, I am... actually we're brother and sister," she finally blurted.

Mark's eyebrows rose. "Pardon me?"

"We have the same mother," Charlene explained. "Miranda Riley?"

Mark felt like he had been gut punched - again. He couldn't seem to find any words as he tried to digest the information.

"I'm sorry," Charlene offered. "It came as quite a shock to us, too."

"Us?" he finally managed.

Charlene nodded. "Me and my younger brother Scott. We had no idea we had an older brother or that our mom had been married before she met Dad. She'd kept it all secret."

Mark didn't know how he felt about that bit of information. The little boy that still resided within him somewhere was suddenly very hurt. "I see. So how did you find out?"

"Mom secretly kept a scrapbook full of all kinds of articles about this famous archaeologist named Dr. Mark Graham. I was helping her pack after she and Dad split up a few months ago, and I found it. When I asked her about it, she wasn't going to tell me anything. But I could tell there was something up, so she finally broke down and told me everything. About her first marriage and how when her husband got custody she just decided to up and start a new life altogether."

Not exactly the way he'd heard it, Mark mused blackly. And what was up with everybody keeping a scrapbook?

"I can see this is quite a shock for you," she said again.

"Yes. To put it mildly."

"I was really choked at first, you know? Like I felt betrayed or something," Charlene said. Mark knew the feeling. "But then I started thinking I wanted to meet this famous brother of mine. And so, after I did a little more research of my own, I flew out here and here I am."

"Just like that," Mark stated.

"Um, yeah. I guess I could have called first, but I didn't know if you'd see me."

"No, it's... fine." Mark cleared his throat and sat up straighter. "So you flew here. From where?"

"Calgary," Charlene replied. "That's where I live with my husband, Tom. Mom and Dad still live there, too. And Scott." She hesitated. "Um, you want to see some pictures?"

She didn't wait for a response but began digging in her handbag.

An unreasonable fear clutched Mark's heart. He wasn't sure he wanted to see any pictures, but Charlene already had them out of her purse and was handing them over as she pulled her own chair in closer to the desk. He willed himself to look down.

"This one was taken about a month ago at my son's birthday party. See, there's my husband Tom, and that's your nephew Cade. He's two." She smiled proudly.

Mark just blinked. He had a nephew.

Charlene continued, "And this next one shows my - I mean our brother Scott holding Cade on his knee. Scott's twenty-one. Cade was born on his birthday."

The same age as Harmony. "How nice," was all that came out of Mark's mouth.

"Yep. He's a pretty proud uncle."

"And how old are you?" Mark asked.

"Me? I'm twenty five."

"I see." So he was just eight years old when she was born, he calculated. Still a boy wondering why he didn't get cards and gifts like the other kids he knew whose parents had split up.

"Here we all are watching Cade and Scott blow out the candles," she went on, referring to the next photograph. She waited for him to peruse the picture before adding, "Oh, and that's Mom there on the right."

Mark swallowed hard, his eyes feeling suspiciously prickly. She was a nice looking woman for her age. She was probably in her early fifties with auburn brown hair done up in a fashionable style.

Mark cleared his throat and handed the pictures back to Charlene. "Yes. Well, thank you for showing me."

"I can send you some more if you'd like. Online?" Charlene offered.

"I don't really do 'Online'," Mark said.

"Oh." There was an awkward silence as Charlene looked down at her hands.

"Perhaps the old fashioned way?" Mark added quickly, seeing her distress.

Charlene nodded. "Okay."

"So…" Mark looked down at his watch. More awkward silence. The minutes seemed to stretch on and on.

"She's not really a bad person," Charlene finally whispered. "Whatever her reasons for giving you up, I'm sure she's thought lots about you judging from the scrapbook she kept. And she was a good mother to Scott and me."

"That's... that's fine." Mark nodded mechanically.

"I'll be in town for a few days," Charlene said. "Tom and Cade came along for moral support. We're staying downtown at the Ramada."

Mark wasn't sure what she expected. "Oh. I see."

Charlene persisted doggedly. "I thought maybe you'd like to meet them. Especially the baby."

"Um..." He focused on a stack of papers on his desk. How was he supposed to concentrate on work when he'd just been thrown a bomb?

"I know you're probably a very busy man," Charlene went on breathlessly, "but we're only in town for a few days..." She trailed off. She looked as if she might cry.

"Of course," Mark said quickly. "I'm still just in shock, that's all. But I would love to meet your husband and son."

Charlene smiled with relief. "Oh, good. I was pretty scared there for a minute. Like you might just kick me out or something."

"No, no. I wouldn't do that."

"Um, and you probably have other family in town. You can bring them along if you like. A wife, kids?"

"I'm not married."

"Oh," Charlene said.

There seemed to be nothing more to say other than to pick the time and location for their next rendezvous.

"So where should we meet?" Charlene asked tentatively.

"You pick," Mark said.

"I don't really know Winnipeg that well," she said hesitantly.

"How about the hotel dining room at, say, seven?" Mark suggested.

"Okay, but..."

"That's probably too late for Cade," Mark said.

"No, it's not so much that as..."

"What?"

"The dining room at the hotel is awfully fancy. Maybe somewhere a little more family friendly? You know how two year olds can be."

Actually, he didn't but he smiled anyway and nodded. "There's a good pancake house on Main that serves kid's meals," he suggested.

"Perfect," Charlene agreed with a grateful smile.

"Alright then. See you there at seven."

Charlene rose from her chair. "Thanks for being so... I don't know. Down to earth, I guess. You're nothing like I was afraid you'd be after reading all those articles about you. I felt pretty intimidated because you sound like such a genius."

Mark just shrugged. "I'm just a plain ordinary man like everybody else." Just an ordinary man with too many problems to count on both hands right at the moment.

"I'm with another group," Mark informed the restaurant hostess. He could see Charlene and her family sitting at a booth across the room and gestured in their general direction.

"Thank goodness!" Charlene said when she saw Mark approaching. "I thought maybe you decided not to come."

"Of course not," Mark assured stoically. He nodded at the man he presumed to be Charlene's husband.

"This is my husband Tom," Charlene introduced. "And this is Cade." She smiled indulgently at the two year old, who was presently stuffing crackers into his mouth.

The two men shook hands and Mark sat down. He had one

side of the booth to himself, since Cade's high chair was at the end of the table in the isle.

"I had some last minute calls to take care of," Mark explained. "Sorry I'm a bit late." More like last minute excuses, he thought.

"That's okay," Charlene said. "I'm sure you're awfully busy. Cade was getting kind of hungry, though. Hope you don't mind that we already ordered."

"Of course not." Mark surveyed his own menu and made a quick decision, ready to catch the next waitress that went by. "So, Tom," Mark ventured conversationally. "What do you do for a living?"

"Electrician. In the patch," Tom answered. He was not quite overweight, but not skinny either, with closely cropped brown hair and glasses.

"Oil industry's still busy these days?" Mark asked.

"Busy enough."

"Good, good."

Mark wasn't sure what else to ask but Charlene came to the rescue. "Tell us more about what you're doing."

"Oh, research. Always lots of research," Mark replied noncommittally.

"You've sure been to some fascinating places," Charlene said. "I was shocked when I read all the articles Mom's been keeping."

There was an awkward moment of silence. "Um... yes."

Charlene looked down at her hands. "I'm sorry. This must be especially - uncomfortable for you. I mean, we know all kinds of things about you and you had no idea we even existed."

Cade started to fuss and Charlene's attention was momentarily drawn elsewhere. Mark was glad for the timely distraction. Of course he was uncomfortable. Uncomfortable didn't even come close to what he was feeling. Shock, betrayal, anger - all mingled together into one indescribable emotion.

"Our, uh... our mother. Does she have other relatives close by?" Mark asked.

"Grandma and Grandpa - her parents - both passed away. They used to live in Winnipeg, I think, but they moved out to the west coast before I was born. We have an uncle out there, too. In Vancouver."

Mark nodded. "I see."

"I should have brought pictures of them, too," Charlene apologized.

"No, that's fine," Mark said with a shake of his head. Knowing he had other siblings was enough. Too much, in fact.

"So, you said you weren't married, but do you have other family? Did your Dad remarry or anything?"

"Yes. Yes he did. I have one other sister."

"Oh. That's nice."

There was more awkward silence. Mark was glad when the food finally arrived and they had something to occupy themselves besides straining for conversation.

"Hey, bro! Fancy meeting you here." It was Harmony.

"Harmony." Mark looked up in surprise. "What are you doing here?"

"I'm meeting Cory, but he's late as usual," Harmony shrugged. "Mind if I join you for a sec?"

"Go ahead." Harmony was already sliding in beside him. "Charlene, Tom, this is my sister, Harmony. Harmony - Charlene and Tom. They're... from Calgary," he finished lamely.

"Hi," Harmony greeted with a friendly smile. She was her usual bubbly self and didn't seem to notice the tension her arrival had caused. "So, I was actually going to call you later. I'm moving into my own place on the weekend and I need your help. Mom and Dad are going out of town."

"You're moving out?" Mark asked. "Why?"

"I am twenty-one," Harmony reminded. "Don't you think it's time I got my own place? Besides, you moved out by the time you were my age."

"True, but I was going on to graduate work in the States. It makes more sense to stay home and save the rent money until you're finished school."

"I was thinking of quitting anyway." Harmony shrugged. "I mean, I've wasted enough of the parents' money as it is and I still don't know what I'm doing with my life. I think I just need some time off. Some space to try and get my act together, so to speak. That and some privacy for a change."

"Because of Cory," Mark noted with a disapproving scowl.

"Oh please!" Harmony laughed. "You're one to talk! Besides, I'm a Christian remember? I don't believe in sex before marriage, so just chill, okay? Big brothers," she said sarcastically to Charlene and Tom. "Hey, I see him. I gotta go. Nice meeting you two, and I'll call you to remind you about the weekend." She planted a quick kiss on Mark's cheek and was up out of the seat and heading toward the entrance where her boyfriend was surveying the crowd expectantly. Mark watched as they embraced before following the hostess to a seat.

"You're a Christian, too?" Charlene asked enthusiastically. "So are we. Wait till I tell Mom!"

Mark almost choked on his water. He shook his head while he tried to clear his throat.

The smile faded on Charlene's lips. "I just assumed... I mean, your sister, she said..."

"Not to worry. I didn't say I *wasn't* a Christian, but to be truthful, I'm in a bit of a questioning phase."

"I hope I haven't offended you."

"Don't worry about it. I'm sure my stepmother would say that God is just trying to get my attention."

"We're kind of new to this Christian thing ourselves," Charlene explained. "We all got saved together. Me, Tom and Mom."

"Then I guess I'm the only hold out on both sides of the family," Mark said.

"I suppose you two are really close," Charlene said off hand, fiddling with her spoon.

Mark frowned. "You mean me and Harmony?"

"Yes." She nodded.

"We did grow up together. She's twenty-one. Same age as your - our - brother Scott, right?"

"Scott would really like to meet you, too, sometime. But he couldn't get time off work." Charlene's face brightened. "Maybe sometime you could come out to see us?"

Mark blinked, not sure how to respond. Sudden attachment for an unknown sister was not something he could just manufacture. And as for some kind of family reunion - that was beyond what his current state of mental health could even fathom.

"Hey, Char, let's not jump the gun," Tom put in quietly. It was probably the first sentence he'd put together the whole time.

"Look, it has been really nice," Mark said. "Surprising, yes, and a bit disconcerting, too. But I can see you two are good people. You just need to know that I am really, really busy right now. I might not have time."

"You don't need to say any more," Charlene said.

"I'm not trying to put you off," Mark said. "I am seriously busy on a dissertation from my last dig. In Africa," he added for good measure.

"Look at you!" Charlene exclaimed suddenly, turning her attention to her son, Cade. "Mommy better take you to the washroom and clean you up. What a mess!" She fiddled with the safety strap on the high chair for a moment and then scooped Cade up into her arms. Mark and Tom both watched her retreating figure as she scurried away.

"I'm not trying to hurt anyone," Mark stated in a low voice. "It's just -"

"She'll be alright," Tom answered. "I'm just glad you agreed to meet us in the first place. It would have crushed her if you hadn't."

"I wouldn't have done that."

"I was worried about this meeting from the moment she got it into her head," Tom admitted. "I'm just glad you turned out to be half decent."

"Only half?" Mark asked with a small grin.

CHAPTER 18

"Anthony," Mark said into the receiver. "How are things going at your end?"

"Excellent," Anthony replied. "I am a genius, if I do say so myself."

"Okay, genius, what have you got?" Mark asked with a laugh.

"I've been able to keep tabs on everything - every scrap of so called data that Laura and John have used to put together their report on the site. It's so full of holes it even smells like Swiss cheese. As soon as they publish, I'll have a counter attack all ready to go."

"Great. But will anybody be listening?" Mark asked.

"Of course, cause here's the good part. You ready?"

"Spill it."

"I've got verification from that Institute in Texas I was telling you about. They are very interested - and I mean very - in backing our study and housing the archaeological display. As long as you can deliver the specimens, like you said, they're all over it."

"Don't worry about my end," Mark reassured. "You just make sure nobody else gets wind of this until we're ready. I don't want this to come out on anybody's timetable but my own."

"Got it," Anthony said.

"I'm actually pleasantly surprised to find out that there are some reputable institutions willing to go out on a limb for true scientific research. Not just try to fit things into their own narrow definition of what could and couldn't take place."

"Intelligent design is gaining in popularity," Anthony agreed. "Of course, this is an institution with a definite Christian bent. Hopefully, the world won't be too put off by that factor."

"We'll take what we can get," Mark agreed.

"Actually, while we're on the topic, did I tell you that I visited my folks last week?" Anthony asked casually.

"No you didn't. Well, that's good news."

"Yeah... uh, did I tell you I kind of, like, rededicated my life to God?" There was silence on the other end. "Mark? Hello? You still there?"

"I'm here," Mark replied curtly.

"It's not a curse, man," Anthony defended. "It's actually pretty cool."

"Well, just don't let it go to your head," Mark cautioned. "I want that display strictly scientific. No reference to faith whatso-ever. You got it? We want to remain credible, not be dismissed as a bunch of religious crack-pots."

"Of course," Anthony replied. "I wouldn't do anything to jeop-ardize the work we've been doing. You know that. Besides, you're the one writing the dissertation, so what's your worry?"

"When you put it that way." Mark consulted his watch. "Lis-ten, I have to go. I'm helping my sister move into her own apart-ment and she'll be expecting me."

"Me, too, man. Laura can be a real taskmaster. Keep in touch."

Mark pocketed his cell phone and stood up. He would just as soon forget about Laura - and John, for that matter. And as far as Anthony's new found faith, it hit just a little too close to home right now.

He'd been feeling the draw of it himself, lately, despite what he'd said to Charlene and Tom. But he wouldn't allow himself to succumb. Not yet anyway. He had to keep his head clear and his mind focused on the task at hand. Vindication.

Mark arrived at his parents' home just as Cory Rantt and Amy Walters were coming out of the house with Harmony's double mattress. Harmony was bringing up the rear with part of the disassembled bed frame.

"Here, let me help you with that," Mark offered, coming to take over for Amy. Their bodies brushed briefly as he secured his hold on the somewhat floppy cargo.

They spent the next half hour making trips in and out of the house with boxes, suitcases and pieces of bedroom furniture. "There's more room in these two vehicles than I thought," Harmony mused. "Maybe we can squeeze it all into one trip. Unless I find some other odd furniture that the parents wouldn't mind getting rid of."

"Better ask first," Mark cautioned.

"You're no fun," Harmony quipped with a grin. "I think I can fit the rest into my own car later. I'll have to bring Mom's van back anyway."

"I can bring it back," Mark suggested. "I'll have to come back for my vehicle when we're through. Why don't you just take your car now?"

"Cause I want to ride with Cory in the truck," Harmony stated matter-of-factly.

"Oh. Right."

"You and Amy can ride together in the van," Harmony called, already jumping into the passenger seat of Cory's borrowed truck.

Mark got into the van and waited for Amy to get her seatbelt fastened before backing out of the driveway. He was hyper aware of her presence, which was ridiculous seeing as they were just helping his sister move.

"You know the way, I presume?" Mark asked.

"I put it on my GPS."

The ride turned out to be less awkward than Mark had feared. They chatted about school, the weather and the Blue Bombers chances of winning the Grey Cup as Mark manoeuvred his way through the streets. Amy turned out to be a die-hard football fan and went to every home game the Bombers played.

"I never would have guessed," Mark said with a laugh. "I mean, you just don't look like the type to follow football that closely."

"Are you kidding? My Dad is a Bomber fan from way back. He used to take me to games when I was just little. I thought you knew that."

"I guess there's lots we really don't know about each other."

"I guess," Amy replied softly and turned to look out her window.

Mark glanced over at her for a moment. She really was very pretty. Soft and feminine - almost cherub like. And young. Very young. His jaw clenched slightly and he kept his eyes on the road for the rest of the trip.

The foursome unloaded both vehicles expediently enough, hauling everything up the one flight of stairs into Harmony's new one bedroom apartment. They were all exhausted by the time they were finished. Harmony flopped down upon the carpet.

"You're going to need more furniture," Mark mused, surveying the room as he lowered himself onto the floor.

"You wouldn't let me, remember?" Harmony stuck out her tongue.

"You can't just take stuff from the house without asking," Mark replied.

"We should have brought some drinks to put in the fridge," Cory said, still breathing heavily.

"We can go out," Harmony suggested. "There's a pizza joint just around the corner."

"We should help you unpack a bit, first," Mark said.

"Naw, I don't feel like it," Harmony said, shaking her head. "I'll do it tomorrow. Although it might be kind of nice to have the bed put together. Mark, why don't you and Amy work on that while Cory and I get the entertainment system back together? The rest is all stuff I can do on my own."

Mark agreed nonchalantly, although on the inside he felt decidedly awkward about the task. The last thing he wanted was to make up a bed with Amy Walters.

"And that's when I burst out laughing and spit my coke all over him," Harmony finished her story with gusto. "Isn't that right, Cory?" She leaned into him playfully as the others laughed. The foursome had gathered at the pizza restaurant as planned and were sitting in a booth. Mark had no option but to sit next to Amy - not that he minded - since Harmony and Cory were cuddled up across from them.

"That still doesn't explain why you started dating," Mark said. "Sounds more like a nasty cold shower to me."

"Seriously, I felt so bad - I ruined one of his best T-shirts - so I had to start being nice to him," Harmony explained.

"Instead of teasing him all the time," Amy added.

"Funny I don't remember any of that," Mark mused. "I mean, you two not getting along so well when you were younger."

Harmony shrugged. "You were so much older and definitely too preoccupied. Or gone already."

"Right." Mark looked down at his plate for a moment, feeling ancient.

"You know," Amy said conspiratorially. "Maybe Cory didn't mind all that much."

Cory just shrugged his ascent, and the rest of the group laughed. The good-natured banter continued, Harmony carrying most of the conversation.

Mark snuck a sidelong glance at Amy. Her blonde curls framed her face and she was smiling and laughing easily. Definitely not affected by his presence the way he was being affected by hers.

He turned back to the conversation and laughed along with Harmony's next anecdote. He really needed to get a grip.

CHAPTER 19

"Hello," Mark said absently after picking up the receiver. He was actually much more interested in the information displayed on his computer screen and hoped whoever-it-was would be quick.

"Mark? Hi, how are you?"

Mark blinked momentarily and then frowned as recognition dawned. "Laura?"

"Who else? You haven't forgotten me that quickly, I hope."

"What do you want?" he clipped.

"Goodness. That hardly sounded very friendly."

He let out a pent up breath. "What were you expecting? We hardly parted on good terms."

"True," Laura noted. "I thought maybe we could get past all that. John and I have almost finished up here. The exhibition is opening soon. I thought you might like to be there for it."

"Exhibition?" Mark's heart leapt in his breast. "I thought all the artefacts went back to Africa already."

"Most of them did, but we've got great digital photos of everything and a power point presentation like no other. Amazing what one can do with technology these days."

"I'll bet."

"So? You interested?"

"What do you think?" Mark asked sarcastically.

"You're being very juvenile, Mark."

"What?" Mark snorted. "I'm supposed to be happy about the fact that you sabotaged my work - you and someone I thought was my friend."

"Better friends than you are to yourself," Laura countered. "In fact, you should be pleased that John and I took over when we did. Your credibility as an archaeologist is still intact. And, if it'll make you feel better, your name is still very prominent in all the findings."

"I don't want my name associated with a lie," Mark grated.

"Mark, be reasonable," Laura said, as if talking to a child. "Nobody is lying. It's simply a different interpretation of the findings than what you wanted. But in the end, it's the most plausible. I had hoped that you'd see that now that you've had a little time to think it through."

"My time to think about it, as you say, has only convinced me that the international cover up is even more deeply entrenched than I thought."

Laura laughed. "Now you're sounding positively melodramatic."

"Whatever."

"In any case, I wanted to let you know that there are no hard feelings on this side of the border, and we would really like to see you at the opening, if you can see your way to coming. I... I miss you."

"Don't hold your breath."

There was a moment of silence before Laura spoke again. "You never used to be so petty. So unfeeling."

"Maybe you never really knew the real me."

"Apparently not."

"Although, I must say, I'm surprised at you, as well, Laura. I never thought you could be bought so easily."

"What is that supposed to mean?"

"We both remember Sangeruka's threats. But you don't seem to be too bothered by that right now. I suppose your findings line up perfectly with whatever he told you to say."

"That's ridiculous," she scoffed. "Time and distance have put Sangeruka well out of the picture. Not to mention a change in authority back in Harare."

"Oh?" Mark asked, his curiosity pricked.

"I'm surprised you hadn't heard. Sangeruka is out. We're dealing with a much friendlier official now."

"The man at the top is still the same."

Laura sighed heavily into the receiver. "I forgot just how paranoid you've become. Look, sorry for bothering you. The invite still stands, in any case, not that I'm expecting anything."

"Thanks, I guess."

"Alright, then. See you around." She hung up.

Mark held the phone aloft for a moment before slowly lowering it. Definitely not the best start to his day, he mused. He went back to his computer screen, trying to regain his earlier train of thought. Easier said than done, apparently. The sentence he just read made absolutely no sense and he had to read it again.

With a sigh he sat back and rubbed his eyes. How did he feel? Angry, betrayed... a bit nostalgic. That should be his presentation; his day in the spotlight. Instead, here he was holed up thousands of miles away, hoping that someone - anyone - would listen to his version of the story. And if he did tell it, would he be safe in doing so? Sangeruka's threats still rang quite clearly in his head, no matter what Laura said.

And what about her declaration that she missed him? Thankfully, he felt decidedly neutral on that score. If he'd ever had any feelings for Laura, they'd been put to rest. Unfortunately, he still had not reconciled his present feelings for a certain someone else or the wisdom of pursuing the object of his affections.

The telephone cut abruptly into his thoughts. So it was going to be one of those days. With a sigh he answered it.

"Mark, good news!" Anthony fairly panted with excitement on the other end of the telephone.

"Yeah? What might that be?" Mark asked.

"The faculty want you to be there for the opening of the exhibit." There was silence for a moment on the other end. "Mark? Buddy? You still there?"

"I'm here."

"So? What do you think?"

Mark shrugged. "Big deal. I'm not coming. Besides, I knew that already."

"You did?"

"Mmhm. Laura contacted me earlier."

"Laura?"

"Yeah. She was very friendly - quite civil. She says they're still giving me credit. Probably just trying to save face, since the whole archaeological community knows I was in charge of that dig. It wouldn't look too good to let people know there was mutiny among the ranks."

"And what did you say?" Anthony asked.

"I told her to shove it," Mark replied. "In a manner of speaking."

"I don't know. We might be able to use this to our advantage."

"Really? How do you figure?"

"Got a minute?" Anthony asked.

"I'm all ears," Mark said, sitting up straighter.

"Let's just say you accept the invitation," Anthony said. "All nice and legit, like. So when you do show up they can't turf you."

"I already told you I wasn't going to that opening. Under any circumstances."

"Even if it comes *after* your own presentation at the Institute in Texas?"

"Just what are you getting at?" Mark asked.

"They want the whole schpiel - you and whatever artefacts you've got." Anthony hesitated a moment. "You did say you had some actual artefacts?"

"Yes."

"We'll have to keep your dissertation under wraps as much as possible. They've already agreed not to mention your name in any of their publicity until after the event. I told them it would add to the hype and all that. People are so gullible these days. Always looking out for whatever will get them the most dollars."

"Whoa, whoa, whoa! Hold on a minute! You're getting way ahead of me, here, buddy," Mark blurted. "Sounds like you have the whole thing planned. And what's this about dollars?"

"Oh, I told them you had an anonymous sponsor that was willing to fund the project under the condition that the publicity was low key until after the opening," Anthony explained.

"Great. And just who might that be?"

"I'm still working on it," Anthony replied easily.

Mark sighed. "I'm not liking the sounds of this."

"Don't sweat it. I've got it all under control. Besides, now that I'm a Christian and all that, would I lie to you?"

"You're really not making me feel any better," Mark replied. "Okay, so then what? We present our findings in Texas, the world gets a hold of it and...? "

"Your name gets attached, then you show up in New Mexico - if they still have the balls to go through with their presentation - and kind of rub their noses in it."

"Or start one heck of a law suit."

"A bit of controversy never hurt anyone."

"So says you," Mark replied.

"Okay. Difference of opinion never hurt anyone," Anthony conceded. "Dialogue is healthy."

There was silence on the other end of the phone as Mark considered everything Anthony had said. "You think we can be ready in time?" he finally asked.

"Ready when you are," Anthony replied. "How soon can you pack?"

Mark's telephone rang. Again. He sighed and thumped his desk with his fist. This was getting down right ridiculous. Just how many phone calls were going to interrupt his train of thought in one afternoon? He glanced at the call display. Harmony. She usually wouldn't be put off.

"Hello."

"Hi. I hope you're not busy this evening because I've made plans for you to join Cory and me. It's our anniversary."

Mark pinched the bridge of his nose and adjusted the phone to the other ear. "That's silly, Harmony. It seems to me that a nice romantic dinner for two is more appropriate for your anniversary, don't you think?"

"But that's just it. It's a surprise, and I need you and a bunch of other people there so Cory doesn't suspect."

"Look, I'm really busy, okay?" Mark tried again. "It's been a crazy day all around and I've got some pretty important new developments to work on."

"But poor Amy! This will make her feel terrible," Harmony wailed.

"Amy?" Mark repeated curiously. "Why will she feel terrible?"

"I told her you'd be there to kind of look out for her, you know?"

"No, I don't know. What on earth are you talking about?"

"Well, there are a bunch of other people coming that she doesn't really know that well, except for this one guy that I know has a crush on her. The only problem is, she can't stand him. She was afraid he would be trying to hit on her all night, or something, but I said you'd be there for her to talk to and that she could kind of, pretend like you were kind of going out or something."

"Harmony!"

"Not like she'd be falling all over you, or anything like that, but just like, if she needed to, you know, call on you for moral support." Harmony's voice took on a touch of pleading. "I mean, she is an old friend."

Mark shook his head, a smile playing on his lips. "Harmony Graham, you can be a real pain sometimes, you know that?"

"Why?" Harmony asked quickly. "I mean, it's not that bad, is it? Pretending to like Amy, I mean."

It was absolutely the opposite of bad. But he couldn't let his little sister know that. "No, no of course not. That's not what I meant."

"Good. Then you'll be there?"

Mark hesitated for another second or two, looking over at his computer screen. "Sure. I'll be there. Just let Amy know I might need to call in a similar favour one of these days."

"Oh?" Harmony asked, all curiosity. "What do you mean?"

"Nothing." Mark laughed. "Now get off the phone so I can get some of this work done before I have to meet you."

"Thanks, Mark. You're the best. Oh, and I forgot to tell you. You should dress up."

"Dress up?" Mark repeated.

"Yeah, you know, a suit or something."

"Whatever you say. Sounds like you have it all worked out."

"Absolutely," Harmony agreed.

Okay, Mark admitted to himself after hanging up the telephone. The prospects of seeing Amy Walters again so soon were not that bad. In fact, it was probably just what he needed to rid him of any niggling doubts about his upcoming presentation.

CHAPTER 20

Mark entered the dim interior of the upscale restaurant and scanned the room for his sister. No sign of her. She could be running late. That wouldn't be unusual for Harmony.

He tugged at the suit jacket and straightened his tie. He didn't much like suits, but he did own a couple. Doctors of Archaeology had to make speeches on occasion and they came in handy once in awhile. The last time he'd worn this one, though, was at Jack's funeral. Probably not the best comparison for tonight's event.

"This way, sir," the hostess said, leading him further into the interior of the building. Mark was surprised when the hostess stopped and he was confronted with Amy Walters. Alone.

"Hi." She waved and smiled.

"Um, where's everyone else?" Mark asked, looking around.

"Harmony just called. She said they'd be late. Cory's car wouldn't start."

"They could always take a cab," Mark suggested, more to himself than to her. He sat down across from Amy and glanced her way. There was definitely something different about the way she looked. Her hair was swept up off her neck in an elegant style and the dress... spaghetti straps, low V-neck - nothing indecent, but definitely not the demure type of clothing he was used to seeing her wear.

He cleared his throat and fixed his gaze on the tabletop instead.

"Is everything okay?" Amy asked.

"What? Oh, absolutely," Mark replied and tried for a relaxed smile. "I was just - I mean, you look different this evening. That's all."

"Oh." The syllable sounded flat.

"I mean, in a good way. Nice... but different."

There was more awkward silence. Amy let out a long and heartfelt sigh. "I, um... I don't think I'm very good at this," she admitted.

"Oh? And that would be...?"

"This." She made a vague gesture with her hand.

"I'm not following."

Amy sighed. "Harmony planned this whole thing. She thinks we would, you know, make a good couple or something. It was all her idea, and I didn't stop her. I'm really sorry because now I feel so stupid for going along with it."

Mark's eyebrows rose slightly as he took this information in. "So, I take it she and Cory aren't actually coming?"

Amy shook her head, her gaze focused on the table top. "No." She looked up and captured Mark's gaze with her own. "I feel so embarrassed right now I could die."

"It's me, remember? We're old friends." Mark smiled in what he hoped was a casual way. His own heart was actually pounding in his ears and he wondered if she could hear it.

"I know. That's what makes it so silly. You probably still think of me as that foolish little girl. You sister's little friend."

"No. Not exactly."

"If you want to we can just leave," Amy said, looking down.

"You probably think of me as the ancient older brother," Mark countered. "Is that it?"

"No!" Amy looked up.

"Good."

"Then you're not mad?"

"Should I be?"

Amy rolled one of her shoulders. "We did kind of trick you."

"I'm a little ashamed to say I fell for it so easily." A slight smile was playing about his features. "I should have known Harmony would be up to something. I hate to think of all the teasing I'm going to have to put up with, though."

"We don't have to stay."

"There's no hurry. Now that we're here we might as well have dinner."

"You're sure?'

"Positive."

"Okay." She nodded and ducked behind her menu.

The rest of their evening at the restaurant went smoothly. There were lots of things to talk about - safe things - like family and football and warm fall weather. When the conversation began to wane and they'd had as many refills of coffee as either could stand, Mark offered to drive Amy home.

"You just need to turn up here," Amy pointed as they neared her street. "Third house in with the blue door."

"I know the way," Mark said with a smile.

"Oh. Right." Amy laughed.

Mark pulled up in front of Amy's parents' home and put his SUV in park, letting the motor idle. There was a moment of awkward silence before Amy made a move to get out of the vehicle.

"Hold on," Mark said, grabbing her hand.

Amy blinked.

The atmosphere in the confined space was electric. "Amy, you must know I want to kiss you," Mark stated.

She worked her bottom lip and nodded.

"But I can't help thinking about the difference in our ages. I mean, you're young. You don't want to get entangled with a fossil like me."

"You're hardly a fossil," she breathed.

"And you're not a little girl," Mark said. "And believe me, I noticed - even without the recent makeover."

"Oh."

There was no more questioning the wisdom of the inevitable. They leaned toward one another and allowed a first tentative kiss. Mark hated to draw away, but knew, for both their sakes, he had to take it slow.

"You know, my sister told me I had to come tonight to protect you from some guy who had a crush on you," Mark said.

"Oh?" Amy asked, blinking.

"Yeah. She said you wouldn't appreciate his advances, so we might have to pretend to, you know... like each other."

"I didn't know she said any of that."

"I'm not pretending," Mark said quietly. She didn't say anything. "And I hope you don't mind."

"No, no I don't," Amy whispered.

"Good." He leaned over for another kiss, this one slower and more deliberate. When they separated, both were breathing more heavily.

"I have a message I want you to give to my sister," Mark said, a slight smile spreading across his face.

"Oh? What's that?"

"Tell her, her matchmaking services are no longer needed."

CHAPTER 21

"I brought that package by," Russ said, stepping into Mark's office.

Mark looked up from his desk. "Hm?"

"The package," Russ repeated. "The one that came to our house by mistake. From…" he read off the package, "Charlene Howard."

"Oh that. Just put it there." Mark gestured to a pile of other unopened mail on his desk.

"Oh. Guess I needn't have bothered then, if it's not important." Russ shrugged. "I thought it might have something to do with the top secret whatever it is you're working on."

"It's not top secret."

"But nothing you can share with your old man," Russ stated, clearly fishing.

"Look Dad," Mark explained. "You already know from what I told you that I'm going to run into some opposition. I just don't want to put you in a compromising position, that's all."

"Who am I going to tell?"

"No one, but…" He sighed. "Look, I might as well tell you. I'm planning to head to Texas next week. I'm still working on putting together an airtight dissertation on that excavation site. Only now it's got to be sooner than later."

"That sounds like good news," Russ offered.

"It is, but I still need to be careful. There are some people out there that won't take kindly to what I have to share."

"Are you being threatened?" Russ's eyebrows descended.

"In recent enough history that I don't want to take any chances," Mark admitted. "I just want to be safe, alright?"

"Are you sure you should go through with this?"

"Not a doubt in my mind." Mark sat up straighter. "Look, I'd love to tell you everything, but I think it's best for everyone if I just keep it under wraps until the actual day of reckoning."

"Sounds ominous."

"Don't worry, okay? Everything is going to turn out alright. But I just think it would be better for you - and Deanie - to know as little as possible. Once everything is out in the open, you might see my reasons. But for now, you'll just have to trust me."

"You know I always do," Russ said, surveying his son for a moment. "Just be careful." He cleared his throat. "Okay. Well, there's the package, anyway." He patted it where it sat on Mark's desk and turned to leave.

"Dad?"

Russ stopped and turned around. "Yes?"

"There's something else on my mind, if you have a minute." Mark smiled sheepishly.

"Okay. Sure," Russ responded, eyeing his son as he sat down.

Mark took a deep breath. "So what was it like for you when you first met Deanie?"

Russ blinked, obviously surprised by the turn in the conversation.

"When you first knew you might have feelings for Deanie," Mark rephrased. "How was that for you?"

"I don't even want to tell you what I thought of Deanie the first time I saw her," Russ said.

"Love at first sight?" Mark asked with an amused grin.

Russ laughed. "Hardly. I thought she was a little tramp."

"Okay. So once you figured that part out, then what?"

Russ leaned back in his chair, considering. "Sometimes she made me so mad. I couldn't really sort my own feelings out. But I knew I couldn't live without her."

"And what about the difference in your ages?" Mark persisted. "Was that a problem for either of you? How did you reconcile that in your mind?"

Russ squinted his eyes at Mark. "Why all the questions all of a sudden? This doesn't have anything to do with Amy Walters, does it?"

"How did you know?" Mark's own eyebrows rose in surprise.

"Your sister isn't that good at keeping secrets," Russ stated dryly. "How old is Amy, now, anyway?"

"She'll be twenty-one pretty soon," Mark replied.

"And you are?"

"Thirty-three."

Russ nodded. "Thirty-four next month, if I remember correctly."

"Yeah. Right," Mark agreed, his tone flat.

"So that makes you thirteen years older than her, give or take a few months."

"I know," Mark said with a grim sounding sigh. "I don't know what's gotten into me."

Russ just shrugged. "I'm almost fifteen years older than you stepmother. Seems to me you're like your old man in more ways than we imagined. We Graham men just take a little longer to decide on a mate, that's all. We're choosey. But when the right one comes along, there will be no other choices."

Mark thought about that for a minute. Amy Walters was his choice. Now he just had to convince her of that fact. "Thanks. That helps a lot."

"Good. Well, I better get going," Russ said, rising.

"Um, one more thing," Mark stopped him again. "About that package. I was debating whether I should say anything or not, but I think maybe I need to."

Russ frowned. "What is it?"

"Maybe you should sit down again," Mark suggested.

Russ did as he was told and waited patiently for Mark to continue.

"I've been contacted by this Charlene Howard person. Actually, she came here with her husband and child not that long ago. I was going to tell you then, but I chickened out."

Russ just raised his eyebrows but didn't prompt any further.

"Yeah... she's actually my sister." Mark could see the change in his father's countenance the moment the words registered. "She's Miranda's - my mother's - daughter," Mark continued quickly. "Apparently she remarried and never told any of them about me - or you. There's a boy, too. Harmony's age."

"And how do you feel about this?" Russ asked tightly.

"Confused, angry, indifferent... how should I feel?"

"I suppose she wants to meet with you," Russ stated. "After all these years."

"As far as I know, Miranda doesn't know Charlene made contact. It was an accident that she even found out about my existence when she ran across a scrapbook Miranda had been keeping about my career."

"I see." Russ rose abruptly from the chair. "Well, you do whatever you want to. I won't stop you. You're a man, after all."

"Dad..."

Russ shook his head and gave a self-depreciating laugh. "After all these years. I thought I was completely over it. I'm surprised at how - vulnerable I feel right now."

"Me too."

"I'm not sure what I'm going to tell Deanie," Russ mused.

"You don't have to say anything if you don't want to."

"Are you kidding?" Russ laughed. "Your stepmother has this

uncanny sense - like radar. She can spot when something's troubling me from a mile away. I'm afraid I'm not that good at keeping secrets. At least not with her."

"Sorry, Dad. For upsetting you," Mark offered.

"I'll get over it. I'm not totally soft, you know."

"So what did you think of the show?" Amy asked as she and Mark strolled hand in hand down the darkened downtown street.

Mark shrugged, allowing a slight smile to play at his lips. "Okay, I guess. I must confess I haven't been to a movie in a long time."

It was only a short stroll from the theatre to Mark's apartment. Their hands had been intertwined almost from the beginning of the movie. As soon as the lights had dimmed, Mark had reached over and taken her hand into his. It fit so perfectly; felt so comfortable.

"Now let's see." Mark stopped by his vehicle, still in its designated spot outside his building, as he dug in his jacket pocket. "I was sure I brought the keys with me when I left. It'll be hard to take you home without them.

"Hope you didn't drop them at the theatre," Amy said.

"They're probably just up in the apartment," Mark said. "You might as well come up for a minute while I go get them. You wouldn't want to stand down here on the street."

Amy nodded. Mark took her hand again and they walked up the sidewalk to the old three story. He led her up the steep flight of steps along the side and unlocked the entrance to his own dwelling. "Not very elegant, I'm afraid," he apologized. "And excuse the mess. I've been a bit preoccupied with work."

It was rather cramped and certainly not new. But as far as any mess went, it looked pretty orderly for a bachelor pad. It was basically one room, except for a door, which led to the bedroom and bath.

"I'll just be a minute," Mark said. "I think I left them on my dresser." He disappeared into the bedroom and was back in just a moment. "Ready to go then?"

"Hm? What's that?" Amy asked absently.

"I was just wondering if you're ready to go," Mark repeated. "Unless you'd like to stay for a bit. I could make coffee..." He trailed off.

"Coffee would be great."

"Okay. You can just throw your coat over that chair if you like."

She nodded again and did as she was told, then lowered herself onto the sofa - one of the few pieces of furniture in the compact room.

Mark busied himself with the coffee maker in the adjacent kitchenette and then turned with a smile. "That should only take a few moments." He crossed to the sofa and sat down beside her. "So... how was your day at school?"

"Fine," Amy replied. "Yours?"

"Fine."

"Good."

There were several minutes of tension filled silence. Mark felt as if his lungs were about to burst until he realized he was holding his breath.

"You're awfully tense," Amy noted.

"Sorry." His arm had crept around the back of the sofa. "Did I tell you how very beautiful you look this evening?"

"Thanks."

"Um... can I kiss you?"

"I thought you'd never ask!" Amy said with a giggle.

Their lips met, softly at first until it heightened into an explosion of light and stars. He leaned into her, pushing her backward onto the couch into a semi-reclining position.

"Wait."

The one syllable was so small, so tenuous, that he almost missed it. He pulled back slightly. "It's okay. Don't be afraid."

"But I am."

Mark pulled away fully, repositioning himself a short distance away. "I would never hurt you. You must know that."

"I know," she whispered. "It's not you I'm worried about. It's me."

"If you're worried about having sex, we can wait if you want to. For as long as you need." He stroked her cheek gently with the back of his index finger.

"Thanks. I - I appreciate that," she said, looking down. "You must think I'm awfully old fashioned. Or naïve."

"I think you are very, very beautiful." He bent his head for another kiss. Their lips met gently this time, tenderly, until the hunger took over again. This time it was Mark who pulled away.

"What's wrong?" Amy asked in a small worried voice.

Mark laughed. "I'm only human. I think I better go check on that coffee." He stole another quick kiss before standing up. He went over to the counter, found two mugs and filled them. "Take anything?"

"No thanks," Amy said, smoothing her hair with her hand.

Mark returned with the steaming mugs and set them down on the coffee table in front of the sofa. "Now if we keep these between us we should be safe," he joked.

Amy took a sip, keeping the mug close enough to her lips to hide their trembling. Mark wasn't fooled. He surveyed her closely, and then with deliberateness he set down his own mug and took hers from her hands, placing it beside his on the coffee table. "It's okay. I'm not going to pressure you to sleep with me until you're ready."

She shook her head. "That's not it."

"Okay. What is it?" He took her hands in his and placed a kiss on each one before returning his gaze to her distraught face.

"I'm... I feel so, so silly," she finally said with a shake of her head.

"Silly? Why?"

"Because you're so... so worldly and I'm such a naïve little duck."

Mark laughed outright at that. "A duck? Now that's a good one."

"I'm serious," she said. "You've been around the world. And you've probably, you know, been with lots of women. And well, I'm not like that. I believe in saving myself, I mean. But you make me want to forget about all of that."

"I told you. I can wait."

Amy shook her head. "Maybe my mother was right. It's too dangerous to be in a relationship with someone who isn't a Christian."

Mark felt his jaw tighten. "So that's what it's about, is it? Religion?"

"It's important," Amy offered quietly.

"For all intents and purposes, I believe the same way you do. I was raised in the church. You know that," Mark stated.

"That's not good enough, Mark. I want you to accept it for yourself. Accept Jesus."

"How do you know I haven't?" Mark countered.

"Have you?"

There was a telling silence.

"I see," Amy said.

"I don't object to your faith, Amy. I know how important it is to you. I don't see how it's an issue."

"Because you don't know Jesus the way I know Jesus. If you did, you'd see where I'm coming from."

"And if I agreed to your terms?"

"It has to be for real, Mark. It has to be sincere."

"Okay. So, say I was sincere. Then what?"

"I still wouldn't sleep with you."

Mark considered this a moment. "Hm. You drive a hard bargain, you know that?" His mouth twisted up at the corner in a boyish grin.

Amy turned away. "I think I want to go home now," she stated.

"Sorry," Mark apologized. "Now I've offended you. I was only teasing. I won't pressure you to have sex. When we make love, it will be strictly on your terms."

"I don't think you've been listening to a word I've said," Amy said with exasperation. "There will be no sex without marriage." She paused for a moment, her eyes welling up with tears. "Oh, I feel so absolutely stupid, now. I just want to go home. This was such a bad idea. Take me home, please." She stood abruptly, dashing at her eyes.

"Amy, wait," Mark said, standing also. "I'll take you home - in a minute. But I think we need to have a talk first. A real, honest conversation about what matters to us and our future."

"I don't see a future," she stated sullenly, but allowed Mark to push her gently back down onto the sofa.

"Because now you're the one who's not listening," Mark teased. He sobered slightly, letting the smile in his eyes be replaced with an intensity of raw emotion. "Amy Walters, you may not realize this, but you are a very powerful woman."

"Stop. If this is about sex, I don't want to hear it. You're making fun of me, now."

"It's not about sex," Mark clarified. "Well, not directly, anyway. I mean, eventually, yes, I hope it is."

"Mark!"

"What I'm trying to say is this. You have, quite honestly, swept me off my feet," Mark admitted. "And you keep saying how naïve and inexperienced you are! Well, let me tell you, I am so grateful for that. Because the thought of any other man, now or in the future, ever laying a hand on you - well, it puts me in a rage!

When I make love to you for the first time, I want to be the only man to ever do it again."

"There you go talking about sex again. I already told you - "

Mark sighed, lifting a hand to silence her. "Look, this is not going at all like I had imagined it."

"I'll bet."

He continued undaunted. "I was going to give you more time. Court you. Woo you. You're young and I didn't want you to feel rushed into anything. It's important that you know your own feelings; that you don't feel pressured. That you're sure. As sure as I am already."

"What are you saying?" Amy asked, frowning.

"I would think it's fairly obvious." Mark laughed.

Amy blinked back tears. "Don't you dare make fun of me."

"I'm not, honest," Mark said, stroking her cheek again. He kissed her gently on the trail made by his finger.

"Mark, don't," Amy pleaded. "I can't think straight."

"Good. Exactly how I want you when I ask you. Now, I do have to admit, I have been around a time or two. And yes, I have slept with other women - a fact I have never regretted up until this moment. But now I wish I could give you the same gift that I hope you'll give me. You have captivated me, Amy. And if waiting for marriage is the only way I can have you all to myself, then I'm asking you. Will you marry me?"

"Mark, you don't know what you're saying."

"Stop telling me what I know and don't know!" Mark exclaimed. "Actually, I am well aware of every word that just came out of my mouth. My Dad said it best. We Graham men are kind of slow, but when we find what we're looking for we fall hard."

"You talked to your Dad about us?" Amy asked, her eyes widening.

"That a problem? By the sounds of things you've been talking to your Mom..."

"But that's different!"

"Why?"

"Well, it just is! Besides, we haven't addressed the issue of your spiritual beliefs."

"I'll believe whatever you want me to," Mark said.

"Mark -"

Mark pulled her to her feet and cupped her head between his hands. "I mean it, Amy Walters. I love you. I've fallen hard. Whatever it takes, I'll do it." He sealed the declaration with a kiss. "You don't have to say yes right away," Mark said when they parted. "In fact, maybe you need time to think on it; take it all in." She opened her mouth to respond, but he quickly covered it with a finger before she could utter anything. "Actually, I don't even want you to say anything right now. Just think on it and in the meantime, know that my intentions are honourable. Take as much time as you need. I'll wait. And now," he said, extracting himself gently from her embrace. "I better take you home before you make a liar out of me."

CHAPTER 22

Mark glanced up from his desk as Harmony walked in after only a pre-emptory rap on the door. She hadn't waited for a response, just entered. He repositioned his cellphone to the other ear and waved her in. "Yeah, I know that, but I thought I told you to be more careful about who you talk to about our relationship." He was talking to Anthony, again.

He paused, looking over at his sister, who was now loitering near his desk. He stood up, speaking more quietly. "We need to be discreet. Absolutely so." He smiled tentatively at Harmony and motioned to her that he was going to slip out into the hall.

A few minutes later, he'd managed to assuage Anthony's fears and returned to the office. Harmony was sitting behind his desk, arms folded.

"Making yourself comfortable, I see." His smile faded when he noticed the distinct frown of disapproval on his sister's face.

"What's that?" She pointed at the computer screen.

"What?" He rounded the desk and stood behind his chair. An open email was on the computer desktop. An email from Laura. "You've got no business reading my personal correspondence."

Harmony stood up and brushed past him. "By the sounds of things, you've got a woman in every port."

"That's not true. And besides that, my personal life is none of your business." He plunked into the office chair and minimized the email.

"Is that who you were talking to on the phone just now?"

"No - and again - none of your business."

"It is my business when my own brother is taking advantage of my best friend!" Harmony stood on the other side of the desk, arms crossed for a fight.

Mark frowned. "Now what are you talking about?"

"Amy really likes you. I know I encouraged her, but now I'm not so sure. For a man who just declared his undying love, you've been awfully stand-offish this last week."

Mark's brows rose in surprise at Harmony's words. "She told you that?"

"We're best friends. Duh."

He raked a hand through his hair. "Firstly, my love life is none of your business. Second, I've been busy this week. If you didn't know, I just got back from a major dig and I have a dissertation to prepare."

"Fine, Mr. Doctor Big Wig. You're so busy you can't even take an hour off for lunch with your own sister or your girlfriend."

"Lunch?" Mark frowned.

"I suppose you've got an excuse for that, too. That's why I'm here. You were supposed to meet us for lunch and you didn't show."

Mark closed his eyes, a sinking feeling in his stomach. "I totally forgot. Tell Amy I'm so sorry. It's just -"

"You tell her. Right now she's probably wondering what she did." Harmony turned to leave but then stopped and faced him again. "Who's Laura?"

Mark's eyes narrowed. "A former colleague. Again - none of your business."

"Why? Because you're off on a rendezvous with a former girl-friend while you leave my best friend waiting by the phone in your absence?"

"That is absolutely juvenile. You've been watching too many movies."

"Well? What am I supposed to think? What am I supposed to tell Amy?"

"Nothing," Mark clipped. "Because you're going to keep your nose out of it. There is absolutely nothing to tell." Harmony still stood with her arms crossed. He sighed and gestured for her to sit. "Laura Sawchuk was part of my team and, yes, we were an item for a time, but that is long over and done with. Whatever else you think you heard - or read into that email - isn't true. Please, just don't go spoiling things with Amy. Okay?" When she didn't respond, he sighed again. "Now, if you wouldn't mind, I really do need to get back to work."

Without a word, Harmony rose from her seat and strode from the office.

Mark opened the email again and read.

"Looking forward to your visit. Very glad you reconsidered. Do I flatter myself that you might miss me after all? No hard feelings on my part. John and Anthony say hi. We'll have a celebration party, just like old times. Love, Laura"

No wonder Harmony had misinterpreted things, especially in light of the conversation she overheard. The fact that he couldn't really explain any of it to either of them made it even harder to swallow. He would just have to trust that things would work themselves out in the end.

Mark leaned back in his chair and stretched his arms backward to cradle his head. He surveyed the computer screen with satisfaction. He was ready. Along with the written dissertation, which was persuasive and well researched, he had a power point presentation that contained dynamic graphics and photographs.

But this was about far more than just empirical evidence. The real kicker was still waiting in his father's garage - the artefacts and samples that he had smuggled off site. Nobody could dispute their existence; nobody could dispute the painstaking care he had taken in testing and identifying each one. The only problem would be the legal ramifications once their existence, and the method in which they were secured, became public knowledge. He would just have to cross that bridge when he came to it. Both he and Anthony were working on an angle, but there were no guarantees.

The tricky part was going to be crossing the US border with the cargo. He still had copies of the original documentation back when the project had started. And, under the auspices of the university, he had secured immunity to transport certain otherwise contraband items for scholarly purposes.

The fact that the said items were not exactly as listed was another matter. He would just have to convince the guards at the border that his cargo could not be opened or tampered with in any way.

Of course, advance permission had already been secured, which was a bit of a worry. The fewer people that knew about his plans the better. Even though it had been some time since Sangeruka's threats, as well as the fact that he no longer seemed to have the influence that he once did, Mark couldn't help but feel a few pangs of anxiety over the safety of his loved ones. It was one of the reasons that he had been so tight lipped about his actual itinerary, even to his father. The less anyone knew, the better off they would be.

Mark glanced down at his watch. It was late - probably too late to call Amy, now. But he felt euphoric, somehow. He needed to share his excitement with someone. All the preliminary work was finished. All that remained was the anticipation of telling the world - and the possible danger of traveling to the appointed destination.

"Hi, Amy," Mark said into his cell. "Did I wake you?" He kept his voice low, as if that would help somehow.

"No, it's okay. I couldn't sleep anyway," she replied.

"I finished up here," he offered, as if that explained everything.

"Oh. That's good news."

"I was wondering, is it too late to meet me somewhere? For a coffee or something? I know it's kind of late, but I was thinking, I haven't had much time for you these past few days, and since I'll be leaving soon..." He trailed off.

"Um, I guess so. I'm not sure what buses are running this time of night."

"Of course," Mark chided himself. "How stupid of me. I'll come by and pick you up."

Amy came out the front door of the Walter residence as soon as Mark drove up. All the lights were off and it struck him how ridiculous it was for a man his age to be sneaking around his girl-friend's house after hours. Like he was doing something illegal or something. Maybe he should suggest that Amy move into her own place for awhile, like Harmony. Or even move in with Harmony.

Wait. Strike that thought. The last thing he wanted was his little sister nosing about his affairs even more than she did now.

"Hi, you," Mark greeted as Amy slid into the passenger seat. A rush of warmth washed over him and he felt definite regret that he had not been able to spend much time with her over the past several days. "You look nice," he said simply and leaned over to kiss her.

His lips barely touched hers before she was pulling away, busying herself with buckling the seatbelt. He frowned slightly, but brushed it off. "Where to?"

She shrugged. "Where ever."

"Somewhere close, I suppose," he said, and pulled away from the curb.

"Or we could just go down by the Forks," she suggested. The Forks, as it was called, was a large park like area in the middle of the city where the Assiniboine and Red Rivers met.

"Forks it is." He reached over and took her small, soft hand into his larger one. "I missed you."

"Me, too."

They were content to ride that way for some time, satisfied in the physical contact without the necessity of words.

Finally Amy spoke up. "Mark?"

"Hm?"

"Why can't you tell me more about what you're doing?"

He glanced over at her and smiled. "If I told you, it would be telling. Which I can't." He noted the slight furrowing of her brow. "Just trust me, okay? I'll tell you all about it someday. I promise." He gave her hand a squeeze.

There was silence again for a time before Amy piped up again. "Mark? Tell me about Laura. Did you love her?"

He scowled. "You've been talking to my sister, again, haven't you?" He released her hand as he turned into the parking lot near the Forks.

"Sorry. I shouldn't have brought it up," Amy apologized timidly.

Mark put the SUV into park with a jerk. "It's okay. I should know better than to trust my sister to get things right." He turned to look squarely at Amy. "Whatever I had with Laura is over and done. Understand? It's finished. Over. Kaput. I thought I made my feelings clear to you the other night."

"Well, yes, but..."

"And about you sharing our personal lives with everyone," he continued. "I'm a pretty private person, and I don't appreciate being the subject of gossip."

"I didn't say anything to anyone," Amy replied, tears brimming. "Well, except Harmony, and then I didn't mean to say anything."

"Ah, but you did," he stated.

"You know how hard it is to keep anything from her," Amy defended.

"I felt like my personal life was being written up in some teen magazine. I'm not interested in that, so you and my sister can stop any time." The moment the words came out of his mouth he realized exactly how hurtful they sounded.

Amy blinked. Her nostrils flared with the effort of keeping the tears at bay.

"Amy, I'm sorry. That was utterly uncalled for," he apologized.

"I'll try to act more grown up from now on," she managed to choke out, her tone sarcastic.

"Oh man," he breathed, closing his eyes and pinching the bridge of his nose between his thumb and forefinger. "I didn't mean that the way it sounded."

"No?"

"No. I just don't want people interfering. I didn't mean anything else by it."

"I suppose you think I'm too immature to be trusted with your secret mission, whatever it is."

"Amy," he pleaded. "That's just -" he was about to say childish, but stopped himself in time. "Silly," he finished.

"Silly," she repeated. "Because I'm just a silly little girl."

Mark sighed. "Okay. What do you want from me? I said I was sorry and I meant it. And I'm sorry that I can't tell you where I'm going or what I'm doing, either. But it's for your own safety and the safety of other people. I know that sounds pretty lame right about now, but it's the best I can do."

"Safety?" Genuine concern replaced any former churlishness. "Why? Are you in some kind of trouble?"

"Amy…" He surveyed her features and reached to run the back of his finger down her cheek. "Even when you're mad you're beautiful, you know that?" he said softly. She didn't reply, but he could see that her features were softening. "Forgive me?"

She nodded mutely.

"Good. And I'll take all the questions as a sign that you care, that's all."

Somehow they managed to find themselves in each other's arms, their kisses urgent with pent up emotion and the knowledge that they would be apart for some time in the near future.

"I'm really going to miss you," Mark said when he pulled away. "I wish we'd been able to spend more time together."

"Mark?" Amy whispered against his mouth.

"Hm?"

"Did you mean it? The other night, I mean."

"Of course. Every word." He kissed her ear and started making a trail down her neck.

"Then I was thinking. Maybe we should go over to your place."

Mark stopped what he was doing and pulled back, just far enough to see her face fully. "Why? What are you saying?"

"Just that, maybe I don't want to wait after all," she replied, her voice sounding small and not quite convinced. She looked down, avoiding his gaze, as heat infused her cheeks.

Mark was silent for a moment before adjusting himself further away from the temptation of her body. Instead, he took her hand safely in his own. "I don't think that's a very good idea."

"Why?" she asked, anxiety catching in her voice.

"Not because I don't want to, believe me. But because I know how important it is for you to save yourself for marriage."

"But I thought... the other night you said you wanted to marry me," Amy said.

"Right. But you haven't answered yet. And I don't want you to, just yet, either."

"But I've already made up my mind," Amy replied quickly. "The answer is 'Yes'. Yes, I want to marry you."

"That is like music to my ears." Mark smiled. "But I'm leaving for awhile. You might feel differently once I get back. Things have been pretty intense between us, not to mention the fact that everything has happened so fast. A little time away from me will help you put things in perspective."

"Or help you put things in perspective," Amy countered. "Maybe you're just hoping that I'll fall out of love with you so that you don't have to get stuck with me."

Mark laughed. "Now that is utterly ridiculous. If anyone is getting stuck with anyone, it's you. I'm practically a senior citizen."

"Hardly." She reached for his collar and pulled him closer for another heated kiss.

"I must admit, you're getting very good at that," Mark mused.

"I'm a fast learner," Amy quipped.

"So I see."

"We could make love right now. In the car," Amy suggested between kisses.

"Not a chance. That would be downright degrading. You're not making this very easy, you know," he breathed.

"I want to make sure you come back," Amy said.

Mark sat back in his seat. "Is that what this is about? You think if you sleep with me I'll be sure to come back to you? Amy, I told you already that I love you. I don't know what kind of crazy notions you've got running around in your head, but let me assure you that it takes more than sex to secure a man's heart. I should know."

The words stung and Mark could see the change in her countenance once again. He let out a gust of frustrated breath. "Man, I just keep putting my foot in it, don't I? What I mean is, you've already got my heart. Don't you know that already? So much so, that I'm willing to wait for you. And if I spoiled that now, even for a wonderful night with you before I leave - something I want more than you can imagine - well, I'd be mad at myself for the rest of my life. You're worth it, Amy. Don't you see? I want to do this thing right, for a change. I want it to be different for us, with no regrets."

"I guess I really am pretty naïve," Amy whispered. "Oh, I'm so ashamed!" She turned away, a tiny sob escaping her lips.

"Come here," Mark soothed, taking her into his arms. He smoothed her hair. "Don't worry about anything, okay? I meant what I said. I'm coming back. I promise."

"And I meant what I said," she murmured into his shirt. "The answer is yes."

He gently bent his head and sealed the declaration with another kiss. "I believe you. Now I better get you home." He shifted in his seat and started the car. "So, this might be it for awhile until I get back," Mark said, steering out onto the street.

"What do you mean?" Amy asked. "I thought you were leaving the day after tomorrow."

"I was. But since I finished up early, I figure there's no point hanging around."

"Oh," Amy responded flatly. "I guess there's nothing here to keep you an extra day."

"That's not what I meant. Of course I'd like to stay and spend an entire day with you. But, on the other hand, too much time with you and we might end up doing something we regret." He glanced over at her and gave her a gentle smile. "Besides, the sooner I get going, the sooner I get back, right?"

CHAPTER 23

Mark arrived very early at his parent's home the next morning. He'd only gotten a couple of hours of sleep, anticipation making it almost impossible to relax. He had already secured the permits needed. All that was left was to load up and leave.

Russ greeted his son at the door, dressed casually in jeans and a sweatshirt, his hair still looking tousled from sleep. "Come in," Russ waved with his free hand. In the other he held a steaming mug. "Coffee?"

"No. I already stopped at Tim's," Mark replied. "Deanie up?"

"Are you kidding?" Russ laughed. "This is even early for me." He downed the rest of his coffee, setting the cup down on a side table by the door before stretching and yawning. "Well, let's get at it, then."

They headed out to the garage. "Is there room for me to back in?" Mark asked.

"If I take my car out, I suppose," Russ said.

"Okay. I think that's the best idea."

Russ surveyed his son speculatively, but said nothing. In a few moments they had made the switch and Mark had opened the back door of the SUV.

"I sure hope you know what you're doing," Russ said.

"You know me. Always got a plan, and if not, I fake it anyway."

"Will you contact us?" Russ asked. "Once you get wherever you're going so we know you're safe?"

"Probably not," Mark replied. "Not right away, anyway."

"I see." Russ nodded stoically.

"It's better this way," Mark explained.

Father and son loaded the vehicle in relative silence. Three sealed crates were safely stowed in the back and covered with a dark blanket.

"Well, that's it, then," Mark said as he closed the back hatch with a firm click.

"Take care, Son," Russ offered, holding his hand out.

Mark shook his father's hand firmly. "I will."

"We'll be praying," Russ added.

"Thanks, I appreciate that." He actually meant it. "Well, I guess I better get going, then. Say bye to Deanie and Harmony for me."

"I will."

"Oh. And tell Harmony, no hard feelings."

Russ raised his eyebrows.

Mark laughed. "It's complicated. She'll understand."

Next stop, the Walters' residence. Russ pulled up in front of the house. He'd called Amy on the way over, waking her. He'd offered to just say good-by over the phone, but she insisted that he stop by instead. He just hoped her parents were still asleep.

He approached the front door and was about to knock when the door swung open. Amy beckoned him inside and shut the door quietly behind him. She was wearing a terry robe and her feet were bare.

"Hi," he greeted awkwardly.

"More like bye," Amy said, her voice already becoming wobbly. Tears glistened in her eyes.

He pulled her into his arms and just hugged her, letting her bury her face in his jacket.

"I'm coming back. I promise." He felt his own throat constricting.

She pulled back slightly. "When?"

"I don't know for sure." He searched her face - that beautiful face that had captured his heart. Why hadn't he made more time for her over the past weeks? He had been so single minded in his need to finish his dissertation that he'd neglected the thing that had become most important - even more than the most intriguing archaeological find of the century. "Amy, I love you," he whispered urgently. "You know that, don't you?"

She nodded and their lips sought each other in a feverish embrace. He could feel her body, soft and pliable against his own. At that moment he wished he had taken her up on her offer last night. He needed her now. He needed to show her, in a physical way, just how much he loved her.

They heard the noise simultaneously, a quiet tinkling of dishes, and parted reluctantly. Someone was in the kitchen making coffee. Mark looked down at Amy and mouthed the words, "I love you."

She took a shuddering breath and stepped back. "Come on," she said quietly, taking his hand. "We might as well go in, since they know you're here anyway.

Both Amy's parents were in the kitchen, still wearing robes. Holly was busying herself near the coffee maker while Brent sat at the island counter, reading. They both looked up when the younger couple entered.

"Good morning," Holly greeted. "Coffee'll be ready in a minute."

"Morning Angel," Brent said to his daughter, rising to give her a peck on the cheek. He turned to Mark. "Mark. Nice to see you again."

The atmosphere was artificially nonchalant, like they greeted their daughter's boyfriend every morning while still wearing their bathrobes. It was decidedly awkward.

"Um, Mark's on his way out of town," Amy offered as explanation. "On archaeology business."

"Oh? This about that big find you made last spring in Africa?" Brent asked.

"Partially," Mark responded.

"Very interesting, from what I recall," Brent offered. "What was it all about again? Dinosaur and human remains found together?"

"I'm not really at liberty to talk about it just yet," Mark hedged.

"Oh. I see. Well, good luck with it, anyway." Brent nodded congenially.

"Take anything in your coffee?" Holly asked as she busied herself pouring four mugs with the freshly made brew.

Mark shook his head. "Um, no thanks." He took the coffee mug from Holly and raised it to his lips. There were a few minutes of silence as the group sipped their steaming drinks.

"So, I take it you and my daughter have taken up with each other." Brent set his mug down on the counter.

"Daddy!" Amy rolled her eyes.

Mark cleared his throat. "Yes. Yes, that's true." He paused, considering his next words. "I was planning to have a talk with you in the near future, but I was going to wait until I got back from my trip."

"Oh?" Brent took another sip and surveyed Mark over the rim of his mug.

"Um, yes. Just so you know my intentions are... honourable."

"I see. And what might that mean, exactly?"

"Daddy! This is embarrassing."

Amy's father obviously wasn't going to make this easy on him, Mark mused. "Just that, even though I'm a lot older, I'm not going to take advantage of her, so to speak."

Brent nodded. "Good, good."

"More coffee?" Holly held the pot aloft.

"I'm fine." Mark placed his hand over the top of his cup. "Actually, I really need to get going now. Thanks." He rose from the stool he had occupied.

They said their good-byes in the kitchen and Amy walked Mark to the front door.

"I'm really sorry about that," she whispered. "I'm so embarrassed."

"It's okay. I'll probably be the same way if I have a daughter." He stopped and looked intently at Amy. "Especially if she looks anything like you." He bent for a kiss. It was hard to keep the intensity at bay, even knowing that her parents were seated in the next room. He extracted his lips. "I've got to go."

"Will you call me?"

"I can't say when, but I'll try. Definitely." He gave her another quick kiss and strode down the sidewalk.

CHAPTER 24

Mark glanced in the rear view mirror and noted the dark green sedan. It had passed him, he was sure, about an hour ago. Probably stopped for gas or something, he mused. He shifted in his seat, trying to stretch as much as possible while still driving. Dusk was descending. He'd been driving pretty much nonstop for the past ten hours and his body was starting to stiffen up.

Thankfully, he had made it through customs earlier that morning with very little inconvenience. Seems his documentation was enough to wave him on through, a blessing for which he was very thankful. He may even have prayed, come to think of it, in a manner of speaking. These days, crossing the border had become a regular comedy of errors. The fact that things had gone so smoothly was truly a miracle.

The landscape across the line was very similar to that of his native Manitoba; flat and dry expanses of farm land, sectioned off with fencing and dotted with small towns and farmyards. He had traveled south on Interstate 29 through the Dakotas and would have to veer west soon, into Nebraska, on a secondary highway that would connect him with the Interstate heading south through Kansas and on into Texas. Of course, that would have to be another day's adventure. He'd be lucky to make it to Kansas tonight.

He was tired already, but the need to make as much progress as possible kept him going. That, and way too much coffee. By tomorrow night, he'd be in Texas.

The green sedan was accelerating again, pulling past him on the left. Apparently, the driver didn't care much about rising gas prices. I guess we've all got places to be, Mark mused.

He had contacted Anthony once during the trip. Everything was, "A-okay and ready to go," Anthony had said. All clear with no suspicion on the part of Laura or anyone else connected. Anthony was scheduled to meet him in Texas the day after tomorrow.

That his presentation was so under publicized was somewhat irksome, to say the least. A find of this nature deserved all the hype available. But, Mark realized, that would have to come later. For now, he must be satisfied that the truth was going to be told.

Several hours later he pulled into an overnight rest area. Unlike the highways back home, the US seemed to have outfitted their rest stops quite thoroughly - bathrooms, plenty of parking, some even had small coffee bars. He'd considered getting more coffee and just carrying on, but decided against it. He had already developed a headache and a slight feeling of nausea from too much caffeine. He'd be better off taking a break and starting fresh tomorrow.

Of course, getting a room for the night was absolutely out of the question. He couldn't leave his precious cargo alone in the car, unattended. After using the restroom, he hunkered down as best he could in the back seat of the SUV and tried for some shut-eye. Fortunately, despite the inordinate amount of coffee and inadequate accommodation, exhaustion finally took over and he did, indeed, sleep.

Not enough sleep, Mark groaned as he struggled to sit up several hours later. But the crick in his neck would not allow further repose.

The morning was clear and he stretched expansively once out of the confines of the vehicle. He would just use the facilities and be on his way to the next town for breakfast.

He stopped in his tracks, frozen for a millisecond with sudden alarm. The green sedan. It was parked just three vehicles over from his. He took a deep breath. Don't jump to any conclusions, he chided himself. Lots of people traveled these highways. There was bound to be someone - probably several people - going in the same direction, at the same general pace. It was just coincidence.

He took a deep breath. Despite his own assurances, he turned back to his own SUV. He could wait to relieve himself. For now, he was hitting the road.

Another hour down the road and Mark felt himself relaxing a bit. The first thing he would do once the cargo was safely off loaded was take a shower. And shave. A full day and a night in his vehicle and he was beginning to feel like he was out in the field again. Out there, he got used to roughing it and hardly noticed the aura of body odour that must be surrounding him by now.

Another hour and he was looking forward to connecting with the next southbound interstate. He glanced in his rear view mirror and nearly swerved. The same green sedan was tailing him. This had to be more than mere coincidence. Mark accelerated slightly and watched with dismay as the green car did the same. That was a definite signal. Apparently, his uninvited traveling companion was no longer trying to be subtle. Okay. What now? The possibility of losing him by taking some other route held little appeal. The last thing he wanted was to end up lost. And judging from yesterday's track record, the driver of that car seemed to know exactly which direction he was headed.

The tension grew more palpable with each passing mile. Mark glanced down at his gas gauge. At some point he was going to have to face the music. He couldn't travel on fumes. According to the overhead signs, he was approaching the next town. Now might be his last chance.

Mark swerved off the exit ramp without slowing down or signalling. He kept both hands on the wheel and held his breath as he manoeuvred the SUV around the cloverleaf and onto a city street. He gunned it through the intersection just as the traffic light turned red and noted with satisfaction that the green sedan was several cars behind, stopped at the light.

Now to find some side streets and try to get lost. He needed gas, but decided it would be better to wait for awhile in some back alley somewhere. He turned into one such likely hiding spot and parked beside a delivery truck. The truck shielded him from one side, but still allowed him to view the intersecting street.

Mark noticed the pounding in his head - his own heartbeat had accelerated and adrenaline was coursing through his body. If that green car had any connection to Sangeruka, he needed to warn Anthony. And he needed to check on his family back home.

Mark waited for several more minutes, listening to the shallowness of his own breathing. Okay. That was probably long enough. He needed to find a gas station and get the heck out of here. He was about to put the SUV in gear when he spotted it again - the green car passing slowly by on the street. He swore under his breath.

Mark took his cellphone out of his jacket pocket and punched in Anthony's number. They had been trying not to contact one another too often via that method for fear that someone would be able to track their communication. But this was an emergency.

Pick up, pick up! Nothing. He wasn't about to leave a message. Well, there was nothing else to do now but take his chances. Mark let up on the break and allowed the the SUV to crawl forward onto the street. Hopefully there would be a gas station nearby and he could be on his way.

He spotted one two blocks down and drove cautiously in that direction, glancing this way and that for any sign of his 'friend'.

Once at the gas station, he went quickly inside to prepay for the gas and then began filling his tank. He watched the meter on the pump as the numbers clicked by interminably slowly. He was just replacing the nozzle when he saw the car again.

He tried to jump into his seat as quickly as possible, but the car was already pulling into the station at break neck speed, blocking his exit. Horns honked as several other motorists made their displeasure known. Well, maybe this was as good a place as any for a confrontation. Sangeruka's thugs wouldn't try anything too drastic right here in broad daylight, would they?

He waited as the driver of the car extracted himself from the driver's seat. There was only one person in the car. That was good. Maybe he could actually take him if it came to hand to hand combat.

The man was approaching Mark's vehicle now. Wait a minute. He looked vaguely familiar. Mark held his breath as his brain struggled to compute.

"Rocco?" Mark asked uncertainly, rolling his window down slightly.

"Geez, Boss. You're not the easiest guy to flag down."

"But... how? Why - what are you doing here?" Mark sputtered. "I thought you were dead!"

"I think we need to find a place where we can talk," Rocco suggested. "That lady don't look too happy about our reunion."

Mark took note of the frustrated face of the woman in the next car. "Right. You lead the way."

"Sure you're not going to take off on me?" Rocco asked.

Mark laughed. "Get going."

Rocco backed his vehicle out onto the street and Mark followed behind. They drove another few blocks to a small diner. Inside, a waitress seated them at a booth where Mark could keep an eye on his vehicle from the window.

"I'm telling you, you really led me on a chase," Rocco said, shaking his head.

"Me? You had me scared to death. I thought Sangeruka had 'sicked' his thugs on me."

"I was going to wake you up last night and talk to you, back at the rest stop. But then I thought I'd take pity on you and let you sleep a bit, first. When I came out of the can this morning, you were already gone."

"So? Tell me everything," Mark demanded. "Right from the moment the truck went off the road. Man, I thought you were dead. How could anyone survive a crash like that?"

"Luck?" Rocco shrugged. "Or maybe providence. I baled as soon as the truck went over the edge and somehow managed to hit some brush that cushioned my landing. The truck exploded on impact at the bottom of the ravine and I guess they figured I got toasted with it. I was pretty scratched up and sore as hell, but no broken bones. Just walked away."

"And the casket?"

"It got hung up in some brush further down, just teetering over an embankment. It took some convincing, let me tell you, to get some locals to help me retrieve it."

"You mean it survived?" Mark asked in disbelief. Renewed hope soared in his breast. "This is fantastic! This is the best news yet! With that as evidence, no one will be able to dispute our findings."

"Hold on there." Rocco held up a hand. "I said it survived, but I didn't say I have it in my possession."

"So who does?"

"Now that is where it gets complicated," Rocco replied. "See, once we got the container safely down from the mountain, there was a lot of curiosity about what it contained. I was afraid that Sangeruka's gang would come after it if they found out it survived. So I had to lie - just a little bit - in order to keep it safe."

"What did you say?"

"I said it contained my grandmother's remains," Rocco replied sheepishly. "I told them she was a missionary in Africa and it was her greatest desire to be buried among the people she loved so well."

"And they bought it?" Mark shook his head. "Surely the markings on the casket itself would bring up some suspicion."

"Only two other men saw the casket," Rocco explained. "It was still well sealed inside the shipping container. I told them she had been fascinated by the old legends and requested her casket be modelled after them. I don't think many people have actually seen artefacts from that far back, anyway. I mean, the legends were there, but as far as actual evidence goes, nobody has really seen it with their own eyes."

"And you don't think there might be some suspicion since we were working on the site that housed the actual evidence? That somebody might put two and two together?"

"I did the best I could under the circumstances," Rocco defended with a shrug.

"I'm sure by now somebody has heard about the military takeover of the site, too. I can't believe it won't go unnoticed."

"Listen, these people are very superstitious, especially when it comes to the dead," Rocco said. "Nobody will want to disturb a dead missionary. They believe strongly in ancestral spirits, and a missionary would have some special connection with God. Nobody will want to risk the Almighty's wrath by desecrating her bones."

"So it's buried somewhere?" Mark asked.

Rocco nodded. "A secret location. Only the two guys I mentioned know where."

"And they can be trusted?"

"Of course. The fact that I survived a near fatal crash, along with Granny's remains, must mean something, right? God must really want her buried there, and who's going to risk arguing with the Almighty?"

"I don't know. I just don't feel good about this," Mark said.

"I guess there's not much you can do about it, now, is there?" Rocco eyed him from over his coffee mug.

"Hm. True. But it's safe for now," Mark repeated. "You're sure of that?"

"Nothing is sure these days," Rocco stated. "By now the international conspiracy might have got a hold of the fact that I survived, along with the casket."

"International conspiracy?"

"Excuse me for being paranoid," Rocco said sarcastically, "but when you've been shot at in order to keep a world changing find from coming to light, well..."

"That could just have been Sangeruka," Mark said. Somehow he didn't believe it, though.

Obviously, neither did Rocco. "Believe me, I've seen enough in my time to know, beyond a shadow of a doubt, that this is much bigger than one wayward African official. I told you before. There's all kinds of evidence out there that has never been shared with the public at large, or has been twisted so much that anyone who tries to say otherwise sounds like a stark raving lunatic."

Mark nodded his agreement. "I know. I've been doing my homework and it's pretty alarming."

"Tell me about it." Rocco snorted. "I have the scars to prove it."

"Right. But we need real proof. Proof that would stand up to the kind of scientific scrutiny that we're sure to face."

"I'm glad you said 'we'." Rocco replied. "Because you just might be the man to shake up the old boys' club once and for all."

"I'm going to try," Mark acknowledged, "I just hope someone is listening. Now, though, if we can actually get access to the casket - get it brought somewhere secure where proper analysis can be done - well, we just might have a chance at blowing this whole thing wide open."

"You better go ahead with your plans as they are," Rocco

advised. "I wouldn't wait any longer. Doctors Sawchuk and Bergman are just chomping at the bit to release their own version of events."

"How do you know that?" Mark asked, frowning. "And how do you know about my plans?"

"I've still got contacts," Rocco said secretively. "I make it my job to know these things."

"Which is why you were able to tail me." Mark nodded absently. He wondered how many other people knew about his plans or his whereabouts.

"Don't sweat it," Rocco said. "I have good intelligence that says you're still safe."

"Now you're really starting to make me worried." Mark laughed nervously. "Good intelligence? You make it sound like you work for the FBI, or something."

Rocco leaned forward, crossing his arms on the tabletop. "I guess I can trust you with this much. There really is an international conspiracy out there - men and women who control the scientific community like so many puppets, releasing whatever information they want to release; feeding them data and facts that support their own agenda. Most scientists are like you - completely unaware that they're being manipulated - played. But there are a few of us, guys like me who've been in the field and know better, who have gotten together and are trying to combat this thing."

"How come this is the first I've heard of it?" Mark asked.

"See, it's like this. We have to be really careful what we say and who we say it to. Otherwise, we look like a bunch of crack pots."

"I've been accused of that, myself. It's still small comfort, though, you know. Knowing that someone has been tracking my movements."

"Consider it free protection," Rocco stated.

"You really think I need it?" Mark asked.

Rocco shrugged. "Who knows?"

"Well, you certainly had me thinking along those lines." Mark laughed. "Don't ever scare me like that again."

"I just hope you're ready once you actually drop the bomb."

Mark sobered instantly. "So you think there might be danger? Even after the fact?"

"I'd just watch my back."

"Makes me wonder if it's really worth it," Mark mused.

"Of course it is," Rocco stated firmly. "That's the whole point. If someone is willing to go to those lengths - even try to kill someone - well, you know it must be worth it."

"Right. I was just joking, anyway. I plan on going ahead. You know that. I've come too far to back down, now."

"Just keep that in mind. We're counting on you."

"So, what's this about Laura and John?" Mark asked. "You said you've got some info on their operation, too?"

"Yeah. Now those two are puppets if ever there were any. Totally bought into the conspiracy's game, if you know what I mean."

"Well, I suppose that's some comfort," Mark mused. "At least they're not the real bad guys."

"Don't fool yourself," Rocco warned. "Neither one of them are exactly innocent. Did you know that John was working to undermine you with the brass right from the beginning?"

"I can't believe that," Mark denied with a dismissive laugh. "No?"

"We've been friends for years," Mark stated firmly.

"Suit yourself." Rocco shrugged. "And your girlfriend. She was the one sabotaging the site all along."

"Laura? You have proof?"

Rocco gave him a withering look. "Remember the cave in? The data collection problems? Delays in sending and receiving important documentation. Even all the mix-ups with the government officials. All her."

"Says?" Mark probed. "Oh, right. Your intelligence network.

Look, I know there were problems, but I can't believe it was all on purpose."

"That's your problem. Always too trusting. I suppose it's hard not to when you were into her pants."

"Hey! That was crude! I always tried to remain professional, you know that. Besides, I had my doubts a time or two, I must admit. But I just can't believe it was so wide spread and so... insidious. That's all."

"Remember that missing wing bone?" Rocco asked. Mark nodded. "Just ask her about that yourself, sometime. See what she says."

"I'm not planning on that opportunity," Mark responded dryly.

"Just don't say I didn't warn you. Sometimes these skirts can really pull the wool over our eyes."

"Talking from experience, again," Mark asked, trying to lighten the almost combative attitude that Rocco had adopted.

"You know it." Rocco winked.

Mark looked at his watch. "Anyway, I really think we need to carry on. There's still a long way to go tonight."

"Now that I finally caught up to you, I'm veering off in another direction for a day," Rocco said. "Say hi to Anthony when you see him."

"You know about Anthony, too?" Mark asked. Of course he knew about Anthony. The guy seemed to know about everything.

Rocco just nodded. He stood up and threw sufficient money on the table to cover both their drinks and the tip. "Drive safe. And don't make any more stops off the main highway."

"Why not?"

"You just need to get your butt safely to Texas in one piece," Rocco said and grinned.

Mark nodded. That was one piece of advice he was definitely going to listen to.

CHAPTER 25

Mark arrived at the university campus in Texas well past two am. He'd already stopped for a stretch not far back, so his plan was to stay put in his vehicle until morning and try to get some shut-eye. It wasn't going to be easy. His mind was racing - and not just on account of tomorrow's prospects. How could he have misread Laura and John so badly? The sense of betrayal cut deep. Very deep.

Somehow, he dozed off. He woke with a start to somebody rapping on his window. Light was streaming in and he could feel the warmth of the Texas sun. He squinted, shielding his eyes for a moment as they adjusted themselves to the onslaught.

"Hey! Wake up in there!" It was Anthony. "What you gonna do? Sleep the day away?"

Mark shifted himself into a full sitting position and rolled down the window. "I see you made it, too," he said amid a huge yawn.

"I rolled in last night about seven o'clock," Anthony nodded. "What time did you get here?"

"About two," Mark replied.

"So you gonna sit in your car all day, or what?" Anthony asked with a grin. "Come on inside. You look like you could use a coffee."

Mark glanced down at his watch. Eight am local time. He really had slept. "I'm not going anywhere until this thing is safely unloaded," he stated.

"Sure. Let's go meet the team, and then they can help us unload," Anthony suggested.

"No, I mean, I'm not leaving the vehicle unattended," Mark clarified.

Anthony stopped for a moment, surveying his friend. "Okay. How about if I go find somebody to show us where to unload and then we can get right on that."

"That would be good."

"You seem a bit... tense," Anthony observed. "Paranoid even."

"You wouldn't believe who I met up with on the way," Mark replied.

"Who?" Anthony asked, eyebrows raised.

"Rocco." By the look on Anthony's face, he was as shocked by the news that Rocco was still alive as Mark had been. "So I take it he hasn't contacted you?"

Anthony shook his head. "You sure?" he asked doubtfully. "I mean, by all accounts, there's no way he could have survived."

"Believe me," Mark stated. "I'll tell you all about it later. For now we really need to get these specimens safely unloaded."

They did just that. Mark was directed to an underground parking area where brief introductions took place. Doctor Tim Hazzard and his assistant George Krasinsky were very excited about the prospects of what this find could do for the credibility of their institution. Mark felt a small pang of anxiety at that. Why did everything have to boil down to some kind of political gain?

They unloaded the precious cargo and took it up to the lab.

"We are very honoured to have you present your findings at our institution," Dr. Hazzard said. He was a man who looked to be in his early fifties, with jet-black hair that was swept back in a definite retro style. He also looked to be in good physical condition.

His colleague, Dr. Krasinsky, was younger, but with much less hair, and he sported large glasses that definitely gave him a stereotypic air. "This could be the biggest break through for creation theory yet. It's wonderful to have someone with your credentials on our side."

"Excuse me?" Mark asked, blinking back to reality. He had been staring at Dr. Hazzard's mop of hair. "Creation theory?"

"Of course," Dr. Hazzard responded. "We are a Christian institution. We teach some very innovative interpretations of the creation model. We've got a very well trained staff with wonderful credentials." He stopped, looking puzzled. "Is there a problem?"

"I... um, no." Mark shook his head.

"I told you it was a Christian Institution," Anthony reminded quietly. "He's probably just a little foggy after such a long drive," he offered to the two other men.

"I hope there isn't a problem," Dr. Hazzard went on. "We pride ourselves on doing everything above board and we certainly wouldn't want you to feel like you've been duped, somehow."

"I was just hoping to present the facts in a nonpartisan way," Mark explained.

Dr. Hazzard nodded his head in understanding. "It's exactly what we do here. Most theory that backs a different timeline for the universe or a different sequence of events than what we've all been told, bases its model on religious creationism. Even though we believe that here, we do try to present all our scientific arguments in just that way - scientifically. We don't want to scare people off any more than you do. Of course, we do have specific classes that teach our findings in conjunction with our religious beliefs. But you needn't worry about that. You can be as nonpartisan as you want." He stopped for a moment and surveyed Mark closely, the friendly smile never leaving his face. "I was simply under the impression that you were a believer also. I didn't mean any offence."

"None taken," Mark replied.

"Well, let's get at it, shall we?" Dr. Hazzard suggested brightly. "How about a tour, Dr. Graham? Dr. Krasinsky would be happy to oblige, I'm sure."

"That would be fine," Mark nodded. He stopped and added hesitantly. "I was wondering if I might go somewhere to clean up first, though? I've just spent two full days and nights in my car and..."

"Of course," Dr. Hazzard said. "How negligent of me. We have a room booked for you. Why don't you go and clean up, have some breakfast or whatever and we can get started after lunch. Does that sound okay?"

"I'll probably be ready long before that," Mark replied. "I'm kind of anxious to get started, myself."

"Excellent," Dr. Hazzard stated. "Don't rush yourself. Just take whatever time you need."

Mark arrived back at the college two hours later. He and Anthony had met for some breakfast in the hotel restaurant after he's showered and changed. During that time he'd been able to fill Anthony in on his little encounter with Rocco.

"I still can't believe it," Anthony was saying as they emerged from the elevator next to the lab. "Not only that Rocco is alive, but all that other stuff about a conspiracy. I mean, sure, there are lots of people out there with an agenda, but do you really think it's that well backed, or that deeply entrenched?"

Mark shrugged. "I don't know what to think anymore. Maybe it would be interesting to get Dr. Hazzard's take on it."

"You think that's safe?" Anthony asked with a grin. "He might be in on it."

Dr. George Krasinsky was waiting for them in the lab. "Dr. Hazzard had a few other things to attend to this morning. I can take you on that tour now, if you like."

Mark hesitated, anxious to get started putting his presentation together.

"Come on. It'll be fun. And informative," Anthony said brightly, looking in George's direction. "Right?"

George nodded. "Uh... right."

As it turned out it was both. Mark was glad he'd agreed. Despite George's rather bland delivery, he was fascinated by what Dr. Hazzard had earlier referred to as 'very innovative interpretations of the creation model'. There was a whole gallery set up for that purpose. Some of the theories, backed up with corresponding evidence, he had already come across in his own research on the subject. But some others were new.

He stopped in front of one particular display. "Explain what's going on here," he said to George, pointing. Inside the glass cabinet was a large replica of the earth with several cut away sections. The earth's atmosphere was shown as a clear canopy which encased the globe. The label said "Creation in Symphony".

"Ah." George nodded. "The work of a fellow Texan. Very convincing research into pre-flood atmospheric conditions."

"Another young earth model?" Mark asked.

"Yes, as most creationist models are," George agreed. "This one speculates that the earth was encased in crystalline hydrogen."

"Wait a minute," Mark interrupted. "Crystalline hydrogen? How is that possible?"

"Quite simple, actually," George replied. "Several Soviet scientists have been able to confirm the possibilities through quantum algebra. The superconductivity of such a substance would also relate to its suspension." He gestured to the model as he continued to explain. "The rakea effect would have intensified colours as well as magnified objects beyond. It would mean that everything outside the atmosphere - stars and so forth - would have been much bigger and brighter to the naked eye. Also, the fibre optic transfer of light and energy would conduct sound waves much like a short wave radio signal. So, solar sounds would have been broadcast during the morning hours - thus the name 'Creation in Symphony'. It's quite fascinating, since the Bible does record such examples in Genesis. The ancients seemed to have been very well versed in astronomy for not having the benefit of modern technological instruments."

"Interesting," Anthony mused.

"It also accounts for the greenhouse conditions that would have been necessary to grow the large specimens that are evident in the fossil record, as well as explain the presence of tropical plants near the poles, etc."

"I suppose so," Mark said. "I have done a bit of reading on that myself. It's hard to ignore some of the discrepancies in present evolutionary theory."

"That it is," George agreed. "Of course, once the canopy began to collapse, a whole series of cataclysmic events would have followed. The hydrogen would have liquefied, the great fountains of the deep would have opened as earthquakes racked the earth and what we know as Noah's flood occurred."

"My favourite story," Anthony said. "Did you know that almost every society has its own version of a worldwide flood?"

"Yes, I knew that," George said. He turned away. "Come. There's plenty more to see."

Mark and Anthony looked at one another and grinned. "Lead the way," Anthony quipped.

What George lacked in delivery, he made up for in knowledge. "Here is some fascinating research done by a very respected scholar, Dr. Robert Gentry. He found that halos in granite, found in the black flakes called 'mica', show evidence of radioactive material that could only have been recorded within minutes of formation - not the millions of years suggested by other scientists. Once again, evidence for a young earth."

Mark nodded. "I have read enough recently that it's hard to dispute, although I must admit, I'm still a bit uncomfortable with the idea."

"Why dispute something when there is so much evidence in its favour?" George asked candidly. "Here's more proof. The geomagnetic field is decaying exponentially, making it impossible for life to exist on the planet past a much younger age. The magnetic field would simply have been too strong."

"I know," Mark responded. "I guess it's just hard to totally throw everything out the window that I've come to hold true for so long."

"Once presented with the truth, it is hard to go back to believing a lie," George said.

"Now that is true," Anthony offered.

"Over and over again, the fossil record shows plants that extend through several layers," George continued. "Look at this. A whale was even found vertically on its tale."

Anthony moved in for a closer look at the display. "Would you look at that? Now if that isn't something else. Poor Moby Dick would have had a hard time hanging out in that position for a few million years."

"Hey, guys," Mark interrupted. "I think I really need to get back to my own work, now." He turned to George. "Thanks for the tour. It was fascinating."

"There is a lot more to see. We've only just started on this section. There is still radiometric techniques, stellar-light velocity and time travel, Pangaea..."

"Thanks, but I think it'll have to wait until later," Mark said. "You could continue the tour with Anthony, here, if you like. Then he could fill me in on the highlights later."

"Can we get to the section dealing with mythological creatures?" Anthony asked.

George looked confused for a moment. "Mythological creatures?"

"Dragons and so forth?" Anthony clarified. "I know there must be some scientific explanation for that. Almost every culture also has dragon like mythology."

The two men had already wandered off, George seemingly more than happy to satisfy Anthony's curiosity. Mark wasn't sure why he'd felt so suddenly uncomfortable. He had been reading and researching many of the same things himself and had come to basically the same conclusions: that there were serious flaws in the present model of how the universe came to be. But there was something different here. Something else that had him feeling antsy, somehow. Probably just tired, he reasoned.

CHAPTER 26

It had been a long but satisfying day. Mark had met with Dr. Hazzard once more to go over the logistics of his presentation, and was able to get everything in order for the next day's event. Then he and Anthony had spent some time together, going over any last minute details. As far as he could tell, everything was on track and running smoothly. It almost seemed silly that he had been worried about anything bad happening.

He unlocked the door to his hotel room and stepped inside. He switched on the light by the door, untying his tie at the same time.

"Finally. I was beginning to think I had the wrong room."

Mark froze. "Laura?"

She smiled, nodding pleasantly as if it were perfectly natural for her to be waiting alone in his room. "You're looking good. I guess a regular shave and a shower can do wonders."

"How did you get in here?" he demanded.

"It really wasn't all that difficult." She shrugged, not moving from her comfortable position in the one armchair. "They should really think about upping their security. I would mention it to the manager if I were you."

"I will, don't worry," Mark said. "Now, may I ask, what are you doing here?"

"Oh, come off it," Laura scoffed. "You didn't think you could keep your little bomb a secret, now did you?"

"Meaning?"

"Don't play dumb. I know all about the presentation you're giving tomorrow, Mark."

"And? What are you planning to do about it?" Mark asked.

"I haven't decided yet," Laura replied, cocking her head to one side. "Nobody else from my team knows. Yet. I guess it all depends on you."

Mark sighed heavily. "Okay. Interpret that, please. I've had a pretty exhausting day and I'm not really in the mood for word games. Just what do you want?"

"I think I should be asking you that question." She rose and moved toward him as she spoke. "Obviously this whole thing is a ploy to ruffle some feathers back in New Mexico. Honestly, I thought you were above that kind of petty need for revenge. You must know that nobody within the scientific community is going to take you seriously. I mean, an obscure college with a misfit bunch of pseudo scholars for backing; artefacts that are questionable in origin, and a definite falling out from the institution that commissioned you in the first place."

"The truth needs to be told," Mark said quietly.

"Right. I forgot how altruistic you'd become." She sighed. "I miss the old Mark. The sensible scientist." She looked at him coyly. "Not to mention one terrific lover."

He felt his insides tighten. Was she trying to come on to him? After all this time and all that had transpired? "I'm going to ignore that last comment," he stated carefully. "Just know this. I *will* present my findings."

"I can't persuade you?" She put her hand on his arm and stepped closer.

"I thought I made it clear that I wasn't interested. In that way." He took a step away, further into the room.

"Really? I'm not convinced." She followed him, coming up behind him and kneading his shoulders.

Mark shrugged her off. "Stop."

"Why? You're so tense..."

"I said stop," he grated, "before I call security."

She dropped her hands. "Look, I'm not that good at playing games, either. Forget the findings for a minute. I'm here because I still care, Mark. Despite everything. The fact that you abandoned us -"

"I abandoned you?" Mark spat, swinging around.

"Yes! Abandoned everything we'd been working on for - for some religiously motivated fantasy."

"Okay, just stop right there," Mark snapped.

"Don't you see? I'm here because I still care, Mark. Plain and simple. I can't stand by and watch you throw your entire career away. Come back to New Mexico with me. We can make a new start there. Together."

"I don't think you get it. There is no chance of 'together' for us. Despite the fact that we're operating from totally different frames of reference, I'm not interested, Laura. I'm seeing someone else."

Laura blinked. "Oh." She laughed self depreciatingly. "I guess I should be more careful about checking my sources."

"Who've you been talking to?"

"Never mind. I just had a tip that maybe you were still, you know - free. In any case, I need to make you understand the importance of cancelling. Don't go through with this. Please."

"I already told you, I have to."

"Mark, if I can't persuade you any other way, think about your own safety. And the safety of your loved ones. Including that someone you're seeing now."

"Whoa. Now you've got my attention. Just what are you getting at?"

"My 'sources', so to speak." Laura laughed nervously. "I have it on, well, reasonably good authority that Sangeruka is still out there. If you do this you could be putting all of us in danger."

"He wouldn't do anything after the fact. Once the information is out there, what would be the point? And as far as your sources go, why should I trust you? I've got some sources of my own." Mark looked her square in the eye.

"I have absolutely nothing to hide." Her gaze flicked downward.

"No? What do you have to say about that wing bone? The very first one found that went missing while I was away?"

"I... I'm not sure. Which one was that?"

"You're lying," Mark stated calmly. "You claimed that you knew nothing about its disappearance. That's not true, is it?"

"I did send it away without waiting for your go ahead," she finally admitted. "But only because I knew it was important and couldn't wait."

"Then why did you lie about it?"

"I was scared when I saw how angry you were. Things hadn't been going exactly as I'd hoped between us. I was afraid you would just call it quits."

"And how did you suppose I would react when I did find out?"

"I don't know." She threw up her hands. "I guess I wasn't thinking straight. Maybe I was afraid of what it actually might be, and I was trying to shelter you. All of us. Look, I think I've made enough of a fool of myself, already, don't you?"

"That's no excuse. I trusted you."

"I know you did." Laura looked down at her feet. "And now, in retrospect, I can see that not telling you was a big mistake. But that was it, Mark, I swear. None of the other stuff that happened on site was me."

"How can I believe that?" Mark asked.

"I don't know. I guess I don't expect you to. I just wish I could make you see. Everything I did - back in Africa and afterwards, was because I care. I love you, Mark. I know I'm a fool to be telling you that, especially now after everything that's happened. But it's true. I love you and there's nothing that can ever change that."

Mark felt his insides tighten, but it wasn't with desire. It was pity that he felt for Laura right now. She was a pathetic creature and he wished he could release her from the hold that she claimed he still had of her heart. "I think you better leave," he said quietly.

"Mark -"

"I mean it. Leave now," he repeated firmly.

Laura turned and left on a sob.

———

Mark woke with a start. It was pitch black in his room and his eyes were slow at adjusting to any light that may have been creeping in below the door or beneath the drapes. He had been startled out of his sleep by what he thought was a noise. But now, listening intently, there was nothing. Probably just edgy after what Laura had said earlier.

He settled back into the comfort of the large bed. Just as he was drifting off again, the telephone beside his head rang shrilly.

"Hello," he said into the receiver. "Hello?" he tried again when there was no immediate response. He was about to hang up when he heard breathing on the other end of the line.

He sat up. "Hello? Who's there?" he demanded.

"Your girlfriend has a nice -" followed by some crude remarks concerning the female anatomy.

"Who am I talking to?" Mark cut in, enraged. "Coward! If you so much as dare -"

"I'm just watching - for now."

Click.

Amy. He had to call to make sure she was alright. He dialed the number and waited impatiently as it rang several times. He swore under his breath. Maybe she had her cellphone turned off. It was late there, as well. He tried to remember her parents' house number but couldn't. He'd never had reason to call it before and it wasn't in his contacts.

Going back to sleep was an impossibility. Who was behind such a threat? Sangeruka? Laura? He hated to think that she would stoop that low, but he wouldn't be surprised by anything anymore.

Maybe he should phone his father. He would at least be able to look out for Amy.

He dialed the number. This time, someone picked up. "Dad?"

"Mark?" There was a slight pause, as if his father was still half asleep. "Do you know what time it is?"

"I know it's late - or early, whichever the case may be. But I need you to check on Amy for me."

"Now?"

Mark took a deep breath. "Someone just called here. They made some crude comments about her. It's probably just hot air, but I need you to make sure she's alright. She's not picking up her cell, but maybe you could call her parents?"

"Alright. I don't relish the thought of waking them, though. Hopefully it's just a prank."

"I hope so, too."

"I take it you made it safely, then. To where ever it was you were going."

"Yeah. I'll be able to tell you more about it after tomorrow. Just make sure Amy is safe. And the rest of you, too. Call when you confirm."

Mark hung up the phone. His worst nightmares were coming true. It was going to be one long wait.

CHAPTER 27

Mark squinted as he stepped out of the hotel foyer and into the light. He had a nagging headache already - not the best start for the day of his big reveal. His father had called back within minutes, saying that everything was alright. Mark had then called Amy himself the earliest he dared and had been relieved that she sounded normal. There was no mention of anything untoward, and when he cautioned, casually of course, that she be careful and not go out anywhere unaccompanied, she seemed miffed. She took it to mean he was treating her like a child again, and it had ended up in what could technically be called their first real fight. He didn't want to tell her the truth - that he had received threatening phone calls concerning her, and so he had to leave it at that. Not a wonderful beginning to his big day.

He reached the spot where he had parked his SUV and stopped. It wasn't there. Maybe he'd parked elsewhere. He looked around the parking lot. He felt a sinking feeling in the pit of his stomach. Stolen? Surely not today, of all days. That would be just his luck, on top of everything else.

He reached for his cellphone, ready to punch in Anthony's

number and tell him the 'good' news. Then he'd have to go inside and report it to the hotel staff and the police.

He stopped abruptly on his way back toward the lobby. There was a vehicle just peeking its nose out around the back corner of the building. It looked to be the same colour as his.

He pocketed the cellphone and strode in that direction. What in the world was going on here? His pace slowed as the entire vehicle came into view.

"What the -?"

Someone had taken what looked to be a baseball bat to the body of the car. Huge dents to the roof and side panels, a crumpled grill, and slashed tires greeted his eyes like yawning wounds. Anger, mixed with a touch of fear, welled up inside. He wondered if the motor still ran.

He approached the vehicle, about to pop the hood, when suddenly he was jumped from behind.

What happened next was a blur of blows. He was punched, kicked and kneed by some unknown assailant with vice like arms and quick movements. He never got a good look at him, although he did note the ski mask over the face, and the grunts of breath being expelled. By the time he came to on the pavement, lying next to his equally battered SUV, the perpetrator was long gone.

With a groan, Mark pulled himself into an upright position. No doubt about it now. This was no random act of violence. Somebody was out to play hardball.

"You're late." Anthony stopped in his tracks. "Oh my goodness, what happened to you?"

"I'm thinking of cancelling," Mark mumbled out of the side of his mouth. It hurt to talk and even more so to smile.

"What? You can't do that. After all we've been through."

"Look at me." Mark gestured to a blackened eye. "It was no phantom that did this."

"What happened?" Anthony asked.

"I was jumped coming out of my hotel this morning. I think I got one good shot in before I got the you-know-what totally kicked out of me," Mark said. "Somebody took a baseball bat to my car, besides. So, let's see. By the time I called the cops and then went down to the hospital, I'd say I did pretty well to show up at all."

"But you did!" Rocco slapped Mark on the back, causing him to wince. "Oh, sorry, Amigo."

"Rocco?" Mark blinked. He turned to Anthony. "Who let this guy in?" He smiled and instantly regretted it.

"He just showed up off the street." Anthony grinned. "Not long before you arrived, in fact."

"I knew you wouldn't let them stop you," Rocco said.

"Who?" Anthony asked.

"The 'International Conspiracy'," Mark supplied glibly, making quotation marks in the air. "I'm not sure it's worth it."

"You can't let them win," Rocco stated. "Not when we're this close."

"This isn't it," Mark said, gesturing at his bruised face. "Last night I received some threatening phone calls, too."

"What kind of threats?" Anthony asked.

"Against my girlfriend back home."

"You've taken up with somebody new?" Rocco asked.

Mark just nodded. "My dad's looking out for her. In the meantime, I'm just not sure it's really worth it. I don't care so much about my own safety, but if anything ever happened to her or to my family, I'd never forgive myself."

"Don't you get it, man?" Rocco asked. "This is exactly why you need to get the information out there, and fast. If it means that much to the international conspiracy, then it must be worth sharing. You're the man of the hour. It's up to you to blow the lid on this thing once and for all."

Mark let out a deep sigh. "Right."

He'd come this far. There was no turning back now.

Mark stepped out of the lecture hall where the presentation had been scheduled for seven o'clock that evening. It was six thirty eight. He'd just needed one last sweep of the place to make sure everything was in order. He felt nervous, but ready. There was little more that could be done now, except hope for the best. That and pray for the safety of his loved ones.

He rounded a corner and noticed Anthony and Rocco engaged in what appeared to be some kind of heated debate. As he approached, he could definitely detect the sound of anger in their whispers.

"Hey, you two. Everything alright?"

"Um, absolutely," Anthony replied quickly. "Just another one of our debates. You know how it is."

Mark nodded. He did know all about it, especially with these two. "Rocco?"

Rocco grunted something unintelligible and turned without excusing himself. Mark and Anthony watched him stalk away.

"He's frowning so hard his eyebrows almost touched his moustache," Mark joked. "What did you do to ruffle his feathers now?"

"Nothing important." Anthony waved dismissively. "You know how he is. Sometimes, I tend to agree with Laura on the subject. The guy is definitely not stable." Anthony sighed and then his countenance brightened. "So? You all ready?"

"Ready as I'll ever be," Mark replied.

Anthony nodded. "Good, good. I hate to admit this, but as much as I've been having a good time, with all the subterfuge and all, I'll be glad when it's over."

"Amen to that," Mark agreed.

"Shall we?" Anthony asked, gesturing toward the lecture hall doors.

"After you," Mark said.

"And now, without further adieu, may I present to you, Dr. Mark Graham." Dr. Hazzard stepped back from the podium to resounding applause. Even though the event had been practically kept under wraps, there was still a good crowd. News traveled fast, apparently.

Mark was seated in the front row and stood slowly. It was now or never. As he approached the podium, he scanned the crowd. He wasn't sure what he was looking for. Potential assassins, perhaps? He put that thought well away. Besides Anthony and the faculty members he had met, there was no one else familiar. Just do it, come what may.

"Good evening, ladies and gentlemen, esteemed colleagues and fellow scientists. I hope you're ready to be amazed, for that is what I was, and still am, after discovering what I am about to share with you tonight. For some of you, it may seem like the stuff of legends; it may rock some firmly entrenched ideas about the history of our planet, as it did for me. For others it will solidify what you already believe to be true. In either case, let me assure you of the most painstaking and meticulous methodology possible. Let me take you now on a journey, to a faraway place in a far away time..."

More applause. Congratulations, handshakes, questions, schmoozing. It was all a blur as Mark was circulated through the room. That the presentation was well received there was no doubt, but then again, this was a Christian institution. Only time would tell how the rest of the scientific community responded.

"Excellent job, partner," Anthony enthused, slapping Mark on the back.

Mark winced, still feeling the bruises from earlier that morning.

"Oh, sorry. I forgot already."

"I haven't, believe me," Mark said with a grin.

"So? When do you think we'll hear from the opposition?"

"You tell me," Mark said. "You're the one who's been hanging around with them all these months." He hesitated. "Did I tell you Laura was in my room last night when I let myself in?"

"No way," Anthony breathed. He seemed genuinely shocked. "For serious?"

Mark looked at Anthony closely. "You mean you really didn't know?" He wasn't sure whom he could trust any more. He would like to think that Anthony was trustworthy, but he had been fooled more than once in the recent past.

"What is that supposed to mean?" Anthony asked, clearly offended. "You think I tipped her off or something?"

Mark just shook his head dismissively. "Sorry. I guess I'm still smarting over Laura and John. Especially John."

"Okay. Apology accepted. If that can actually be classed as an apology. So why didn't you tell me earlier that you'd seen her?"

"I was otherwise occupied, remember?" Mark gestured at his black eye.

"Good thing field archaeologists of your calibre are supposed to look rugged," Anthony said with a smirk, peering more closely at the damage. "So, I'd say that if Laura already had the tip off, she'll be publishing her rebuttal as we speak. Funny she wasn't here herself."

Mark nodded. "My thought exactly, but I didn't see her anywhere in the crowd. Did you?"

"I already said I didn't." Anthony frowned. "But if Rocco is right, there will be plenty of other spies just waiting to fill them in."

"Speaking of Rocco, I didn't see him either. I fully expected him here, you know?"

Anthony shrugged. "Who knows with that guy?"

Mark glanced sideways at his friend. "What were you two fighting about earlier, anyway?"

"I think I offended him when I questioned his secret intelligence sources a little too closely. I mean, I agree that there is definitely something going on that is not above board, but he makes it sound like some kind of 'mission impossible' operation."

"Whoever attacked me and wrecked my car was real enough."

"True."

"Which reminds me, I need to make a phone call."

"Want me to come along?" Anthony asked. "You might need a bodyguard."

"No, that's okay. I'll just find a quiet corner. I won't go too far." He noticed another enthusiastic audience member approaching with more questions. "Take these ones for me, will you?"

"Gotcha." Anthony saluted. "I'll add question deferrer to my list of credentials."

Mark slipped from the room and found an empty corner in a nearby hallway to make his call.

"Amy!" His heart flooded with relief when she answered.

"Mark?"

"I can't tell you how good it is to hear your voice. You're okay? Everything is okay?"

"Um, yeah."

"I really miss you." He waited but she didn't respond. "About this morning, I'm sorry it seemed like I was being over protective. It's just, well, when I get home I can explain everything."

"I should hope so."

Mark frowned. There was a definite edge of annoyance to her

voice. "Listen, Amy. I know you don't want to hear it, but just be careful, okay?"

"Just what is going on, Mark?" she asked point blank.

"I gave a presentation today on my findings in Africa," he tried to sound enthusiastic. "It went well, I think."

"Oh right. You and your archaeologist friends."

"It is what I do for a living." There was silence on the other end for a moment. Mark thought he heard the distinct sound of a sob. "Amy? What's happened? Are you alright?"

"Why can't you just come right out and say it? I thought you had at least that much integrity."

"Amy? What are you talking about? If it's the fact that I haven't told you much about my trip, I promise I'll fill you in when it's safe to do so."

"I'll just bet!"

"Pardon me?"

"When were you going to tell me about her, Mark?" Amy asked, her voice full of despair. "Or were you planning on keeping both of us? A woman in each country, so you'd never have to sleep alone!"

"Whoa! Hold on a minute! Now you're making no sense at all," Mark sputtered. "Have you been talking to Harmony again? I swear when I see her next -"

"Don't lie to me, Mark. You're better than that. Just tell me, honestly. Have you seen Laura since you've been in Texas?"

"Well, yes, but -" Renewed crying on the other end drowned out whatever else he might have said. "Amy, it's not like that. We're former colleagues. Of course we're bound to meet up with one other on occasion."

"But you invited her to your room!" Amy cried. "And to think I almost slept with you!"

"Amy! That's not true. Who told you that? It's ridiculous! It's -
"

"Was she or was she not in your room with you - alone?" Amy asked.

"Okay, now I'm getting angry," Mark said. "Just who have you been talking to?"

"Answer the question."

"Yes, but -"

"I never want to see you again, Mark," she stated. The finality in her voice gave Mark the shivers.

He rubbed a hand through his hair. "Amy, you don't know what you're saying. Did Laura contact you? Is that it?" He let out a frustrated growl. "I can't believe she would stoop that low. I told her flat out that I was not interested in her anymore. That I was seeing someone else now. You."

"Good bye, Mark," Amy whispered.

"Amy, wait," Mark pleaded. "Please, just let me explain."

Click. She'd hung up on him.

All the elation he'd felt after his presentation was now as flat as a deflated balloon. It meant very little, when his heart was breaking.

The urge to redial was strong. If he could just get her to listen to reason. Her phone rang until the voice mail picked up. He listened intently to the sweet sound of her voice telling him to leave a message. What could he say? He ended the call without saying anything and pushed off the wall with his shoulder.

Just as he turned, he saw Dr. Hazzard approaching, and nodded.

"Well done!" Dr. Hazzard enthused. "Your colleague said you had just slipped out to make a call. Everything all right?"

"A family emergency," Mark said.

"Oh? Not too grave, I hope?"

"It'll keep till tomorrow," Mark hedged.

"Good, good. So many people have so many questions. Your findings are absolutely ground breaking. Shall we go back inside?"

"Yes, of course," Mark replied woodenly.

"About that incandescent lighting in the antechamber..."

Mark followed the professor back into the room, nodding like an automaton to passing well-wishers as he tried to concentrate on what the doctor was saying.

"Dr. Graham?"

"Yes?" Mark snapped himself back to attention.

"I thought I had lost you there for a moment." Dr. Hazzard laughed good-naturedly.

"Oh, sorry," Mark apologized.

"Thinking of that family emergency?" Dr. Hazzard asked sympathetically.

"Uh, yes," Mark agreed with a sheepish grin. "And the irony of this whole evening."

"Irony? What do you mean?"

"Well, it does seem a tad ironic that a fence sitter like me should be the current hero at a Christian university."

"Ah." Dr. Hazzard nodded. "Of course, the difficulty with the creation model for most people is not the logic behind it, or the evidence, for that matter. Quite simply, if one believes in the creation model, then one must also believe in a Creator. And there, as they say, is the rub." Dr. Hazzard's eyes twinkled.

"Indeed," Mark agreed flatly.

"No pressure." Dr. Hazzard slapped him on the back, bringing a wince from Mark. "Just think on it later, after you've enjoyed your accolades."

"Do you mind if I excuse myself for just a minute? I find I'm in need of some fresh air."

"No problem," the doctor said. "This party isn't going anywhere."

Mark pushed his way through the crowd, avoiding eye contact that might lead to more questions. Once outside the building, he let out a pent up breath.

He believed it himself, deep down. Of course all the evidence pointed to God - to the Biblical model. It was wearing him out trying to justify his findings and still not put his faith in the one who created it all. So why was he still resisting? It's what his family wanted. What Amy wanted. Why was he so stubborn in not just doing it?

Accept Christ now, idiot!

He looked up at the night sky, glowing orange with the artificial light of urbanity. It was a far cry from the African sky, bejewelled each night with diamonds from heaven. It was a far cry from what the ancients would have seen, magnified tenfold under the canopy of crystalline hydrogen.

What would it have been like, he wondered? To live back then, so close to the beginning of creation? Men were as evil then as they are now. They didn't believe, even though the evidence was right before their eyes.

Mark blinked. Okay, so it wasn't an audible voice, but if ever he'd felt like God had just talked to him...

He shivered.

"Okay, God," he said aloud. "I can't deny your existence any longer. But like Dr. Hazzard said, if I believe in the creator, I have to take the whole package. You know I'm kind of stubborn, though. So you're going to have to help me in that department. P.S. Can you help me win Amy back?"

He smiled, a very surreal peace coming over him. Should he go back inside and field more questions? Naw... he'd talked enough for one night. He just wanted to go back to his hotel room and mull this new faith thing over a bit. Wait until he told his folks.

Until he told Amy, if she would listen.

He dialed the cab company he had used earlier that day.

Let whomever come and beat him to a pulp while he waited. He didn't care about much right at the moment, except basking in this strange light that had nothing to do with the urban glow.

CHAPTER 28

Mark opened his eyes gradually to greet the morning light that was filtering through the partly opened drapes in his hotel room. He hadn't slept this well in weeks, he realized. With a satisfied smile, he stretched languorously and relaxed back against the pillows, arms behind his head. It was his first day as a brand new person. Despite all that could happen, he felt strangely peaceful about the future.

He should probably call his folks. Then he would work on Amy. Or maybe he should wait until he got back home and deliver the good news in person. Yeah, that seemed like a better idea. But Anthony - now that guy deserved a bit of gloating time, even if it was way too early in the morning. That would be half the fun. Mark smiled at the thought of what Anthony would say, and reached for the phone.

After trying both Anthony's room and his cell, Mark called the front desk. "Did Anthony Vanguard check out by any chance?"

There was a pause as the woman consulted her computer. "No. He's still in room 309."

"Oh. Okay. Did he leave any messages for me?"

"I'm afraid not, Sir," the woman at the front desk replied.

"Thanks," Mark said and hung up. Maybe he was back at it already, although it wasn't like Anthony to be up and about this early in the morning.

For his own part, there was no going back to sleep. He was ready to face this new day and was anxious for it to begin in earnest. Dr. Hazzard would be pleased by his new found faith, he was sure. Now he just needed some help in remembering what to do next. He knew reading his Bible and praying was part of the deal. His parents had drilled that into him. There was probably one of those Gideon Bibles somewhere in a drawer. He'd start with that.

He found the Bible in the bedside table and opened it to a random page. Romans 8. He scanned the page and noticed a break in the text with this heading: "Our Victory in Christ". Sounded good...

"And in the same way the Spirit also helps our weakness; for we do not know how to pray as we should, but the Spirit Himself intercedes for the saints with groanings too deep for words; and He who searches the hearts knows what the mind of the Spirit is, because he intercedes for the saints according to the will of God."

Hm. That was good. He certainly didn't know what to pray right at the moment, or even how to pray, for that matter. "Okay, God. I'm taking you at your word. Help me out here. I want to do Your will, so You're going to have to show me how to do this. " He continued reading.

"And we know that God causes all things to work together for good to those who love God, to those who are called according to His purpose. For whom He foreknew, He also predestined to become conformed to the image of His son, that He might be the first born among many brethren."

Mark stopped reading and thought about that for a moment. He'd heard that verse before - the one about God working all things out for good. His parents had quoted it often enough. Did that mean *all* things? Even all the mess with the archaeological dig? Getting mugged? The present falling out with Amy? He looked at the verse again. It said ALL things. And it was pretty awesome to think that God knew about it all, even before it happened. He was predestined to be a child of God; to be counted among 'the brethren'. Yes, he could believe it. It was what he had been moving toward his whole life.

He closed the Bible and said another quick prayer, this time for guidance in approaching his career in this new frame of light. God knew everything, including what his next step should be in that regard.

Just as he was putting the Bible back into its nest, the telephone rang. Probably Anthony.

"Hello?"

"Mark?"

Mark smiled. He'd been right. "Wait until I tell you the news," Mark began.

"Hang on," Anthony interrupted. His voice sounded weak and far away, like he was gasping for air.

Mark frowned. "You alright, buddy? You don't sound too good."

"Can you come to my room right away? And maybe call an ambulance first."

"It's okay if I don't make it," Anthony whispered. "I know where I'm going."

"Stop being melodramatic," Mark chided good-naturedly. "The doctor says you'll be fine. A couple of broken ribs; a few bruises. You'll be fixed up in no time and outta here."

Anthony lay on the emergency room gurney, waiting his turn in the already busy ward.

"Doesn't feel like it. I'm glad I'll be seeing you in heaven, though. That is good news."

"Just stop it. Nobody is going to heaven today."

"How do you know? The cost just might kill me."

"You've got insurance." Mark looked Anthony square in the eye. "You do have insurance?"

Anthony nodded, and then winced. "Geez, that smarts. Not like you spoiled Canadians and your Medicare."

Mark ignored the gibe. "Where are you going to stay? I'm sure Dr. Hazzard won't mind putting you up for awhile until you can travel."

"I hate to put him in danger."

"Quit being a martyr."

"And you? How long will you stay?"

"Just until I can get packed up. I've got some - business to take care of back home."

"Lady business?" Anthony asked.

"None of your business," Mark clarified with a grin. "Man, for a guy with multiple injuries, you sure talk a lot."

Anthony smiled before groaning in pain once more. "I feel like crap. You sure I'm gonna live?"

Mark nodded. "Doctor said so. He should be turfing you shortly."

"Did you check the papers yet? I wonder what the reviews say. Or if there's any rebuttal from New Mexico."

"I haven't had time. I've been otherwise occupied," Mark said with a grin.

"Yeah. Likewise. Did I say thanks for rescuing me?" Anthony asked.

"Yep. What are friends for?" He sobered. "This is getting kind of scary. Maybe Rocco's theories aren't all that off. You got a good look at him, right?"

Anthony nodded. "Too good."

"Oh? You told the police?"

"Yep."

"And you think it might be the same guy who beat me up?"

Anthony hesitated. "I think there are a couple of things I should tell you."

"Like what?" Mark asked, his eyes narrowing.

"I should have said something earlier, but I didn't want to worry you unnecessarily right before your presentation."

"Just spill it."

"It's about Rocco."

"I'm listening."

Anthony took a breath and winced again. "That argument you saw between me and Rocco. He was asking me some pretty funny questions."

"What kind of questions?"

"Questions about you and your girlfriend. He seemed to think she might be a distraction. I told him it was none of his business."

"Which is exactly true," Mark responded. "How does this have anything to do with what happened?"

"I'm not sure. Just some other stuff he said. Random stuff about you and Laura and the conspiracy." Anthony hesitated before continuing. "I think the guy has gone loco, Mark. Like, stark raving mad."

"Whoa. I'm not really following you."

"I think Rocco is the one who beat me up. Who beat us both up," Anthony said.

Mark blinked. "Why?"

"I recognized his voice," Anthony replied. "At least I think it was him. And even with his face covered, he had the same build."

Mark thought for a minute, grasping for a shred of recognition that was trying to form in his own brain. "There was something familiar about the guy. It all happened so fast, but..." He snapped his fingers. "He said something in Spanish! The guy who beat me up. It was just the kind of thing that Rocco would say when he was frustrated."

Anthony nodded.

"But why?" Mark asked, his brow furrowed. "I thought he was on our side."

"I think he was trying to scare us. Scare you, anyway, to make sure you were taking his conspiracy theory seriously. And me? Maybe he thinks I'm still on their side; a double agent, so to speak."

"Do you think he's on his own?" Mark asked. "That this whole conspiracy is a fabrication and he's just a vigilante, trying to take matters into his own hands?"

"I'm not sure," Anthony replied. "But I'm worried about Laura."

"Laura?" Mark glanced over as the attending Doctor approached. "What about her?"

"I'm not sure," Anthony said. "Just something he said the other day during our argument. Maybe you should check into it. Warn her. She might be in danger."

Mark nodded. "I will." He stepped back as the Doctor greeted them.

"You're very lucky, Mr. Vanguard. One rib came very close to puncturing a lung." He held up the x-rays for inspection.

"But he's going to live, right?" Mark asked with a grin.

"A long life, I would suspect," the Doctor agreed with a smile. "Now, I'll make a final wrap on those ribs, write you a prescription for the pain, and you can be on your way."

———

Mark helped Anthony out of the cab in front of Dr. Hazzard's home. It was a gracious Southern two story with large trees in front almost hiding the house from the street.

"Pretty easy for a guy to cloak himself in the trees, if he wanted to try to break in," Anthony mused.

"Yeah. We should warn Dr. Hazzard," Mark agreed.

The man himself appeared in the doorway. "Come on up. You need a hand with your belongings?"

"Everything's back at the hotel," Mark replied. "I'll have to go back for it and check out."

"No use spending money on a cab," Dr. Hazzard said. "I'll drive you over later myself, or I can lend you my car, for that matter."

"Thanks," Mark replied.

"My goodness," Dr. Hazzard clucked. "If I didn't know better, I'd say you boys have made some enemies along the way. First Dr. Graham's car accident and now this. What exactly happened anyway? Did you trip on the stairs or something?"

"Um, maybe we should go inside," Mark advised. "We didn't want to alarm you with the details over the phone, but I think there are a few things we need to straighten out."

"This is grave indeed." Dr. Hazard shook his head.

Mark grasped his hands as he sat forward in the wing-backed chair he occupied in Dr. Hazzard's sitting room. "We should have been up front with you right after I was attacked. Before that - well, I didn't want to alarm you with mere speculations. But afterwards - I apologize. You had a right to know the truth."

"We didn't want you to cancel the presentation," Anthony offered from his semi-lounging position on a nearby sofa.

"I wouldn't have done that," Dr. Hazzard replied. "Maybe taken some extra precautions with security..."

"But now I don't know what to think," Mark continued. "If there really is some kind of international conspiracy to hide the truth about creation, then you and your institution could be in danger. Not to mention, the artefacts."

"I doubt that's a problem," Dr. Hazzard said. "We've dealt with this kind of thing before. We have a very tight security system. Besides that, now that the truth is out, the opposition wouldn't dare sully themselves further with anything too obvious."

"You mean there really is a conspiracy?" Anthony asked.

"In a manner of speaking, yes," the doctor replied. "Although, I'm not sure it's quite as insidious as your friend Rocco says. It's more a war of words. There are certain factions that have out and out lied on more than one occasion. Changed the facts, rewritten the texts, taken evidence completely out of context. It's a mega game that the opposition takes quite seriously. There are millions of dollars of government funding at stake. Evolutionists can't afford to have the truth come out. It would mean an end to their steady pipeline of money."

"That's just not right." Anthony tried to sit up straighter and then gasped.

"Maybe you should lie down," Dr. Hazzard suggested. "My wife Mabel has already made up the guest room. You should be comfortable there."

"Maybe you're right." Anthony nodded. "Those meds are starting to make me feel pretty drowsy."

"Just down the hall and the first door to the right. The bathroom is right across the hall. Do you need help?"

"No, I should be fine," Anthony said, rising from the sofa with difficulty.

"You sure?" Mark jumped up to lend a hand.

"No, I'm good," Anthony replied, waving gingerly.

"I'll bring your stuff over as soon as I can," Mark called after Anthony's retreating figure.

"Just watch your back," Anthony mumbled.

The two remaining watched him disappear around the corner.

"Did you see the morning paper?" Dr. Hazzard asked.

"No, I didn't," Mark replied. "The reviews are in already?"

Dr. Hazzard nodded. He reached behind his chair and retrieved a jumble of newspaper that was already in several pieces. "Let's see. Here's the section. Quite a good piece, I would say.

Certainly not the kind of thing the 'conspiracy' would appreciate. The facts are quite well represented, I would say."

Mark took the paper. The headline read, "New Finds In Africa Lend Credence to Noah's Flood". He scanned the article, noting the mention of his own credentials and the 'good work' he'd done in the past. It outlined the find in most of its particulars, including the Pterodactyls and 'giant men' found together, the advanced technology in the antechamber, and the fact that it was sealed off by layers of sediment that helped preserve the specimens.

"So what do you think?" Dr. Hazard asked.

"Generally very accurate," Mark conceded with a satisfied nod. "It almost makes me suspicious. There were no major details left out and not even a hint at sarcasm. I was at least expecting a small dose of scepticism."

"My feelings exactly. I'm surprised the opposition hasn't come out with a rebuttal yet. I checked on line and there was nothing so far. All in due time, I suppose."

"Yes. I'll be interested in what my former colleagues back in New Mexico have to say." Mark hesitated for a moment, remembering Anthony's warnings about Laura. "Um, actually, speaking of which, would you excuse me while I make a phone call?"

"Go ahead."

Mark let Laura's cell ring until her voice mail picked up. What kind of message could he leave? "Watch your back"? He ended the call instead. He'd try again later.

"So tell me more about this Rocco fellow," Dr. Hazzard said.

"He was always a hard worker. Very knowledgeable. Up until recently, I trusted him completely, but now... Anthony seems to think he's gone crazy. I know he talked to me before about people out in the field not telling the truth and it really frustrated him. He says he hooked up with some others who want to rectify the injustice, but to do the things that we think he might be doing...?

I just don't get it. It makes no sense. It's working against us, if anything, not for us."

"People can commit heinous acts, all motivated by good intentions. Take, for instance, the attacks on abortion clinics over the years," Dr. Hazzard mused. "Harming those involved doesn't stop the killing of babies. It probably furthers their cause, if nothing else."

Mark nodded in agreement. "Two wrongs never make a right."

"And as for your friend Rocco, I guess we'll have to leave it to the police to find out whether he's involved. In the mean time, you and Anthony should probably both stay here."

"I don't know," Mark said hesitantly. "I really do want to get back..."

"The family emergency?" Dr. Hazzard asked. He smiled.

Mark narrowed his gaze but he smiled in spite of himself. "Just what has my colleague been telling you?"

Dr. Hazzard shrugged. "Something about a love interest, that's all. If it's real, it can wait. I would think the young lady in question would rather have you home in one piece."

Mark laughed. "Once Anthony recovers, I'll kill him." He sobered slightly and added, "I wouldn't want to put your family in any danger."

"Don't let the homey-ness of my property fool you. I've got quite an advanced security system in place," Dr. Hazzard assured. "I think we should alert the police, though, so they can check around periodically."

"And you're sure everything will be safe?"

"Absolutely. You can rest assured that the artefacts are completely secure."

"Okay. I guess I'll have to take you on your word, Doctor."

"True enough. And since you'll be my guest for the next few days, please call me Tim."

"Right. Tim it is, as long as you call me Mark."

"Agreed. Now, may I suggest that we go over to the hotel and retrieve your belongings?"

Two days passed and still no rebuttal from New Mexico. Other scientists and interested individuals entered the fray online, some for and some against. Some tried to downplay the creationist connection and explain the findings in other more 'plausible' ways, while others attached their own religious biases to such a degree that it made Mark cringe.

Even though he was now a believer himself, it was downright embarrassing the way some fundamentalists carried on. At the least, his presentation had generated some debate, which meant it hadn't gone completely unnoticed. But the fact that there was nothing - not a peep from New Mexico - had him worried.

Maybe it was their way of distancing themselves; shunning him, so to speak. If they didn't even bother to reply, then it would show the world that they really didn't put any credence in what he had to say.

Or maybe there was a more sinister reason.

Mark had tried Laura repeatedly since Anthony's warnings, but there was still no answer. He'd even stooped to leaving a message for her to call him back. He hadn't quite steeled himself to call John, though. That betrayal was still a little too raw.

There was little more that he could do here. The debate online continued and he had even received a request to talk on the local radio station, which he had done earlier that day. But now he was anxious to go home. He had more important things on his mind that needed reconciliation. He planned to head out first thing tomorrow.

He was lying in bed in the room that Tim and Mabel had prepared for him. It wasn't that late, but he felt the need for some solitude. He kept going back to that passage he had read in Romans the other day. The one about God working everything out for good. He was clinging to that promise right now. He also liked what it said a little further down in the chapter, in verse 31.

"If God is for us, who is against us?"

It seemed like God's hand had been with him so far in presenting his findings to the world. There was very little opposition, which still surprised him. He just hoped it didn't fade into obscurity; just another quack Christian trying to tout his own beliefs.

His reflections were cut short by the ring of his cellphone. He almost let his voice mail answer it, but decided against it.

"Hello."

"Amigo! Congratulations! I see everything has gone off well with your presentation. Now maybe those sceptics will take us seriously, eh?"

"Rocco?" Mark asked, sitting up fully.

"Of course it's me. Who else?" Rocco laughed.

Relief and fear mingled inside Mark's gut. Rocco wouldn't be calling if he was actually guilty, would he? But then again... "Hey, buddy," Mark said with forced cheerfulness. "Where have you been these last few days? I thought you'd want to be here to celebrate."

"Sorry about that, Amigo. I had some other business to take care of."

"We missed you. Both me and Anthony." Mark paused to see if the mention of the other man's name had any effect. Nothing. "Anthony met with a bit of an accident, I'm afraid."

"Oh?"

"Yeah. Kind of similar to my accident, if you get my drift."

Rocco chuckled - an unexpected response. "About time that Mama's boy got toughened up a bit."

"Excuse me?" Mark questioned in disbelief.

"He'll mend," Rocco continued. "A couple cracked ribs never killed anybody."

There was silence for a moment as Mark digested what Rocco

just said. "How did you know about his ribs?"

"I've got my ways, remember?"

"So you said."

"So, I've been keeping up on the debate. I'd say we're coming out on top about 80% of the time."

"Yeah, right," Mark responded.

"Hey, you don't sound too pleased," Rocco noted. "What's the matter?"

"I'm just a bit concerned about who our supporters really are," Mark said. "If there really is an international conspiracy, why aren't they more vocal? And who exactly is on the other side? How do I know I can trust them any more than the opposition?"

"I'd say it's pretty obvious that the conspiracy is alive and well. Look what they did to you and Anthony," Rocco reasoned.

"Did they?" Mark asked point blank. "Was it really 'the conspiracy', as you call them, or was it some other well meaning vigilante trying to convince us of a conspiracy?"

There was hesitation on the other end for a moment before Rocco laughed again. "Whoa, now! I'm not sure what you're getting at, but don't bite the hand that feeds you."

"What is that supposed to mean?"

"Look, things are working out perfectly for our cause. Who cares how it came to be? Just bask in it, Amigo. Grasp it and run with it."

"Did you or did you not attack Anthony?" Silence. "I see."

"It was for his own good. He was playing a double game, you know. It just helped to put the fear of God in him, so to speak. I don't think he'll be wavering over to the opposition again anytime soon."

"Did it ever occur to you that that was all part of our plan?" Mark asked.

"Either way, no harm done," Rocco said. "It still makes the bad guys look worse and the good guys look better."

"In some people's minds," Mark said. "Okay. So you admitted

that much. What about me? And don't try to deny it. I know it was you." There was more silence. "Rocco? Answer me, damn it!"

"Look man, you don't even know half of what I've done for you," Rocco said, his voice sounding hard; foreign. "You should be thanking me for spurring your ass into action. For saving you from distractions -"

"You mean Amy?" Mark cut in, his throat constricted. "It was you that told her I was still seeing Laura?"

"Hey, I couldn't look that kind of a gift in the mouth. When I tipped Sawchuk off about your presentation, I had no idea I could use her for more than one purpose."

A chill ran down Mark's spine. "You tipped her off. But why?"

"Lots of reasons. It would keep her close by, where I could keep an eye on her."

"Rocco, tell me once and for all. Is there really an international conspiracy - the kind you've been warning me about? Or is this just some giant fabrication that you've come up with to further your own cause?"

"Oh, it's real enough," Rocco responded. "I'm just helping bring it to light a little quicker, that's all."

Mark closed his eyes. The man really had gone loco. "Look, Rocco. Thanks for all your help, but I think you should just back off for awhile now, okay? We don't want anyone else to get suspicious."

"I was planning on it anyway. That last job got a little messy. I'm going to disappear for awhile, myself. I think you can handle the rest from here."

"What do you mean?"

"Don't worry about it," Rocco laughed. "I took care of every-thing. You won't be hearing any slander from New Mexico. Gotta go, now. Take care, Amigo!"

"Rocco? Rocco!" Mark called into the receiver. Nothing. The man had already hung up. Oh no. What had his former friend done now?

CHAPTER 29

Laura Sawchuk and John Bergman were added to the missing persons list and a warrant was issued for Rocco Cortez's arrest. Three days later, Laura's body was found in a shallow grave near the college grounds in Texas. Another four days, and John's body was found floating down the river.

My God, my God, why have you forsaken me?

It pounded through Mark's brain like a mantra after each grisly discovery. Several days of a fog filled existence moved Mark forward through time, each day making the necessary motions to eat, sleep, and talk with the police. Tim and Mabel Hazzard became the solid foundation upon which he and Anthony relied. In all, it was like a dream, surreal in its clarity, but distorted beyond reason.

"I'm really sorry it's turned out this way," Tim was saying. They were standing at the doorway of the Hazzard home, Mark and Anthony both ready to take their leave.

Mark shook his head. "Yes. You and me both."

"And you?" Tim turned to Anthony. "You're sure you're fit to travel? You're welcome to stay on longer if you'd like."

"No, it's about time the prodigal son made his way back home again." Anthony grinned. "Besides, I miss my Mom's cooking, no offence to your wife."

"None taken." Mabel smiled. "It's been a pleasure to have you both, even under these trying circumstances."

"Just remember, God is still in control," Tim declared.

"I'm trying to remind myself of that daily," Mark said.

"Hopefully we'll both make it home in one piece," Anthony noted. "I mean, Rocco is still at large."

"I'm sure the police will ferret him out soon. He can't hide forever," Mabel reasoned.

"His type don't stay underground long," Tim agreed. "Always looking for publicity. It's unfortunate that we've gotten some bad reviews out of it, though. The connection between you and Cortez has certainly shed some questionable light on your discovery. Not in my mind, of course, but the critics are getting a hold of this and eating it up, I'm afraid."

"I guess Rocco's plans backfired pretty badly," Anthony said. "Looks like he's played right into the 'conspiracy's' hands."

"If only it was just our reputations that were lost," Mark added.

The others nodded.

"Yes. A very sad outcome," Tim offered.

Sad could not nearly describe what Mark was feeling. Despite what had taken place in the recent past, these people had been his friends, his colleagues. John had been his most trusted confidant, and Laura? Well, she had even shared his bed. His stomach turned inward with another spasm of inner pain. It was time to go home.

"Thanks again for everything," Mark said, shaking Tim's hand solemnly.

Mabel gave him a heartfelt hug instead. "Anytime you're in Texas, feel free to look us up."

"I'm sure we'll want some follow up on your work once the dust settles a bit," Tim added.

"If my reputation isn't in complete tatters," Mark said with half a grin.

"Trust," Tim advised, looking Mark straight in the eye. "Sometimes God puts us through the refiner's fire to make us more useful."

"I'll keep that in mind."

The quartet waved their final good-byes and Mark and Anthony got into the waiting cab. Mark settled back into the seat, shutting his eyes in an attempt to block out the rush of emotions that continually threatened to overtake him when he thought about recent events. Maybe he never should have pursued this thing in the first place. If he had only listened to Laura, to the Director of Archaeology back in New Mexico - to any voice of reason, maybe none of this would have happened. Maybe then, Laura and John would be alive. Was telling the truth really worth such a cost?

"Hey, you awake?" Anthony nudged Mark in the shoulder.

"Hm?" Mark opened his eyes.

"Check out the car behind us," Anthony said. "Or should I say, the driver of the car."

Mark turned around and peered out the back window of the taxi. He let out a gust of air.

"No way. It can't be."

"The guy certainly has balls, I'll give you that," Anthony said.

"Hey, driver." Mark leaned forward. "I think we're being tailed. You got a police band on your radio?"

The driver looked in his rear view mirror. "Who are you? I don't want no trouble." He moved into the far right lane. "I'll drop you off. That'll be eleven fifty. I don't want no trouble."

"Whoa! Wait a minute," Anthony interjected. "We don't want trouble either. Just keep going. But faster."

"I don't want no trouble," the cabby repeated.

"Then keep going," Mark advised. "I'll call the police myself." He dialed the number.

Rocco had pulled up beside them on the left and was gesturing for them to pull over.

"Ignore him," Mark said, waiting for the police to answer. "Hello? Yeah, I've got a location on a guy named Rocco Cortez. There's a warrant out for his arrest." There was a pause. "Yeah. He's headed down the freeway now, going south toward the airport. Right. He's in a green sedan..." The police took the rest of the pertinent information and Mark hung up the phone.

"Okay," he said more to himself than anyone else. "If we can just keep him with us, the police should be able to head him off at the next overpass."

"I don't want no trouble," the cabby said again, almost whining as if he was trying to convince himself now.

"You're doing a great job," Mark assured.

"Yeah. Consider it your civic duty. The guy's a nut case. A criminal."

The cab driver gripped the wheel even tighter as he rounded the next bend, Rocco staying close by on his left. Suddenly, Rocco swerved toward them, side swiping the cab with enough force to make it momentarily veer into the sidewall and bounce off again. "I don't want no trouble!" the cabby shouted, almost in tears.

"Keep driving," Mark shouted back. He looked at Anthony, who was holding onto his side. "You okay?"

Anthony nodded, grimacing. "I just hadn't braced myself, that's all. I'll be ready next time."

"There better not be a next time," Mark said through clenched teeth. "Can't you go any faster?"

There was a next time. This time he could see the sparks fly with the impact.

"He's crazy, I tell you," Anthony muttered.

Mark nodded. "I know."

They were rounding another curve, this time to the left, when Rocco hit the taxi once again. This time, the force of the impact sent the cab over the edge, air born for a millisecond, before landing with a jarring thud on a grassy section amid the spaghetti factory called freeway. Rocco's green sedan bumped afterward, coming to an abrupt halt ten feet away.

The cab driver ejected himself as quickly as possible from the driver's seat and took off running. Anthony lay slumped in the back seat. For his part, Mark had taken a bump to the head, which was already forming into a goose egg, but was none the worse for wear. He checked Anthony's pulse. His friend let out a groan. That was a good sign. Glancing to the side, he saw Rocco's stocky figure looming in the back window.

"Get out, turncoat," Rocco growled as he jerked the rear door open.

Mark had no choice but to comply, being half jerked out of the back seat by one of Rocco's powerful hands. He held a pistol in the other.

"All I did for you," Rocco ranted, waving the gun. "Everything. And you turn on me. What kind of a friend is that?"

"You turned on yourself," Mark countered, raising his hands slowly to chest height. "How could you do it, man? Laura and John were innocent."

"Innocent?" Rocco spat. "How can you say that after what they did to you? To all of us. To the cause."

"I don't know what cause you're talking about," Mark said. He tried to keep his voice calm, though everything inside of him was screaming with adrenaline. "Maybe they had different views, but that doesn't mean they deserved to die."

"We all die one day," Rocco countered philosophically. "Some just sooner than others."

Mark shook his head. "I thought I knew you. Thought you were my friend. But this - this monster that you've become! What happened to the Rocco I knew?"

"He got stomped on one too many times. Oh yeah, you were my friend - when you wanted to be. But do you know what it's like being bossed around by a bunch of young intellectuals that think they know more than you just because they got a piece of paper that says 'Doctor' on it? Man, I been around longer than any of you. And I know my job, too. But, I always had to bow to what the 'experts' had to say."

"So that's it? You were jealous?"

Rocco snorted. "Jealous? Naw. Just fed up. I been on too many sites where the truth gets covered up with fancy theories that don't add up. It was time someone told the truth. I thought you were the man."

"I was. I am," Mark said. "You heard it. The truth was told, so why did you have to go and commit murder?"

"It wouldn't be long before they twisted everything you had to say and made it sound like a fool's fairy tale. I know how these things go. I had to stop them before they had a chance."

"But there are other ways, Rocco. Legal ways," Mark reasoned, as if talking to a child.

Rocco snorted. "I've tried that. Doesn't work in the end. The only way is to eliminate the problem."

"By committing murder?"

"I did what I had to do." Rocco shrugged. "And I'm really sorry, Amigo, but I'm afraid you're going to have to join them." Rocco had steadied himself and was now pointing the gun straight at Mark's head.

"What would that prove?" Mark asked. "You're just digging yourself in, deeper and deeper."

"You think you're pretty smart, don't you Dr. Graham? You think I've gone off my rocker and you can somehow sweet talk your way out of this one, don't you? Well, let me tell you a little secret. You're not as smart as you think you are. I was able to keep pretty close tabs on everything - even your secure files."

"What files are we talking about?"

"Everything. In Africa... North America... It wasn't very hard, my friend. You really should have chosen a better password. I mean, 'saxophone'? How hard was that to figure out? For a Doctor, I'd say you're not too bright."

"Okay. So what was the point of that? I would have told you anything you needed to know."

"Ah, really? For one thing, I found out that the government was getting a little too nosy. That Sangeruka fellow was starting to push his weight around."

"Sangeruka," Mark repeated. "Just what exactly did you have to do with him?"

"As little as possible," Rocco admitted. "Although I did try to throw him off the trail just a bit."

"Meaning?"

"Missing artefacts, the cave in... my own little insurance should he and his cronies come snooping around."

"What? I don't see how that helped -"

"Of course you don't," Rocco cut him off in a reasonable tone of voice. "That's because you're not seeing the bigger picture. I was looking forward to what I knew would be the next great cover up. Oh yes, I knew as soon as I laid eyes on that first wing bone that we were heading down another one of those trails. I just had to make sure that when the time came, you'd have enough firsthand experience to believe me."

"That doesn't make any sense," Mark said. "You're sick."

"Watch it." Rocco laughed. "This sicko is the one holding the gun, remember?"

"So what about my arrest? Did you mastermind that as well?"

"That didn't go quite as planned," Rocco admitted. "Especially not the part about me getting chased and losing the casket."

"So that part is true?" Mark asked. "The casket is still intact, buried somewhere?"

Rocco nodded. "Of course. Why would I lie about that? Too bad you won't be around when I retrieve it."

Why indeed. "So how did I manage to get released?" Mark asked.

"That I don't know. Maybe the good Lord was looking out for you even back then." Rocco shrugged. "In any case, it's time for you to meet your maker now."

Rocco's gaze flicked to the side, momentarily distracted by the distant sound of sirens.

Mark heard it, too. "Give it up, Rocco. The cops'll be here any minute. You'll never get away with another murder."

Rocco focused on his victim once again. "Might as well go out with a bang, then." He laughed at his own joke; a sickening maniacal sound. "Any last requests?"

Wham! Rocco toppled to the ground as the simultaneous sounds of a grunt and the bark of the gun mingled. Pain shot through Mark's body and he fell backwards. He grasped for his shoulder and blinked past the heat at the sight of Anthony sprawled on top of Rocco. The gun lay on the ground and Anthony scrambled to pick it up before Rocco could get to his feet.

Still on his knees, Anthony trained the weapon on Rocco. "Mark, you okay?" he rasped, holding his side with one arm as he tried to keep his other arm steady.

"I've been hit," Mark groaned. "I think it's my shoulder."

Sirens blared as a police car arrived on the scene, bumping its way over the rough terrain.

"Put your weapon down!" a commanding voice shouted over a megaphone.

Anthony dropped the gun and put his hands in the air as far as he was able, bending forward slightly with the effort.

"He's not the one," Mark tried to shout. His own voice sounded disturbingly far away.

Suddenly everything went black.

CHAPTER 30

Mark lounged in front of the TV, letting the white noise cradle his consciousness like he was cradling the sling that encased his injured arm. It was good to be back in Winnipeg, in the comfort of his parents' home. With his injured shoulder, and all the other trauma he'd suffered recently, it didn't take much convincing to stay with them for awhile. He could use the pampering.

"How's the shoulder today?" Russ asked, coming into the room and sitting in the chair beside Mark.

"Mending, I suspect," Mark responded.

"What's on?"

"Um, I'm not sure," Mark said honestly. "I guess I wasn't paying much attention."

Russ nodded. They were silent for a few moments, staring at the TV with glass eyes.

"You know, Son," Russ finally said. "You did the right thing. Telling the truth about your find, I mean. No one could have predicted what would happen after that."

Mark nodded. "I know. But I'm still coming to terms with that, I guess. It just seems so senseless, now."

"God's truth is never senseless," Russ stated.

"Even when innocent people die?" Mark asked.

"I don't pretend to know all the answers. Just know, that in His sovereignty, God does."

"I know that. Really. I'm very grateful that you and Deanie never gave up praying for me."

"That's what parents do." Russ smiled.

"It does hurt, though, that the dig is getting so much bad publicity. I mean, I could handle it if it was just my own reputation that was getting slammed, but the whole dig is being discredited. It makes Laura and John's deaths seem even more pointless."

"Satan will have his day," Russ mused. "But I believe that what Satan means for harm, God can still use for good. Someday you'll be vindicated. And there are still lots of people out there who believe you."

"Anyone that will give me job?" Mark asked with a sardonic grin.

"Give it time," Russ advised.

"True. Dr. Hazzard is still on my side, anyway, although I'm afraid he's taking some flack for it."

"God works all things out -"

Mark cut his father off and finished the sentence. "For good to them that love the Lord."

"You got it."

"Don't you two just look cozy, sitting in here together having a man to man chat?" Deanie stood in the doorway to the family room.

"Well, hello there," Russ said. "Come sit with me. There's room for two." He gestured to his lap.

Mark smiled. He had hoped that someday he could share that kind of lasting relationship with someone. With Amy. They had only spoken once since his return, and despite his revelations about his new found faith, she seemed distant.

"Actually, I was just coming to tell you that we have company,"

Deanie said. "Amy Walters," she added, giving Mark a knowing look. "Her car just pulled into the drive."

"In that case, I better leave you alone," Russ said, standing up. "We'll send her right in."

Mark's heart was pounding in his chest. Amy had come to see him. It was the first time they would meet face to face since his arrival back in Winnipeg. He straightened himself in the chair a bit and then winced with the effort.

"Mark," Amy greeted, entering the room. Mark made a motion to stand and grunted. "No, please! Just stay sitting. I was so worried when I heard you'd been hurt." She perched on the edge of the seat that his father had just vacated.

"Were you?" Hope soared in Mark's breast. He settled back down into the comfort of the cushions.

"I was," she stated. "I was grateful when I found out you'd be okay. And when I heard everything else, too." She trailed off, looking away.

"Amy, you have to believe me when I say there was nothing going on between me and -" he almost choked on the last word. "Me and Laura."

"I believe you," she said quietly. "I'm so sorry, Mark. About everything."

He nodded, unable to speak for fear he would burst into tears in earnest. What must she think of him? That he really cared for Laura in that way? Somehow he needed to reassure her. "Honestly, Amy. It was long over between us. But that doesn't mean she deserved to die."

"I know that, Mark. It must be very hard for you."

He nodded again.

"And I was very happy when I found out you had given your life to Christ. Sorry if I sounded kind of - distant - the other day when we talked on the phone. I guess I was still in shock over everything that's happened."

"I wondered about that," Mark said, trying for a feeble smile.

"I was going to call the very night I accepted Christ, and then I decided I'd wait and tell you in person. Probably not that smart, considering everything else that took place in between."

"But the bottom line is, you've made a decision for Christ," Amy stated.

"Yes. Yes, I have, Amy. It's the genuine thing, not just a way to get you to marry me."

Amy looked down at her hands, clearly flustered. "Mark -" she said hesitantly.

"Amy, you must know, my feelings haven't changed. I still love you and want you to marry me. If you'll have me, now that I'm a bit defective." He gestured at the wrapping on his arm.

She smiled. "It's not that."

"Then what is it?" Mark asked. "I get the distinct impression that this is not going the way I had hoped. Is there someone else?"

"No. Of course not." She sat up straighter. "Look, Mark. I still care about you, but I've had some time to think about things while you've been gone. And well, maybe I am too young to know my own mind about something so important."

"Who told you that?"

"Nobody," she defended. "I've come to that conclusion all on my own. See, that's part of the problem. You treating me like a child. And maybe in some ways, I am. I'd like to grow up, Mark, on my own terms. Not because you tell me to."

"I see. You think I've been overbearing."

"No. You were sweet and attentive and made me feel desirable -"

"Because you are," he interrupted.

"Let me finish! I just feel like I need to see the world. Follow my own dreams before I settle down. You've traveled the world; followed your dreams. Surely you of all people must understand how I feel."

"What are your dreams, Amy?" Mark asked quietly.

"To be a missionary. To help people. To tell people about Jesus," she replied just as softly.

Mark surveyed her angelic young face. Tenderness overwhelmed him. "Then you should follow your dreams, Amy Walters," he said finally. "I won't stop you."

"Thank you," she barely whispered. She jumped up and rushed to his chair, kissing him on the forehead, the way a schoolgirl would kiss an aging elder. Then she swept from the room on a sob.

Mark sat for a moment, blinking back his own tears. It was the most profound act of love he had ever shown her - setting her free.

Was this how God worked all things out for good? Two friends dead, another criminally insane, and utter rejection from the love of his life. And yet... he couldn't help going back to the next part of Romans 8.

"But in all these things we overwhelmingly conquer through Him who loved us. For I am convinced that neither death, nor life, nor angels, nor principalities, nor things present, nor things to come, nor powers, nor height, nor depth, nor any other created thing shall be able to separate us from the love of God, which is in Christ Jesus our Lord."

CHAPTER 31

"Um, Dad? Can I talk with you a minute?" Mark asked from the doorway of his father's study.

Russ looked up from the book he was reading. "Sure. Anytime. Come on in." He removed his reading glasses and placed them on the desk.

"I've been in contact with Charlene Howard again, since I've been back." He scanned his father's face for recognition. "My... sister in Calgary," he finished, hesitating on the word 'sister'.

Russ nodded. "I see."

"I was thinking I might like to go out there. To meet with her and... and the rest of the family." He stopped, holding his breath for his father's reaction.

Russ steepled his fingers, rocking back and forth in his chair.

"I know you don't approve," Mark rushed forward, "but I think I might need the closure myself after all these years, and -"

Russ silenced his son with a raised finger. "Mark, I think you should know that Deanie and I have talked about this. We knew it was coming. And... well, we both think you should go." He looked squarely into his son's eyes.

"You're sure?" Mark surveyed his father closely.

Russ nodded. "Absolutely. Whatever demons I need to exorcize in relation to your mother are mine and mine alone. You shouldn't be held hostage by my shortcomings."

"But -"

"And besides that," Russ cut him off, "it's time I faced up to the facts. I was not totally blameless in my first marriage. I wasn't the husband I should have been. I was controlling and bitter and I see that now. I've been carrying this offence way to long. It's time I gave it over to the Lord once and for all. You deserve to know the rest of your family. It's simply the right thing to do."

"Thanks, Dad. I appreciate it."

———

Mark paid the driver then stepped out of the cab. Another wave of anxiety hit him as his stomach tightened into a hard ball. Dr. Mark Graham, renowned archaeologist, world traveler, and a man who had faced death - shaking in his boots.

He was in Calgary, where the other half of his 'family' lived. Charlene had given him the address to her home and the rest of the family would be there, waiting. Charlene, Tom, and little Cade; Scott, the brother he hadn't met yet; and - her. The woman who had given him birth. He took a deep breath. Well, no use in stalling any further. Might as well face the music.

It had been a long journey around the world and back again, but somehow it seemed that this was the culminating moment, when all the questions about his own worth as a person - his own purpose on this earth - would be answered. No matter what the outcome of the meeting, he knew God could use it for good as he put his new found faith to the test once again. Perhaps it was symbolic of his life in general. He had no idea what his future held. It certainly was not what he had expected or even hoped.

And yet... in the midst of all the devastation, he felt the hand of God, and for that, despite everything else that had happened over the past year, he was grateful. Maybe that was all that really mattered.

EPILOGUE

Despite the khaki hat, the African sun beat down mercilessly on his head as Mark strode down the sidewalk. Mid afternoon was no time to be out in Harare. He needed to find some shelter. He spotted a small sidewalk café across the street, and headed in that direction, dodging the slow moving traffic that clogged the street.

He ducked under the awning, feeling the immediate reprieve from the punishing rays of the sun. Most of the tables were occupied already. He spotted one with a lone woman - a white woman at that, sitting against the brick of the building.

"Excuse me? May I join you?" he asked. His heart literally stood still as recognition dawned. "Amy? Is that you?"

She looked up, clearly as taken aback as he was. She nodded mutely, then managed to squeak out. "Please sit down."

He did, the chair scraping along the cement as he pulled it out before sitting.

"What are you doing here?" they both asked at once and then laughed.

"You first," Mark said politely.

"I'm working at an orphanage for victims of Aids," Amy informed.

Mark nodded. "Of course. And telling the children about Jesus, no doubt," he added with a grin.

"Naturally," she said with a smile of her own. "And you? Are you working on location somewhere near?"

"Sort off," Mark said. "I'm not really sponsored by anyone in particular. I'm just here on my own to do a little follow up."

"Oh? What about?"

"Just a tip off a friend gave me once," Mark supplied. "About a certain Granny that might be buried somewhere in the mountains."

"A Granny?" Amy raised her brows.

"Long story. I'll tell you about it sometime."

"I'd like that."

"I can't believe we've run into each other after all this time. In Harare, of all places." Mark shook his head. How many years had it been now? Four? Five? He'd lost track. But Amy... Amy Walters was as beautiful in his eyes as ever. He stole another glance and noticed she was surveying him just as intently.

She looked down. "Yeah. Imagine."

There was a moment of silence before Mark spoke up again. "Harmony and Cory had a son. He's about six months old."

"Yes, I heard."

"Of course."

"You must be a very proud Uncle."

"Indeed I am."

"I'm sorry I didn't make it to their wedding. I was working with 'Doctors Without Borders' at that time, and was somewhere on the Pacific."

"You were missed. By more than one person," he added, trying to catch her eye.

She kept her gaze down. "Oh. I'm still trying to get used to the African sun. It's so intense."

"Amy, look at me, please," Mark said.

She looked up, her breath catching in her throat.

"You know, you are still as beautiful as I remember you."

"Mark, don't," Amy pleaded. "After all this time -"

"I've never stopped loving you, you know. There has been no one else since you, you know that? I've pretty much resigned myself to a life as an eccentric old bachelor. But now, seeing you again, I feel this small glimmer of hope. Tell me there's hope, Amy."

"I... I don't know what to say," Amy faltered, clearly flustered. "I mean, I've grown up a lot in the past five years, Mark."

"It's been that long?" he asked. "It seems like only yesterday I was gazing into your beautiful eyes."

"Things have changed. I have changed."

"I see." He looked down at his hands. "Then life as an eccentric old bachelor it is."

"I mean, I've matured, both as a woman and as a Christian," Amy continued. "I'm not the shy, naïve little girl you knew back then. I've traveled the world for myself, Mark. I've seen things, some of them pretty horrible. And yet my faith is still strong. I've been able to make a difference in the lives of these people. And I can't believe that God would want me to sacrifice all of that to satisfy my own feelings."

Mark looked up. "You still have feelings?"

Amy hesitated before nodding.

Mark's eyes filled with tears; uncharacteristic and yet fitting. He let one roll unchecked down his cheek. "I'm a believer, too, Amy. Remember? I told you that way back when I got home from the States."

"I know. I guess I just needed to know that it was for real. Not something you said or did just to satisfy my requirements."

"No, Amy. It's for real," Mark reassured. "I've been through enough to know that no matter what - whether you take me back or not - God will never leave me or forsake me."

"Is that what you think I did? Forsake you?"

"It felt like it. But I think God had a plan. He knew you

needed time to grow up, to live life on your own and to make a
difference in the world. And I needed to grow up, too. Spiritually.
I needed to make my faith my own, not just something my
parents handed down to me."

"But what about my career?"

"What about it?"

"I like what I do," Amy said defensively. "I don't want to give
that up."

"And why should you? I mean look at us. Here we are,
meeting up in Africa of all places after all these years. I'd say we
both have a bit of the wanderlust in us. Surely God must have a
niche somewhere for us, where we can work together."

"Do you really think so?"

"God works all things together for those who love Him,"
Mark quoted. "My favourite verse. I think He can do the same for
us, Amy."

"I'd like that." Amy smiled.

"Then I take it your answer is yes."

"To what?" she replied coyly. "You haven't asked a question
yet."

"Right. Okay, Amy Walters, for the second time – or is it the
third time? Anyway, Amy will you do me the honour of becoming
my wife?"

"I thought you'd never ask!"

After a prolonged kiss, Amy pulled away with a giggle.

"Now what are you laughing about?" Mark asked. "I haven't
lost my touch, have I?"

"No, that's not it. I was just thinking how worried I was that I
was destined to be an old maid missionary."

"You're kidding, right?"

"No. I guess you weren't the only one who had resigned
himself to life as a single. I mean, I kept telling myself that I was
still young, that someday someone else would come along and
sweep me off my feet. That I was too young when I fell for you

and it was probably just a crush. But deep down I knew. There would never be anyone for me besides Dr. Mark Graham."

"Now that is music to my ears." Mark laughed. "If Jack were here right now, he'd be playing a celebration tune on his saxophone."

"Maybe he is here," Amy mused. "Looking down on us from heaven with his own four thousand piece jazz band."

Mark nodded. "Yeah. And somehow, I think he approves."

Read about Mark's parents in the prequel
PLAY IT AGAIN - a romance set in the rockin' 80s.

Join my mailing list and get up to date info on all new releases, promos and giveaways when they happen. You'll also get a free book!

https://tracykrauss.com
- fiction on the edge without crossing the line -

If you enjoyed this novel, or any of Tracy's books, please consider writing a review online. Reviews help readers find books they'll love and are tremendously helpful for today's authors. Thank you in advance!

ABOUT THE AUTHOR

Tracy Krauss writes contemporary Christian romance with a twist of suspense and a touch of humour. Her books strike a chord with those looking for a hard hitting yet thought provoking read. Her work has won multiple awards and has been on Amazon's bestsellers' lists. She also writes stage plays tailored to a high school audience, and has contributed to several anthologies, devotional books, and one illustrated children's book. Tracy has a Bachelor's degree from the University of Saskatchewan and taught secondary school Art, Drama and English—all things she is passionate about. She is a member of ACFW, The Word Guild, and Inscribe Christian Writers' Fellowship, a Canada wide organization for writers of Christian faith. She and her husband have lived in five provinces and territories including many remote and unique places in Canada's far north. They have four grown children and now reside in beautiful Tumbler Ridge, BC where she continues to pursue all of her creative interests. Visit her website for more: https://tracykrauss.com

ALSO BY TRACY KRAUSS